one woman short

A Novel

nelson george

Published by Simon & Schuster
NEW YORK LONDON TORONTO SYDNEY SINGAPORE

Simon & Schuster, Inc.
Rockefeller Center
1230 Avenue of the Americas
New York, NY 10020

Designed by Colin Joh
Text set in Electra

Manufactured in the United States of America

ISBN 0-7394-1097-0

Dedicated to
Bill and Tanya Stephney
and
their full house

1

I was in a wedding. I wish my momma could have been there. I wish my sister could have seen. I wish all those women who said I'd never, ever be anywhere near a chapel could see me standing in front of a church in a blue suit and ruffled white shirt with neo-Elizabethan flavor.

But none of those people were there. Not my momma, who's not feeling very well. Not my sister, who chided me as a frivolous, immature dog just a few days ago. Not any of the women I'd disappointed by not "acting right."

None of them were here 'cause this wasn't my wedding. Right next to me in a blue suit that looked even more Elizabethan than mine was Timothy Waters Jr., whose lips wore the tight smile of a nervous contestant at a spelling bee. All his emotions, every bit of dread he felt at the prospect of husbandhood, were right on my friend's kisser.

There were moments at the bachelor party when, despite the bottle of Moët in his hands and the incredibly buxom stripper squirming in his lap, Tim's face had this same look.

When he glances over I whisper, "If you wanna make a break for the door, I got your back, homie." For a moment he actually seems to be considering an escape.

The wedding march commences and we turn our attention to the back of the church, where bridesmaids in the faux Elizabethan dresses Bernice Wilson chose to fulfill some childhood fantasy stride toward us like comely members of the English court in *Shakespeare in Love*, albeit looking more chocolate than the Queen Mother was used to.

Caron, the bride's maid of honor, a beauty with bronze

7

skin, aimed an incandescent, toothy smile my way. I was contemplating the possibilities when Bernice and her father, Dr. Thomas R. Wilson of Sherman Oaks, strode toward us. To my jaded mind Bernice and her pops appeared to me as ritualistic executioners marching to send an innocent man to an unjust reward. I glanced again at Tim, seeking confirmation of my apprehension, but my friend of ten years was seeing something else.

The strained look had evaporated. The tension in his body was gone. A look of immense satisfaction filled his brown face. His mustache twitched happily. Tim wasn't resigned to his fate; he was joyful in anticipation. By the time Bernice stood at his side Tim Waters Jr. looked beatific. Whatever had troubled him about the loss of freedom, the assuming of responsibility, plain old growing up—Tim had suddenly made peace with. His transformation was startling, and so, to me, was my reaction. I was jealous.

Up until that moment I'd felt sorry for my man. After all our years scoping out honeys at ski summits, getting acquainted with MBAs at Martha's Vineyard beach parties, and macking coeds at the Howard homecoming, he was giving it all up for permanent residence in monogamyland, a place I'd never imagined he'd reside.

Bernice changed all that for Tim. Stability. Consistency. Sweet potato pie. Since he'd met Bernice, three years ago, Tim's options had slowly disappeared. Like an aging basketball player Tim no longer could go to his left and his right. Now he had only one move to the hoop and it always ended as a layup into Bernice's arms.

Now my man's face was shining like new money. Throughout the ceremony he held Bernice's hand, squeezing it tightly and even swinging it at one point like a giddy kid on his first date. When Reverend Myers announced, "You may kiss the bride," Tim tongued her down like the chapel was a short-stay motel out by LAX. Tim and Bernice got so into it people started whooping as if the ceremony was an episode of the *Def Comedy Jam.*

Before I knew it Tim and Bernice were striding down the church steps in a shower of birdseed—nineties PC replacement for whole-grain rice—while I was organizing chauffeurs, rounding up groomsmen, and otherwise seeming the attentive best man, despite feeling dazed. As we stood out on the church's lawn with the Santa Barbara sun cutting through the haze and a nice ocean breeze making our Elizabethan ruffles sway, I etched my professional-publicist smile across my lips while the wedding photos were taken. In my job I'd long ago learned the enduring value of an insincere smile, though I knew there was something unseemly about employing it at your best friend's wedding.

All through the reception I wore my insincere mask to guard my fragile self-esteem and do my duty for my now ecstatic friend. "I didn't think it would feel this good, Rod," he whispered to me before the toast.

"You look happy as hell, Tim."

"Yeah," he agreed, "I really am. Can you believe it?"

My toast, thankfully written before this unexpected burst of envy, actually sounded quite heartfelt. "In every person's life," I said, "there are people you date, people you become lovers with, people who romantically affect your life in profound ways. But there is only one true love—one person who makes you whole, who completes you, who is your spiritual link to the future. Bernice and Timothy are two people lucky enough to have found their other half. Let us toast their good fortune."

Afterward I got patted on the back for my words. I wanted

to respond, "Well thanks, but that's what I do. Hype is my middle name." Instead I did the right thing—I smiled and said, "Hey, what's true is true."

What's actually true is that I didn't believe much of what I said even when I was writing it. I've always believed there were any number of good matches in the universe and that life was about exploring as many of these possibilities as possible. I'd lived my thirty-three years this way. So had Tim.

Of course, a year ago Tim had decided to marry Bernice, which was the end of his quest, though my take was he'd just gotten tired and that this whole showy ritual was less about exhilaration than exhaustion. Now, after all this time Tim and Bernice had dated, the months they'd been engaged, and the Elizabethan splendor of the day, I was having to doubt myself.

Even when Caron, that beauty of a bridesmaid, scribbled her pager number on my wedding program, my mind was elsewhere. All these thoughts of true love made the prospect of trying to pick up girls at a wedding seem roach. So when Caron asked, "You gonna page me?" I said, "Sure," way too halfheartedly.

"Don't say it like it's a favor."

"Oh, I'm sorry," I said, trying to recover. "I sure didn't mean it that way."

"Whatever," she said. "I heard you were trifling but"—she gave me an appraising up-and-down—"I figure if Tim can become a good man, you can too." This kinda pissed me off but I let it slide since, I guess, she was paying me a sideways compliment. I too, she was saying, could one day be a husband. "When you learn to act right, use that number." Then she turned and somebody's aunt came up and gave her a big hug. The combination of intense jealousy and low self-esteem I was feeling would have been an appropriate way to end the day.

Yet my day was far from over. There were still things to do—making sure the bridal suite at the hotel was ready, that the limo would pick them up in the morning, that the tickets to Bora Bora were in Tim's travel bag. Even as Tim and Bernice were cutting the wedding cake I was in the kitchen paying Reverend Myers along with Bernice's father.

About 1 A.M., after the toasts and the cake cutting and dances with strangers, I was lying on my hotel bed in my rented tux, staring at the ceiling. I remembered the night, some three years ago, when Tim and Bernice met. I was there. I was right there. The NAACP Image Awards in Pasadena. We were in the lobby of an ornate old Hollywood theater, Tim and I tuxed out and side by side again, glasses of wine in our hands, as we checked out the room.

Bernice strolled by. Classy beige dress. Elegant stride. The gleam of intelligence in her brown eyes. And a smile. A smile at two brothers in tuxes holding wine. I smiled. Tim smiled bigger. A half hour later Bernice and Tim were looking into each other's eyes and it was on.

Maybe if I'd smiled wider, better, bigger, things might have been different. Maybe tonight I would be making absolutely legal, religiously sanctioned, enthusiastically matrimonial love in the same hotel I was now laid up in with my tux disheveled, brain strained, and my mood as dark as late night over the Pacific.

"Things might have been different." That sentence rolled around my dome for a while. Then stronger, and as insistent as a nightmare, were the words I'd uttered so glibly that afternoon: "But there is only one true love—one person who makes you whole, who completes you, who is your spiritual link to the future."

It was all hyperromantic bull. I knew that when I scribbled it down in my notebook. I felt that even as it flowed smoothly from my nut brown lips. I knew that. Yet what I knew was having no impact on how profoundly lonely I felt.

Then a curious thing happened. I reached over to the hotel nightstand and picked up the peach-colored notepad next to the phone. Next I picked up the white-and-peach-colored hotel pen. The white-and-peach-colored pen moved haltingly across the peach paper, and in thin blue ink, a named appeared. Peachina Evans.

Twenty years ago, when I was a skinny adolescent with a sprinkling of acne and long, embarrassingly girlish eyelashes, Peachina, best friend of my cousin Becky, brazen beyond her fifteen years and quite taken with my eyelashes, took me into a toolshed behind her father's Newport News, Virginia, house. That day in the toolshed, amid rakes and hammers, garden hose, and a big bottle of carefully marked rat poison, Peachina showed me what El DeBarge called "the ways of love."

I remember it in flashes. Her mouth on mine. My zipper going down. Her fumbling with her bra. My terror at her father's possible sudden appearance. Her smell filling my nose with a ripe, pungent scent I hated, then learned to love. My body quivered like a coed in *Scream*. Our bodies, awkward, frantic, moaning, and breathless, experienced a fleeting exchange of energy and then separated, guilty and proud, out of the shed and into a strange and woozy early evening.

Peachina Evans. She was the first name on my list. Or was I just the third or fourth on hers? Either way I just kept on writing. Name after name after name. When I'd finished racking my brain it was nearly dawn.

2

My hotel wake-up call was right on time, at 10 A.M. Soon as I got myself together I dialed Tim's room. When Bernice answered I said, "Good morning, Mrs. Waters." She replied, "You mean Mrs. Wilson-Waters."

"Oh," I replied, "is Mr. Wilson-Waters available?"

"He's in the shower. I heard you asked Caron for her number."

"If you mean we talked about getting together, we did, though I don't know how seriously I should take a beeper number and not a home number."

"You know, Rodney, it's really time you got serious."

"Yeah," I agreed noncommittally. This lecture was not how I wanted to start the day. But then screaming on my best friend's bride wouldn't have been cool either. So as pleasantly as possible I said, "Well, just let your husband know the limo for the airport will be downstairs in half an hour."

After I'd finally, mercifully, peeled off my tux, showered, trimmed my goatee, and slipped into jeans and a T-shirt, I was down in the lobby handling my final best man duties—checking out the honeymooners, confirming the limo with the concierge, and calling the groomsmen about returning their tuxes as soon as possible.

Tim and Bernice came off the elevator holding hands, trailed by a bellhop and a cart filled with bags. Bora Bora was seven and a half hours away, but judging by their demeanor the vacation had begun.

"And how was last night?" I asked, which was our old way of asking, "How was the boning?" Tim just looked at me piously and replied out of Bernice's earshot, "This is my wife, Rodney."

"Sorry," I said as respectfully as I could to a man who used to describe his sexual heroics like each encounter was the Super Bowl.

"What's going on?" Bernice wondered, and Tim reassured her, "Nothing, honey." Then he flipped it. "So, Rod, I heard you and Caron might get together."

"We'll see" was my conservative reply. Tim cut me a look, the old raffish look I knew so well, and said, "Well, Rodney, you know whatever you do, you better act right." This was uttered with a touch of irony, so I knew that somewhere, buried inside Bernice's husband, my old running buddy still breathed.

A few of Bernice's relatives appeared in the lobby. Much hugging and kissing ensued. For a few moments Tim and I stood side by side, our first private moments since he'd become a husband. I took the opportunity to put a question mark in my voice: "Wilson-Waters?"

"Yeah." He spoke the word slowly, stretching it into two syllables as he glanced at his bride. "It makes sense for her, Rod. It doesn't take anything away from me and it makes her happy. And you know, that's the gig."

"Three weeks in Bora Bora?"

"Yeah," he said as slowly as before. "I researched this spot. Got a satellite dish at the bar that pulls up NBA games and *SportsCenter*. My plan is to watch sports, fish, and make a baby."

"Wow, you are married."

"Rod, I hadn't had sex without a condom in four years— until last night."

"So you're just happy to be home," I observed.

"You got that right. Besides," he added as he turned to smile at his bride, "I love her like a Babyface song."

I hugged my homie. I kissed his wife. I watched them enter a limo and drive off in the direction of Bora Bora. I sat in the hotel's breakfast nook and watched as members of the wedding party checked out. Uncles and stepdaughters, second cousins and nephews, childhood pals and ex-lovers disguised as friends. Caron, the maid of honor and possessor of the telegenic smile, sauntered up to the front desk, her walk as sultry as a Georgia night, and I debated intercepting her.

But as I haven't done that often in my life, I let that romantic/sexual impulse pass and watched Caron walk her beautiful self alone out of the hotel's front door. It was almost checkout time and I hadn't even packed. My duty to my friend and my reaction to his joy had left me strange and funny, like someone had told a joke I didn't get.

Back in my room I slowly gathered up my things, stuffing them in my duffel bag with the delicacy of a retiring garbageman. Then I remembered my list. On the nightstand next to the phone was that peach notepad with names written down in my ugly scrawl. Women's names. Names so dear. Names from the past. Names I should have forgotten, like bad dreams.

Peachina Evans remained at the head of the class, but the enrollment was long. I counted up 133 names. An odd number, 133. Nothing special about it. Certainly nothing sacred. I knew men with many more names than me. So many that they weren't names anymore—just body parts and situations and smirks. But predatory Peachina had a name. So did all the other women who had blessed me with their bodies. The question was, why? Why did this list exist and what did it mean?

Woodrina Perkins. Woodrina had woolly red hair, freckles,

a lime green jumpsuit, and platform shoes. She used to hold my head in her hands and look into my face with glassy, amused eyes.

Charlotte Hughes—Carla—was another publicist. She stumbled into my bed one night after I'd helped her write a press release and listened to her talk about her absent boyfriend. We were both embarrassed in the morning and never ever acknowledged it had even happened.

Yim. She was the only Asian woman I'd ever been with. Met her with Tim at a trip hop lounge in Hollywood. Beneath glasses and a fluffy sweater was a lovely yellow body. We devoured each other one long May night, and in June she got deported in a tragedy of epic proportions.

Before I spent all day reminiscing I folded the list up, slipped it into my back pocket, and headed down to the lobby.

3

I took the Pacific Coast Highway from Santa Barbara. It was the long way home but the view out of the right side of my car—Cali at its prettiest—was worth the extra time. Far west was Hawaii, where Tim and Bernice would land briefly before experiencing the whiter, cleaner sands of Bora Bora. I thought about them, hugged up in first class, making plans for the house in the gated community she wanted in the Valley. Perhaps sneaking into a lavatory to join the mile-high club.

Jealous again, I pulled out my list, rubbing the names with my fingers as if I could feel the women through their names. Nina Rodriquez was twenty-one when I was twenty-three and only did it 'cause I kept asking. Afterward I felt guilty every time I saw her face—which is why I avoided her face.

I exited the PCH in Santa Monica instead of going home and found myself wandering across its pier, past fast food seafood joints, carousels, a Ferris wheel, and an amusement arcade filled with games that predated video games. The pier was a product of the mid–twentieth century, which now looks like a much more innocent time. Perhaps that's what I was looking for.

I sat at a small table next to a neon Budweiser sign and a fake nautical window, nibbled on fried shrimp and french fries, sipped a flat Coca-Cola, and slipped out my 133 names in search of meaning. At first it seemed a collection of erotic images of seduction, conquest, and fun. A simple, silly list of trophies. Yet the longer I looked at it the sadder I became. The truth began to fill me up with sorrow and I realized that the list truly represented only one thing—my emotional failures.

Somewhere among those 133 was my wife, and in between my immaturity and my dick, she'd gotten away. I had watched her get dressed, reassured her I'd call, and then never spoke to her again. I had let her tell me she couldn't see me again unless I got serious, and remained mute as she strolled away. I had let casual sex remain casual when nothing that good should be so damn leisurely.

I knew some of their bodies—could still remember which had hair on their nipples, which had lovely suckable toes, and which favored Massengill. But who were they? Why did Sandra Rutt cry so easily? What did Gail Neal mean when she said I was too passive? Was Carrie James really frigid, or was that just an evil excuse to slow me down?

This was, I concluded, the list of a fool. One hundred and thirty-three names over thirty-three years came out to about four women a year. But the real math began when I was twenty-two and I got an apartment on Adams off Crenshaw and a late-model but well-maintained Mustang. Tim was my roommate and my fellow predator. Between our graduation from USC at twenty-two and right now, ten years later, I'd exchanged intimacies with most of these women. Somewhere in there I had an amazing year where I'd bedded twenty-odd women. It's remarkable how persuasive you are when every stitch of your self-image is tied up in one simple thing.

Now, looking out at the dark Pacific, thinking about Tim and Bernice jetting toward Bora Bora, I felt like George Clinton's Atomic Dog—just not as funky. Every time I told myself this self-pity was bullshit I saw Tim's puppy-happy face and I had to retract my arrogance.

My wife.

Which one of these ladies was my wife?

It was 11 P.M. before I left that table and headed for my car.

Couples, mostly young and Hispanic or Asian, strolled around me with stuffed animals, cotton candy, and the giddy intimacy of young lovers. A sexy young black girl in a clingy brown dress and hugging a stuffed pink dog to her waist caught my eye. I looked away to act like I wasn't staring and when I turned back a beefy Chicano wearing sunglasses at night had his arms around both the pink dog and her waist. I really wanted to play Air Hockey—the Santa Monica Pier was one of the few places left in town with that old game—but I was alone and Air Hockey was made for two.

The lovey-dovey atmosphere was beginning to nauseate me. Not what the kid needed right now. All those couples were at the start of something—their evening, their love affair, their life together—and I was now obsessed with endings.

By the time I'd taken the 101, gotten off at La Brea, passed Flora Kitchen, and parked the car in the garage in the back of my apartment, I'd gone through more bad endings than a hack scriptwriter. I recalled last kisses. I remembered being cursed out. There were times they said, "Speak to you next week," and they never did. There were times I walked into a party and saw them in a corner with another man.

I went through my 133 names, making notes next to each, on the hows and whys of our endings. Melani DeVoe had bad breath. Sue Fallon didn't think I was focused. Rocena Briggs moved to South Africa with a white actor back before Mandela was released. Tonya Lee watched too many soap operas. Melissa woke up screaming at night about unspoken childhood traumas. Every name was a story. A beginning, a middle, and an end. Except for three—Belinda Myles, Amy Davis, and Sabena.

Belinda was a wild child who gave cool parties in the no-man's-land of downtown L.A. She was the first woman I knew to have a tattoo on her breast—a neon green rose—to have her navel pierced, and thumb rings on both hands. Despite her outward manifestations of trendy freakiness, Belinda was a great businesswoman who always seemed to be on the edge of what was next—I first heard of techno raves, trip hop music, and the return of the cigar bar by eavesdropping on her conversations.

When I last saw Belinda she was wearing matching leopard pants and halter top, with her hair slicked back and shiny as a gigolo. I didn't think Belinda was my wife, but damn, I was happy with her, though always a bit wary, as if one morning I'd wake up in her bed covered with tattoos. That last night she'd been peeved because I was leaving her party to have drinks with a client. She cut me a dirty look and sucked her pretty teeth, and then, in full diva form, turned her back. I bid good night to her leopard-clad behind and was going, going, gone.

My mother loved Amy Davis, a black girl as normal as fried chicken and Sunday school, which she sometimes taught. Her day job was working as an L.A. transit dispatcher, and at night she took classes toward a business administration degree. Amy lived in Leimert Park in a bachelorette house filled with glass tables, faux African art, and a gold-embossed Bible she kept by her collection of John P. Kee CDs.

If the stomach was really the way to a man's heart, Amy should have been married three hundred times. Dinner with her was like that *Soul Food* movie come to life. It got so that Tim, who devoured any leftovers I'd bring home, would join me at Amy's for dinner, bring a date, and eventually even some frat brothers. No one went away from Amy's hungry, though I was never satisfied.

Amy was devoted to God and as chaste as a true believer should be. I respected her. The lady had integrity. The lady had principles. The lady had very strong hands. So strong that they kept this sinner at bay for half a year of church attendance—not every week but a lot. After six months she'd absolutely convinced me her husband would be the next man she'd make love to, so I stopped pressuring her. I felt I was being gallant. Still, I could not be as chaste as Amy. If Amy knew I had others she didn't say, though toward the end even she wondered why I wasn't bothering her anymore. Guess she missed twisting my fingers.

The last time I saw Amy Davis was outside the West Angeles Church on Crenshaw. She was going inside for choir practice. I sat in my car and watched her hips roll up the church's steps, eyeing them like a foolish teenage boy. She was so healthy and I was so weak. It was just too much to take. Like a sucker I drove off and I never came back.

Sabena (aka Bridgette Brown) was a tall, lanky beauty with a model's body and a truly giving personality. She was a nurse at Cedars-Sinai Hospital in Beverly Hills, where she was always being propositioned by producers and agents who wanted to take her away from all the sickness and pain. I know that's true because I tried that rap myself.

Kind as she was, Sabena took pity on me and let me, slowly, into her life. At Cedars-Sinai, where she worked with sick cancer patients and talked sweetly to the elderly with Alzheimer's, Bridgette Brown was an angel of mercy who used her given name. At home on Cashio Street off La Cienega Boulevard, she transformed into Sabena, a dreamer in Danskins and hard bare feet with two goals—one, to found an Afro-Cuban dance company, which was fine, and two, to perform in the New Year's Day Tournament of Roses parade, which seemed a little weird to me.

Belinda, Amy, and Sabena were all lovely blasts from my past that, for whatever reasons—jealousy at my friend's marriage, despair at my own love life, and my mother's condition—I now thought about contacting. That night I contemplated this strange fact lying on the brass bed of my mid-Wilshire apartment when my sister, a woman of strident opinion and abrasive voice, rang to pull me back to everyday reality.

"Rod-nee!" In her mouth my name is broken down to its phonetic roots. "Rod-nee!"

"Yes, Roberta."

"You going tomorrow." This sentence had no question mark.

"What time?"

"Just be home at eleven."

"Okay."

4

The Sunday sun is always a little brighter than the sun of any other day. That's true even in Los Angeles, where the sun is brighter than in most other places, even when the smog conspires against that brightness. But even in L.A., where the Sunday sun is so bright, my sister, bless her stout heart, burns brighter than any sun.

My door can't stop the sun. Can't stop it from creeping underneath and around the sides. Nor can my door stop my sister. Even after I ignored her phone calls, her pages, and turned a deaf ear to the tapping on my bedroom window, Roberta Hampton somehow penetrated my front door, and now, just like the bright Los Angeles sun, she wakened me.

"Rod-nee! Rod-nee! Get up!" My sister, Roberta, is broom-handle skinny, yellow with hazel freckles on her shallow cheeks, and has limp, forlorn hennaed hair. She doesn't appear at all powerful. Yet there is a fierceness in her dark brown eyes and a willfulness in her soul that make my sister a force of nature. "Rod-nee!"

"How did you get in?"

Roberta held up two keys, said, "They're Ma's set," and then grabbed my right foot and jerked me out of my bed onto the floor. Next my best beige suit, a white shirt, and a brown belt plopped onto my stomach. From the floor I saw my sister's feet in shiny black patent leather church shoes stomp out of my room.

"Don't you want me to wash!" I yelled.

She yelled back, "It wouldn't change who you were, Rod-nee. It would just change the way you smelled. Why bother?"

23

Despite Roberta's observations I decided water and soap would be a nice touch. After I showered and dressed I exited my bedroom for the kitchen, where Roberta sat sipping coffee and gazing with amused eyes at my 133 names.

"Rod-nee, you are a mess."

"Yeah?"

"Little brother, you have way too much free time on your hands."

"Can I have that back, please?" I tried to snatch it from her but Roberta was too quick.

"I remember a lot of these sad girls. *You* fucked Tashana Fields?"

"Those are just the names of people I dated."

"Please, Rod-nee. I know you and your doggish heart. This is a list of women who you somehow fooled into spreading their legs. All of them thought you were a nice guy. A sad bunch of silly girls like Tashana Fields. And Rod-nee . . ."

"What?"

"You fucked Amy Davis! I thought she was saved!"

Moving quickly, I snatched the list out of her hands. "You don't listen to me," I said. "This is just a list of women I dated. That is all."

For the next half hour after we'd left my place and she drove us downtown across Wilshire, I listened as my sister amused herself by giving her biased, one-sided view of my love life. "Rodney, if you weren't my brother and my only source of non-interest-bearing loans, I would never ever speak to a man like you. You meet women, you act like you are a nice guy. Sensitive, hardworking, and all that shit. Yet you a D-O-G right down to the way your tongue dangles when you look at a woman."

"You're just mad your girlfriends liked me."

"That goes to show you how doggish you are, Rod-nee. You went into my bedroom, stole my diary, and Xeroxed copies just to get Jasmine to touch your dick. You would do that to your own sister just to get with a ho."

"She was your best friend, Roberta."

"It just took time for her to show her true colors, that's all. See, it took a D-O-G like you to bring it out."

"Roberta," I said, "let me once again explain something to you about men and women. Every woman is a princess to some man, and every woman is the nastiest ho to some man. Same woman, different men. Different relationships, different dynamics."

"So what, Rod-nee? You just bring out the ho in women?"

"Unfortunately the answer is now no. To be honest, I'm really slowing down."

"Don't tell me you've reformed, 'cause I don't believe it."

"No," I said quickly, "I'm not saying that. Just that I'm slowing down."

"Oh, your boy got put in the kennel yesterday, so now you getting all philosophical and shit, right?"

"Maybe."

"Maybe my ass. You want to know what your life's about? It's Rebe Hampton. That's what your life's about." At that truth I just fell silent and looked out the window.

5

The Saint Mary of Genova senior citizens' residence was an aging Depression-era building on the edge of downtown, tucked away behind some skyscrapers and a freeway. It wasn't our first choice—we'd wanted somewhere by the water or out in the Valley. But after procrastinating for so many months, Saint Mary's was the only place we could afford on short notice. It made me guilty to go there, and it should have. The most important woman in my life should have been treated better.

Up on the second floor, in a dayroom filled with seventies furniture and the faint scent of mildew, Rebe Hampton sat in a wheelchair by the window looking out at that bright Sunday sun. Roberta and I turned her wheelchair around, and in her eyes—eyes once warm and clear, now milky and dazed—I searched for flickers of the woman that raised me. Her skin was sagging as if ready to slip off her bones, and her black-and-white dress hung loose upon her. A white skullcap kept her hair in place just above the ruby earrings she wore, glistening relics from her previous life.

Every time I saw my mother like this—a sack of flesh on feeble bone—I got weak kneed. It was hard to speak to this shadow of Rebe Hampton. I knew this was my mother. I told myself that. Yet it always felt like we were just visiting the last vestiges of her soul.

"Look who came, Ma." Roberta shifted Ma's wheelchair to face me. I leaned over and kissed her with love and dread. To my lips her cheek was soft and waxy, as if some medication was flowing through her pores. I tasted her discomfort on my lips and then swallowed an overwhelming sense of guilt.

In a whisper I heard her say, "Rodney, my baby," and almost lost it. Roberta put her hand on my shoulder and guided me into a chair just as she used to when I was a toddler and she was a loving big sister. For the next two hours Ma, Roberta, and I sat in that room and spoke in the hushed tones of a Catholic confessional. We spoke of medicine. We spoke of Medicaid. We spoke of the moon over Inglewood.

Ma had always been a night owl. She'd been a nocturnal type who loved life under moonlight, especially after Daddy's death. It's not that Ma had been a party girl, though she did know her way around a disco floor. Ma would gladly take night jobs—waitress, cashier, cook—that allowed her to be up and around at four in the morning. So, often she would come home in time to wake us for school. She'd usually sleep from 9 A.M. to 2:30 P.M., pick us up from school, prepare dinner, and head off to work around 8 P.M. This unconventional schedule made her happy. "There are only three things I loved," she said in a voice I barely recognized, "and that was you two and the nighttime."

"You know you loved Daddy," my sister added hopefully.

"Not as much as the night," my mother said, and then there was a long pause as we all recalled that long-lost man. My daddy. A picture on a mantel. A vague memory from my baby days. He in a black suit in a coffin, gatted by a junkie for his fake Rolex watch at a taco stand on Western. For me Daddy was always a flicker, never a true flame.

"Rodney." My mother woke me from the past in a voice that finally sounded like Rebe Hampton. "You know, you're one woman short."

"Ma, I don't know what you mean."

"You have your sister, who loves you to death—when she's not scolding you." Ma chuckled when she said this and so did I. "You have me, who loves you even when you're not here." Ma chuckled again but neither my sister nor I could find the humor in it. "But what you really need, what you need to finish you as a man, is someone else to love you and forgive you for being you."

"So I'm one woman short?"

"That's what I think." She reached out and held my hands. Through the milky eyes she stared at me. "I think about it a lot, Rodney."

Ma," my sister cut in, "he ain't never gonna find her. He can't see that good." Now Ma and Roberta enjoyed a nice long laugh and I sat back in my chair and put on a small smile, wondering if my list would improve my vision.

6

My sister and I crawled along Wilshire Boulevard past MacArthur Park with Marvin Gaye's *Here, My Dear* flowing from the speakers. "Rod-nee," she said, not looking at traffic, "did you understand what Ma was telling you?"

"Yeah," I said absently, "keep looking."

"And?"

"And what?"

"And that she's dying."

"What," I said excitedly. "Did the doctor tell you something?"

"No," she said quietly. "The doctor didn't say anything. It's just something that I feel."

"Roberta, don't say dumb shit like that. Don't even put that idea in the air."

"Rod-nee, I know this is uncomfortable for you. I know you ain't real comfortable with your emotions."

"What," I said, pissed off, "are you talking about now?"

"Ma wants you to have a woman before she passes."

I replied stupidly, "I've had women."

"Come on, Rod-nee, stop playing and come on up here with the adults. She's worried about you."

"I know that, Roberta." I looked out the window a moment. "You saw the list. You see it's been on my mind."

"But it needs to be in your heart, Rod-nee. Sometime you got to let somebody in your heart."

Who was she to lecture me on love? The girl's got three babies, three babies' fathers, and never had one good job.

But—and I had to admit this—Roberta knew love, she knew love hard. Without equivocation or reservation, when my sister gave her heart she did it deeply and truly. Just two sides of a coin, my sister and I. Each of us seeking love—she sure of its life-affirming value, I too easily satisfied with flesh alone. I sighed and told Roberta, "I'm doing the best I can. I really am."

She smiled sympathetically. Her harsh, judgmental face softened. Then she said quietly, as if praying, "Do better, Rodnee. For Ma you have to do better."

The rest of the ride I was quiet. I listened to Marvin's suite of songs about his ex-wife—a bittersweet payment for long years of marriage and strife—and contemplated my own love life. Though Marvin's marriage to Anna Gordy ended in a very public manner, it was still a sign of deep passion. Nothing in my life had generated that kind of intensity. It struck me then, as it had at Tim's wedding, there was an emptiness in my life, a level of self-expression and giving I simply had not experienced yet.

My love life had been defined, in a way, by my career. I am, by nature, a juggler. I like keeping balls in the air. I usually have five or six clients hovering at any time. Some are on their way down, some on the way up, all of them in a perfect, ever rotating, constantly moving, asymmetrical circle that is maintained solely by my dexterity, speed, and unabashed pleasure in the art of juggling. When I have a client on the cell, a client on the phone, a client paging, and another in the office, I feel as comfortable as a burger on a bun.

It's the same with women. I love them circling around me, some going down, some going up, and a couple right in the palm of my hand. They whiz by my face and I feel molecules of air shifting as my hand speed increases to move them more rapidly around me. I get so intoxicated with the act of juggling that it becomes an end in itself. From my clients I receive payment—dollars that keep the doors open, pay Pacific Bell, and provide loans to my sister.

Women, however, are not as easily juggled as work. After a while they become very aware that your hands are full. That you are not pausing to caress them. That it's just one hard squeeze and they're up in the air again. With an insecure woman, of whom there are far too many, this peculiar performance art can last for months, even years. They can be satisfied with flying through my hands, circling in an orbit of my choosing.

The speed varies but the sensation of the arch—up, up, up to a peak—brings them back to me. The fall—fast, straight, unavoidable—appears to have its appeal as well. After all, I always catch them before they hit the ground. And for a moment or two they rest lightly on my fingertips, cradled but not clutched. As if involved in a circular soap opera, these women come back to see what'll happen next, despite knowing the motion as well as I do.

I think the reason Sabena, Belinda, and Amy stick out for me is that, quite simply, I dropped the ball with each. I don't know if I lost control or got distracted, but one minute they were in my rotation, the next they'd hit the floor, bouncing rapidly away.

Now, I've dropped other balls. A few have hit my feet. After all, one can juggle only so many balls at a time. When new balls are added, others must go. But with those three dropped balls—the sound of their bounce resonates. Yes, they were gone, but they were not replaced. Perhaps they were irreplaceable.

7

first studied the circus trick of juggling lovers back during my sophomore year at USC. Sometime during my nineteenth year on earth it became clear that listening, not rapping, was key to getting in the game. Making women feel you cared about what happened to them—how much they hated their brother, how nasty their ex-boyfriend treated them, how they wanted to decorate their dream house, and how they felt about all these things—was crucial to getting their confidence and (pardon the expression) pussy.

However, listening did not guarantee horizontal enrichment. Listening too well could get you stuck in Chris Rock's dreaded "friend zone," which for a perpetually horny college-aged male is hell on earth.

So the key was to be sensitive enough to listen, yet to remain aggressive in pursuit of pleasure. Under no circumstances should she forget you had a dick. For me this was the center of my college education. At my best I was a B student. As for Tim, my college roommate and role model, he got A's and showed up only for tests.

You see, the moment Tim walked out of our room he was a woman magnet. Six feet four with chiseled light brown features, a boxer's physique, and a winning smile he refined nightly in our bathroom mirror. In addition, this Harry Belafonte–looking Angeleno was also a genuinely nice guy. Lucky for Tim, he was so damn handsome that being nice wasn't a love-crippling handicap.

I was none of the things Tim was. I was six feet and would be described as "lean" by those not wanting to offend me and "skinny" by my sister and others who didn't give a fuck about my feelings. God didn't see fit to make me short or pudgy or profoundly ugly, so I thank him for that.

Yet compared to Tim's my features were soft and unfocused, my skin neither dark enough to be "sexy" or light enough to be "fine." I was plain brown in a world where pecan or cocoa ruled. My only advantage over Tim was that I wasn't a nice guy, and since women really aren't immediately romantically attracted to nice guys, I cultivated my baser instincts.

Don't get me wrong. It's not that most women will consciously go for the un-nice (or if you insist, bad) guy. Most will say they want a decent, respectful guy. But if you sit on a college campus, in a club, or in an office cafeteria and watch women around arrogant, un-nice guys—drug dealers, basketball stars, con men, investment bankers, judges—you understand how titillating a bad boy can be.

Back then I was a college student with no portfolio. How was I to manifest my slick, un-nice tendencies? The revelation came in communications class during my junior year. Professor Weekly had invited a guest speaker in to enlighten us on the ways and means of publicity. Her name was Trudy Sims—a redhead in a sharp pinstripe pants suit and round, dramatic glasses with frames that matched her hair color, who spoke in a crisp, authoritative voice.

Her agency handled a slew of Hollywood players. You could see why Trudy was doing well. Everything about her was edgy—the crease in her pants, the severe haircut, the direct way she moved through the presentation and answered our questions.

She'd made some passing comment about "the necessity of fabrication" and I asked her, with youthful, smart-ass petulance, "Excuse me, Ms. Sims, but by 'the necessity of fabrication' do you mean you lie for a living?" That generated a few chuckles from my classmates but Trudy surprised us all by acknowledging, "Fabrications, exaggerations, and sometimes outright lies are, at least on a limited basis, a tool a publicist sometimes employs to protect and serve a client.

"After all," she elaborated, "lies are simply stories. At their essence that's all a lie is. Some bit of narrative that distracts people from reality. Okay, that's disingenuous. Lies are weightier than that. They can have larger consequences than a mere story.

"But," with a stern smile she added, "a good liar doesn't dwell on those consequences. He lies because it's often simpler than the truth and certainly a lot less emotional. Besides, lies are creative. Someone who can concoct a believable pack of lies is as much an artist as any writer, rapper, or poet. They are stories that alter reality. They are distortions that can become a parallel universe with a life of its own.

"When I tell clients that 'everybody lies,' they agree with me. When I tell clients, 'Lies can get us through a tough day,' they nod their heads, 'Yeah, you're right.' They tend to be less supportive when I urge them to 'tell a lie a day, just to keep in practice'—they act as if I've gone too far.

"I've decided it's one thing to acknowledge lying happens. No one can escape that fact. But to advocate lying, to say out loud that there's a true, necessary, life-enhancing value in lying—well, most people just can't be that honest with themselves. Me, I'm not a hypocrite, I'm just a liar—at least, I lie for my clients. Moreover, they want you to lie. They just don't always want to know how."

Professor Weekly was upset by Ms. Sims's frankness. After she'd taken her edgy self back to Hollywood the professor warned us about internalizing "fabrication as a tool." But her words struck a chord, both professionally and personally. Number one, it made me see publicity differently. It wasn't just kissing ass, it was a game. You were given a project—a record, a toy, a candidate—and you made it what you needed it to be. Whatever it really was could be remade, at least for a time, into your projection of it. Eventually its true nature would emerge. You couldn't hide a thing's true nature forever, or for even a month. Good or bad, mean or muddled, whatever a thing was would become evident. No question about that. But between now and then—well, you could have big fun until then.

But even deeper, I realized that the same was true of romance. Who you were could be camouflaged. The more skillful you were, the longer the illusion could last, though no illusion lasts forever. If you smiled a lot but were actually mean as hell, you'd one day scream at your mate for no good reason. If you were irresponsible with money but talked about saving cash, well, one day you'd be borrowing money. If you were a restless lover—if somewhere inside you were always anxious to board the next passing ship—then protestations of fidelity wouldn't stop your relationship from sinking. But think of all the fun that could be had until then. And as a result, I became someone who always kept a lifeboat handy.

8

On the top shelf of my bedroom closet there's a small trunk. At the end of every year I throw in my date book, my kitchen calendar, and usually my telephone book if it's worn down enough. I've done this religiously since I was in college. Occasionally, on late lonely nights, I've been known to sip from a bottle of good northern California merlot and sift through life's accumulated numbers. This is one of those nights, except that this particular trip through digits and dates isn't without direction. I'm in search of big game—a three-headed beast of lost love.

Nineteen ninety-one. That was the year I toiled at Def Jam publicizing Russell Simmons's awkward attempts to sell gangsta rappers from Compton by way of New York. I even appeared in a music video wearing rock-hard denim Dickies and swinging a twelve-gauge Mossburg shotgun like I was an OG. That same video shoot, in the great tradition of record-biz weasels, I wooed a vide-ho with loose talk of a record deal. Jeneva was her name. She worked nights as an orderly at Charles Drew Medical Center in Compton, where the victims of drive-bys (gang bangers and innocents alike) bled nightly onto the floor of the trauma unit. Jeneva eventually lost interest in me, dumping my hypster ass for a real OG in a wheelchair who ran a rather lucrative music production company.

Nineteen ninety-one was also the year the house I grew up in disappeared in smoke and Ma's spirit started to wither away. Until then I felt like a missing character in *Boyz N the Hood*—one who stood firmly between Ice Cube's ghetto pragmatism and Cuba Gooding's collegiate aspirations. Angela Bassett's ma was my ma, but with Daddy dead there was no Laurence Fishburne to backstop her. When our house burned down to its foundations Ma drifted into a depression like that Public Enemy lyric, "comatose walking around," and aged decades before our eyes.

Yes, 1991 was a bad year, filled with sad days. The one exception was December 11. According to my date book that was the day I met Sabena. I had three numbers listed for her—an apartment on Cashio off La Cienega, a dance studio where she taught classes, and her beeper digits at Cedars-Sinai. A triangle of home, medicine, and performance defined Sabena's life then.

What defined her now? Did any of these numbers still work? Would she return my call? Did she even remember me? Brothers in barbershops had schooled me that if you loved a woman right—I mean really curled her pretty pedicured brown toes—she'd always have love for you. Even if that was true, it raised another question. Did I truly curl Sabena's toes back then, or did she just curl mine?

We'd met at Sushi on Sunset one blustery December night. I had stopped by in search of hot sake and cold California rolls. I was lounging on the second floor of the restaurant, sunk down into one of the gray futons perfect for hugging, huddling, and surreptitious sensuality between friends, when long, brown, leather-clad legs carried a lean chocolate woman up the steps. She was model tall but had a loose, lanky gait that announced she was a dancer. Her hair was cut short and her eyes were small, dwarfed by slim, powerful eyebrows and a full, stunning mouth. I grinned shamelessly and she nodded a polite acknowledgment.

Following close behind this goddess was a short, muscular

white man in an extra-expensive black leather jacket and shiny cowboy boots. Had on trendy big-framed yellow-tinted shades and a little blunt mustache. Had an actor vibe about him—like he'd been a heavy in *Die Hard 4* or something of that ilk. He cut me an "I see you, now fuck off" look and guided his date to a futon in the corner.

My attitude toward white-male/black-woman hookups was, I thought, quite liberal. I had no problem with it—as long as the sister wasn't too fine. Not only did this chocolate goddess cross the fine line, but making it worse was that, for that brief moment our eyes met, I'd felt chemistry.

So while I did my best to respect their privacy, I used the corner, side, and back of my eyeball to peek as they dined. My reading of the scenario: this was a first or second date; she liked him but wasn't sold; he was trying hard, perhaps too hard, to close the deal; and my looking pissed off cowboy boots.

To my disappointment the chocolate goddess was quite respectful of her date, ignoring my leer and being attentive to her white companion. So after finishing my third sake I decided it was time to go. After all, I'd come for the sake and that's what I got. I paid the bill. I stood up and stretched loudly, aimed one last glance over at salt and pepper, and headed downstairs.

I slid into the men's room, unleashed some recently processed sake, and headed out the door, where the chocolate goddess was ending a call. "Sure, I can come in tonight." She spoke in a soft, surprisingly sad voice. "Gabby covered for me last week, so it's all good. See ya soon." After she hung up I went for it.

"Excuse me, miss."

"Yes," she said, surveying me. I really didn't have a play

designed. No slick fakes. No power moves. So I went with a traditional give-and-go. "You look like you might be an artist," I said while pulling out ye ole business card, "and I'm in the business of helping them out." She clutched my card and looked me in the eye. "So I look like an artist, Rodney Hampton."

"Yes, you do, Miss—"

"Sabena."

"Yes, Sabena, you do. If you ever have an event to publicize or a show you may be doing—"

"Call you, right?"

"Or if you just want to have sushi."

That got a smile out of her, which is all I wanted. I'd flattered, flirted, and shared a human moment with my new friend Sabena. Under the circumstances—with cowboy boots waiting upstairs—that's the best I could hope for.

Part of me would have been disappointed if she'd given me her number. It would have been disrespectful of the guy upstairs and certainly would have made me question her trustworthiness in the future. As far as I knew she would later throw the card away or show it to cowboy boots for laughs over sake.

"I hear you, Rodney Hampton," she said, easing my heart. "I may just call you."

"Sushi," I replied, "is on me."

I shook her lovely chocolate hand and then watched as the chocolate leather goddess ascended the steps. We got together a week later and were inseparable for six wonderful months, and it all went wrong and I never heard from her again.

Nineteen ninety-four. Spent much of that year dressed in black. Following a trip to New York I got caught up in that town's downtown vibe and made black the backbone of my wardrobe. Some thought this a strange choice of color for a

Cali native, but Ma was living with Roberta and the girls by then, growing increasingly withdrawn and uncommunicative, which made me so somber that black seemed an appropriate color.

Maybe it was my black clothes. More likely it was the cloud of torment my mother's condition sent hovering over me (women love rescuing tortured men). Whatever the reason, I had plenty of women that year—the AIDS epidemic did nothing to inhibit this longtime latex devotee. The one that stuck was Belinda Myles, club promoter, lover supreme, and dreamer extraordinaire. Belinda was someone you could always touch, yet getting a grip was like snatching at a butterfly in June. Sometimes Belinda and I wore black together—two ebony swatches cutting through brightly lit L.A. parties and then through each other. It was all good until the night I flipped the script and unraveled our unresolved plot.

Belinda's Meow party was always held at some unlikely looking space known only to true club crawlers, hard-core dancers, and others seeking a libation way after hours. In L.A., despite its glamour, last call for alcohol is one-thirty. Then at 2 A.M. they snatch the glasses right off your table. The thirsty or lonely then sought out Meow for sustenance and seduction. There Belinda, in all her florid loveliness, would greet you with a hug, a salty wisecrack, and if she really liked you, a tab of X to keep you smiling till dawn.

We'd bonded one morning around 3 A.M. My workday had just ended, as the lead singer from some impossibly hot, incredibly mediocre Atlanta vocal trio I'd been squiring around all night had just been led out of the club by his bodyguard. The singer, Devon Lewis, a little shaky after two bottles of Cristal, a joint, and a tab of X, had left with an actress who played the nubile teenaged daughter on a WB sitcom. In my role as publicist/flunky I'd introduced them a mere three hours ago and then watched the hormones fly, with Devon and the actress each vibing off the other's celebrity and counting up the pop quiz points they'd receive for bedding down the other.

Now that they'd moved their negotiations to the Hotel Nikko, I was having one last glass of merlot before heading home. B.I.G.'s "Nasty Boy" was flowing through the speakers when Belinda appeared next to me and rested her petite, perfect little face on my shoulder.

"So, are you through working, Shaft?" "Shaft" was her playful take on "Rod."

"You call what I do work?"

"Baby-sitting was always work to me, and you seem to do a lot of it."

"I've been in here a lot, huh?"

"So much that I've been thinking about asking you to work the door on alternating Tuesdays."

"Thanks for the offer, but I like what I do."

"The pay's good?"

"Not as good as yours, judging by how packed this joint is."

"Well, if I'm clocking like that, why don't I buy breakfast?"

I'd met Belinda maybe six months before this conversation but that morning was the first time we'd really talked. As the sun rose over Sunset we sat at a table in Duke's, indulging ourselves in their legendarily light pancakes. At first I'd fallen into the publicist's trap of the hard sell—"I've worked at Def Jam. I've lived on both coasts. I know Russell Simmons. Hype. Hype. Hype."

Then it hit me that I was already doing fine if she'd invited me to breakfast, considering the number of men who leered at her nightly. So I slowed my roll and got into one of those relaxed conversational flows—who is doing who, who is in rehab, and who definitely, absolutely no longer means anything.

That was all good. Then my insecure nature reared its head. Instead of slipping on my shades against the rising sun and letting her run the show, I had to be intrusive. So under the guise of trying to be smooth, I said, "So, isn't this the part of the conversation where one of us asks if we're seeing other people?"

"It could be," she replied, studying me to see how much of a sucka I might be. "But it's a pretty short conversation. You're seeing a lot of girls. Even one or two women."

"Thank you, I think."

"And I've been seeing a few people and will continue to do so."

"Honesty can be scary," I said back.

"I don't like games unless I'm committed to playing. And I'm just, like, I'm not into total possession, Rodney. I make my own decisions about who I am and what I do."

"No traditional romantic connections interest you?"

Belinda replied, "The life I have now is the one I've always wanted. If you want to win in this town, you've got to feel that way. Babies. A house. A nine-to-five-type mate. Where I come from that's a no-brainer. And for a woman the rules for that life are real basic: dress up, shut up, and know recipes. It's like something Chris Rock would say. My mother did that, and God bless her. My sister does it, and she can kiss my sweet black ass. That's all well and good, but it's not me. I don't wanna live having settled for that."

"Well, it sounds to me that I could be an asset in continuing your lifestyle."

"Every night I like to watch one particular person. See how they move when they're on and when they think no one's looking. Tonight I was watching you, Shaft. About two-thirty you got this look. You stared at your wine and then at the dance floor, and I knew you wanted to be anywhere but where you were, doing what you were doing. You were desperately trying to hide it but it was screaming out from behind your unusually curly eyelashes."

"Do you enjoy your parties?" I asked, not because I wanted to know but because her words undressed me and I needed time to recover.

"You got to look close, Shaft. I smile. I joke. But I'm doing all that with my mouth. Just like you do it. You smile. You joke. You hype. You do it all with your mouth. Everybody can lie well if they really want to. But lying with your eyes—that's a special breed. And me and you don't belong to it."

"Since we're two of a kind, what do we do now?"

"Right now I'm going home and going to sleep. But Monday nights I always go to see the big band at Atlas over on Wilshire. It usually starts around eight. I'll be there at seven. Usually I sit at a table on the right side of the bandstand."

"Would this be a date?" I wondered out loud and she, with admirable slyness, replied, "It would definitely be a meeting."

That was Belinda. Perceptive. Sensitive. Direct but indirect. Always one step removed from my grasp. In my time with her—one month just over a year—I was never in control and rarely on top of things. That was literally true when it came to sex. Belinda didn't view the missionary as her salvation. Sideways. On the edge of tables. With my head on the floor and hers facing the sky. She'd pull out a handkerchief or grab a towel afterward to cleanse the sweat off my brow and chest, which I came to view as a kind of benediction, a blessing from one filled with divine intensity.

Tim saw Belinda a bit differently. "She's a psycho bitch,

homie. Simple as that. You in over your head." My man had never been as consistently negative about any woman I'd ever dated. He thought she was playing me. When Belinda wasn't throwing parties professionally, she partied like a pro. He saw her around when I wasn't and decided, with uncharacteristic naïveté, that somehow she was disrespecting me. This from a man who used to say, "Out of your sight, out of your control," to describe the relationship between his girlfriends and fidelity.

The problem was, and Tim would never admit it, that he had the hots for Belinda and she, at best, tolerated him. Usually women, even ones who really liked me, made some complimentary remark about Tim—his looks, personality, blah, blah, blah. Some of them—churchgoing Amy, for example— were constantly trying to hook Tim up with one of their friends as a way to displace their lust. Belinda wasn't impressed with Tim, which at first I loved and then later distrusted. It was so unlike the other women I knew. So much so that I started to believe Belinda was playing me.

Belinda was very much a new-school woman. In retrospect I realize that her being so up-front about her attitudes ended up making me nervous. I'd trained myself to believe that relationships were manifestations of gamesmanship and an unending desire for control. Belinda subverted all that and it slowly ate at me. It made me realize I was way more traditional than I knew. That reality, exacerbated by Tim's criticisms, led me to walk out on some of the best pussy west of the Rocky Mountains. Meow indeed.

Nineteen ninety-six. A year of penance and earnest attempts at self-salvation. Roberta and I finally agreed to sell our burnt-out shell of a family homestead. We used part of that cash to place Ma in Saint Mary's, a place I'd searched out, selected, and now can barely stand to look at. And it was one smoggy Sunday that August that I accompanied a client, a veteran R&B vocalist contemplating a career in gospel, out to black Hollywood's preferred church, West Angeles, out on Crenshaw.

On any given Sunday Denzel Washington, Magic Johnson, Angela Bassett, and scores of thespians, singers, and sepia-toned entertainment industry functionaries filled West Angeles's first two rows. The VIPs entered through a special side door after dropping off their expensive rides in an exclusive parking area. West Angeles's congregation numbered in the thousands, so services were held, like tightly timed stage shows, at eight, nine-thirty, and eleven. This was one smooth-running institution of religious devotion, so it was good business to have clients turn up in one of the church's front rows to affirm their Christianity and confirm their celebrity.

Amy was sitting two rows behind the celebrity section when we first exchanged eye contact, and I found myself twisting and turning throughout Dr. Charles E. Blake's sermon to smile at the lovely caramel sister in the cream-colored hat. She had slightly slanted oval eyes, suggesting a bit of Asia in the DNA, and a small, pert mouth that parted slightly when I mouthed the words "Meet me outside."

I wasn't sure what she'd do. I'd met women in a lot of places, but this would be my first romantic encounter in church, so I wasn't sure of the etiquette. After the service I slid out the VIP door along with my client when it hit me that the caramel sister would be exiting out the front door into the teeming multitude of West Angeles parishioners coming and going. So, after placing the singer in his beige Beemer, I ventured out to Crenshaw Boulevard toward the church's entrance in search of a black angel in cream.

At most African-American church services there were

many more women outside than men. So the sight of me peering intently at women while wearing my best silver-fox gray Sunday-go-to-meeting suit turned a couple of heads. Just not the one I sought. After about ten minutes of surveying I admitted defeat. I'd thought those pert lips parted for an invitation when they'd likely been the beginning of an interrupted yawn.

My car navigated my disappointed soul out of West Angeles's VIP section as the eleven o'clock crowd rolled in. A block away from West Angeles I saw a lovely caramel body encased in cream slide into the driver's seat of a white Ford Festiva. With the daring of Sandra Bullock in *Speed* I wheeled my ride between a Lexus and a Range Rover, so that as she was starting her engine, I was right beside her.

"Good morning, sister!" I shouted through my open passenger window, and then smiled, using every molar at my disposal. The half-parted mouth that enchanted me earlier reappeared. Her driver's side window rolled down. Now I'd see that smile's true nature.

"Good morning," she replied, tossing the rhetorical ball back at me.

"My name is Rodney Hampton. I saw you at church."

"Oh," she said. "I wasn't sure if you were looking at me or had a nervous twitch." Couldn't tell if this was a joke or a bland observation. Undaunted, I pushed on.

"Have you had breakfast yet?"

"Yes, I have."

I was kinda stuck there. My little adventure in religious romance looked doomed. Then she parted her lips a bit wider. "I always eat before I go to service. Pancakes, bacon, and grits."

"Well, now that you've made me hungry, you could at least

do me the courtesy of coming to watch me eat. I tell you, sista, it's very entertaining."

Here was her moment of decision — sink or swim, hang up the phone or make the connection. She parted those lips again and offered, "I know a place."

"Okay," I happily agreed. "By the way, what's your name?" Amy Davis, she told me, then she and her little white Festiva pulled off, guiding me over to Stevie's on the Strip soul food spot and into her life for six spiritually uplifting months.

In my phone book I found Amy's home number. She lived in a pink house in Leimert Park that was full of sewing needles, gospel tapes, and a big old Bible that I flipped through the many times I slept on Amy's pullout sofa.

That was it. Now I had Sabena, Belinda, and Amy's numbers conveniently listed in my current date book under "Things to Do," right alongside all the relatively normal activities I was pursuing at the start of the new millennium. But then, trying to find love (even if it's in the dog-eared pages of forgotten date books) is, I guess, what we're really here for. At least that's what I muttered to myself as I placed my past back on the upper shelf of my closet.

9

Monday morning, two days after Tim embarked on his new life, I'm deeply mired in my current one. Two press releases to write. Checks to cut to Pacific Bell, Jackson Limousine, American Express. Hit my sister off with some cash. Five invoices to be mailed to deadbeat clients— all at least three months late. Avoid hints from my extremely loyal assistant, Miss Adele Hopkins, that a raise would help keep her bigheaded boy in Nikes. Try for the sixteenth or seventeenth time to get Joseph Kwanza, the head of the local Urban League, to reply to my proposal for their Black History Month fund-raiser.

On the walls of my office I have little inspirational slogans printed up, like HYPE OTHERS—NOT YOURSELF; DON'T BELIEVE THE HYPE—SELL THE HYPE; HYPE IS A DISEASE—ANALYSIS IS THE ANTIDOTE. Over my desk, right above the postcards, telephone numbers, and press releases pinned to the wall, is an enlarged *New Yorker* cartoon that reads "We believe in words not deeds."

My work space, for which I pay $600 a month, is smaller than the walk-in bathrooms at the Peninsula hotel. My one window faces the west and grants me a wondrous view of sunsets over Sunset. I savor any small pleasure since I am in public relations, a business where clients are flaky, demanding, and aren't satisfied with anything less than an hour on *Oprah*. Unfortunately, my best contacts are not in syndicated television but at the area's biggest black weekly, the *Los Angeles Sentinel*. When I'm particularly charming, I can get a listing (with picture!) in the *L.A. Weekly*.

Mostly I represent entertainers. Low-level entertainers.

Jazz organ trios that play Crenshaw bars. Comics who open for Rudy Ray Moore. Non-gang-affiliated Compton rappers who can't get two mikes in the Source.

Thankfully I'm not limited. I represent church groups giving gospel extravaganzas in Torrance. Blockbusters opening in Ladera Heights strip malls. Long Beach swap meets where you're greeted by the Clippers' dancers. You name the roach event and I'll write a press release, place the photo, or get it plugged on public access television. I used to dream about working at a big firm like Rogers & Cowan. Then contemplated building an operation in L.A. that would rival the Terri Williams Agency in New York (I read her book, *The Personal Touch*, five times).

Recently my resolve has weakened and I'm pondering selling perfume or seeking employment at some governmental agency with a health plan. When you run your own business everything is yours—the grandiose dreams and the stream of bills.

Yet in the middle of my business day, when time was precious and work demanded completion, I found time to input my list of 133 names into my aging Apple laptop. My peach-colored paper was becoming worn and crumpled. Grease from my fingers. A coffee stain courtesy of Roberta. So it was time to give it the sense of permanence being saved in a computer file means.

It was strange looking over this list in the logical light of day. I realized how little I knew of these women. I knew their lips. I knew some of their bodies—could still remember which had hair on their nipples, which had lovely suckable toes, and which favored Massengill.

At the end of my inputting I was back where I started—at Belinda, Amy, and Sabena.

I put stars next to those three names and then printed the whole list out. For some reason holding the two sheets of paper in my hand made me hungry. So I told Adele to take messages and I tried to skip out early for lunch.

But my assistant, a highly motivated, heavyset twenty-eight-year-old product of Long Beach University with bright orange hair, matching Hard Candy nails, and a personality almost as lively, wanted some info. "So, how was it, Rodney?" she wondered in reference to the wedding. "You been quiet this morning, so I haven't bothered you, but you can't leave this office without reporting the 411."

"You want the PR version, or what I really felt?"

"PR version first," she said.

"It was a lovely, harmonious coupling of two wonderful human beings."

"And what did you really think?"

"That until the moment Bernice walked down the aisle, Tim was gonna break for the door."

"Rodney, forgive me for saying this 'cause I know this is a sensitive issue for you and all, but I believe your ass is next."

"You think so?" I replied with mock excitement.

"I know it," she asserted with equal mock excitement.

"Tell me when, please. I'd hate to be surprised."

"Sooner rather than later."

"Come on, Adele, if you're gonna be a prophet you gotta give me more than that."

She sighed deeply and patted me on the shoulder. "All right, I'm lying. You are nowhere near ready and I'm not sure you'll ever be."

"That's kind of reassuring, I guess."

"I just said the other thing 'cause I know the wedding upset you."

"That obvious, huh?"

"I've been married twice, Rodney, and been a bridesmaid twice, so I've seen all this anxiety up close and personal. You'll live."

"Thanks."

"You feel better?"

"Yeah."

"So, when's my raise?"

"I'll be back in an hour."

The offices of Hampton Media were on the third floor of an office building on Gower, just off Sunset, near the Hollywood Palladium, KCBS television studio, Pinot Hollywood, and most important, Roscoe's Chicken & Waffles, a black Los Angeles culinary landmark where I dined regularly. It was there that I sat Monday around noon, finishing off my waffle and the last of my four chicken wings, when a woman entered looking as pure, sweet, and caramel as the syrup on my plate. I was sure this was Amy Davis.

Had I conjured her up? Had the list worked like some Southern mojo root, bringing back the lost and lonely? With her back to me she stood at the register looking righteous and lovely, and I did nothing. I didn't move a single muscle. I was immobilized and as silly as a $3 bill. My eyes did all the work. They tugged at the woman's back, forcing her to turn and face me.

I expected a nod. Hoped for a smile. Prayed for an embrace. Instead I got a stare as blank as new fax paper. This wasn't Amy. She was just a woman—a cute woman, but not the one I'd talked myself into seeing.

"Do I know you?" she asked when I continued boring my eyes into her.

"No, you don't," I answered politely. "You just look a lot like someone I know."

"You could do better than that," she replied.

"I wasn't trying to pick you up, beautiful, but if you want to have lunch with me you're welcome." She just smiled and went on her way, which suggested I could have followed up if I wished, but my mind was elsewhere even as I watched her and her take-out chicken wings walk out the door.

10

The nineties, a time people once thought would introduce the paperless office, has in fact been a decade where more trees have been killed than ever before in history. People who can't type a lick now print out at the flick of a key. Which is why I—one of those now-typing fools—regularly drive west on Sunset toward the Kinko's near Crescent Heights. This onetime bank is now a twenty-four-hour temple dedicated to our unending need to copy, print business cards, and rent computers at ungodly hours. On this morning I was stopping at this holy shrine to see how many more oaks I'd sacrificed.

As I entered Kinko's, Kenya Murray, the store's adorable Hershey-dark assistant manager, gave me the "Hold up!" sign and then cut her eyes toward the manager, Mr. Antonio Spillner, a round, ruddy-faced man whose body resembles a fill-in-the-blank oval on a multiple-choice test. While Spillner stared testily at some invoices, I slid back out the door as my friend nodded her approval. This was a problem. Somewhere inside the Sunset Boulevard Kinko's were my new business cards and two-color promotional piece, for which Kenya and I had outlined a "delayed payment" arrangement Mr. Spillner wasn't privy to.

"Rodney!" It was the voice of fair Kenya exiting Kinko's. Though it was early summer she was wearing a blue peacoat that bulged in the front in the most unorthodox way. Kenya's eyes, small and piercing, looked like almonds in the cocoa swirl of her skin. And her smile, well, it was so wide and deep that I can't imagine a metaphor that would communicate its intensity, so I won't even try.

"You're getting fat, sweetness," I joked. "Why don't you let me help you?" I reached down for the box under her coat and she pushed my hand away. "You can help," she replied playfully, "by buying me a burger."

A few minutes later Kenya was toying with lightly greasy fries and my self-control at the All-Star Burger on Sunset. "So when are you gonna hook me up with an audition?"

"I'm not a producer, Kenya."

She rolled her eyes, dipped a fry in ketchup. "But I know you know some," she suggested. "Without an agent, I hear about everything after the fact. You won't take me out, so the least you can do is help me."

"Okay, I do have a meeting coming up with this producer about doing unit publicity on a movie."

"Yea, team!" she said in a cheerleader's voice.

"But I don't have your head shot."

With a smirk Kenya pulled the lid off my box of promo papers and, surprise, there was a very sunny, sexy head shot of Kenya. She leaned forward and batted her eyelashes at me. "I'm always prepared."

"Stop flirting with me. You're too young for me."

"I am not too young for a thing, Rodney."

"Kenya, if you were a fish I'd have to throw you back."

"Fuck you."

"You wish, little girl."

"Oh no, you'll wish, Mr. Hampton. So for now you just take my head shot and get me a job. You'll beg later."

Kenya wasn't really that young. Twenty-three going on twenty-four. However, in the white three-stripe Adidas, black sweatpants, and the blue Dodgers baseball cap, the girl could look fifteen. Good for her acting career. Bad for my rep. Pedophilia was never my thing. Nor was becoming a daddy surrogate for a young woman.

As a rule I tried dating women no more than five years older or younger than me. Sure, I violated that rule a time or two (or three). Still, I kept it in the forefront of my mind, feeling that within that ten-year swing the cultural references, states of mind, and physical plants were relatively compatible.

Outside that zone weird things can happen. You mention records your mate never heard of, they start using slang you don't understand, and then you one day wake up realizing you wore polyester in high school and she wore Tommy jeans. Ultimately it doesn't all add up. Kenya didn't care much for my rules, though I was never sure if it was true love or the need for conquest that made her continue to jock me.

Sometimes you connect with someone you shouldn't be with. They might have bad breath, bad grammar, or plain old bad luck. Still, there's a spark, some chemistry, some gurgle in the gut, and a certain growth in the groin whenever you see her. I had that with Kenya. But I believe connecting with some people, despite all the potential for pleasure, sometimes must be avoided.

The day we met I walked into Kinko's in a hurry before a meeting at Edmonds Entertainment with Tracy Edmonds. "Hello," I'd said to the cute young woman behind the counter, "I need ten copies." Instead of robotically taking my papers and writing out the order form, she picked them up and read out loud.

"Excuse me," I said forcefully.

"Hold on," she ordered.

"Miss," I said.

"Kenya," she answered.

"Kenya, would you stop doing that?"

"Please"—she glanced at the top sheet—"please let me finish this paragraph. I'm feeling it." In the face of such enthusiasm and her bright, delightful delivery, what could I say? She continued on. When she was finished I said, "You read that well."

She declared, "I'm an actress."

"Oh really," I replied playfully. "I thought you worked for Kinko's."

From behind me a hostile voice said, "So did I." A customer uncharmed by Kenya stood behind me with folded arms. A flash of anger crossed her face and I expected her to shift into the kind of neck-rolling anger only sisters can muster. Instead Kenya suppressed it, answering, "I do work here, sir. Forgive me for inconveniencing you."

Kenya's voice was no longer delighted. Now it was professional, crisp, and efficient. "Excuse me, Rodney," she told me. "Let me handle this gentleman's order first." There was something so theatrical in this shift, so willfully dramatic, that it struck me that Kenya was acting, that instead of flexing on the guy, Kenya was using the moment to play.

Over a couple of lunches and a dinner I learned that Kenya Murray was born in Philadelphia and raised in some transitional suburb where white folks were fleeing and municipal workers, people like her parents, were fulfilling their (African) American dreams. Watching Jennifer Jason Leigh in *Rush* as an adolescent made her want to act, and playing the Lady in Red in her high school production of *For Colored Girls* made her love it. Her father, a hardworking second-generation Jamaican-American, wasn't too partial to this impractical career move. Her mother, a wanna-be buppie from Birmingham, Alabama, toiling for the state welfare department, figured it was just a passing fancy.

Then Kenya went up to New York to visit NYU's Greenwich Village campus. Liberated and excited by the area's energy, Kenya—at great expense to her folks—became a drama major and never gave a thought to job security. It doesn't exist for a thespian—one job is just a stepping-stone to the next. The pay for each is different—from Equity scale to $1 million a flick— but it's all essentially piecework that hopefully constitutes a whole career.

When I encountered Kenya she'd already been in L.A. two scrambling postcollege years. Year one had been spent with two roommates in a tenement in a highly creative, hugely vermin-infested Hollywood apartment as she balanced waitressing with acting auditions. Year two she'd landed a commercial for the California lottery and the Kinko's gig, and a tiny one-bedroom on Sweetzer near the gay mecca of Santa Monica Boulevard.

Kenya was a quirky girl. Because she viewed life as one big audition, Kenya was sometimes overly dramatic. I mean if a strong winter breeze passed her face, Kenya would suddenly be Merle Oberon in *Wuthering Heights*. If she argued with you on some point, suddenly you'd be confronted with Angela Bassett as Tina Turner. You never knew when she was going to flip on you and she loved the uncertainty that caused. Between her drama and her youth, I deemed her an unsuitable mate.

But what I deemed and what I desired were at odds. After my first Kenya encounter I'd continued to go by Kinko's and a ritual developed. She'd take my papers and then, on the spot, read a graph or two aloud, irritating her coworkers, pissing off the other customers, and delighting me. Often Kenya worked the overnight shift and I'd roll in after a party at three or four and talk with her until dawn. We'd talk art. We'd talk acting. We'd talk love. Our bond was more romantic than friends, but much less physical than lovers.

As for Kenya's love life, she vaguely alluded to men she knew and dates she'd had. Nothing too serious was going on—at least that's what she told me. Kenya was way too vivacious to be lonely, so I assumed Kenya told me only half or perhaps a third of the truth. Actually I didn't want to know more. Kenya's vagueness kept her door open. We both knew I was free to walk in.

11

My quest seemed over before it really began. So far Amy hadn't returned my calls and I'd spent two long Sundays sitting in vain through the eight, nine-thirty, and eleven services. I contemplated planting myself in front of her apartment in my car, but that sounded creepy and way more desperate than I really was.

Leafing through the *L.A. Weekly* provided new inspiration. Todd McFarlane, the creator of a comic book character named Spawn, was signing copies at the Golden Apple on Melrose an upcoming Sunday afternoon. Though Amy was overtly as devout as the pope and as chaste as any modern woman could be, she had a weakness for comic books, particularly Spawn, a black CIA assassin whose soul was captured by the devil and enlisted in his battle against God. Spawn, however, was more interested in winning back the love of his widow and child than in fulfilling his devilish destiny.

From this tension came the comic book's essential drama (plus pages of graphic, four-color carnage). The comic's premise wasn't one that any Christian denomination would endorse, which in my estimation was why it so titillated Amy. In her bedroom closet, stacked beneath her Sunday-go-to-meeting hats, was a considerable collection of comics, trading cards, action figures, HBO cartoon episodes, a home video of the New Line movie, and an autographed photo of the macho, monosyllabic actor who starred as Spawn in the flick.

On any list of deadly sins Amy's infatuation with Spawn didn't rate a spot in the top seven. "Thou shalt not read *Spawn*" wouldn't even make an expanded list of the Ten

Commandments. Yet for a remarkably straight girl like Amy, this down-low fixation was wonderfully out of character, and therefore quite precious to her.

So on the morning of the Golden Apple signing I slept late, had a leisurely breakfast of whole wheat pancakes at a spot on La Brea, and then around noon walked west down Melrose from La Brea toward the comic shop. There was a line coming out of the Golden Apple of full-fledged nerds, hipster alternative nerds, and aging nerds, many wearing the obligatory glasses and carrying comic books wrapped in plastic.

Whether white, black, Asian, or Hispanic, there was something dark and bookish about the men and women on line, as if they'd all emerged from the same well-appointed yet grungy basement. None of them looked like they'd just arrived from church, so even if Amy hadn't been one of just a few black women on line, her rose ensemble of jacket, skirt, and like-colored loafers would have definitely stood out. I watched her a moment, dropped in a breath mint, and then made my move.

"Amy Davis," I said, and she turned slowly, theatrically, as if she'd known I was coming and prepared for her close-up. Her lips parted again—half smile, half frown.

"How are you, Rodney Hampton?"

"You may not believe this, but I've been looking for you."

"Well, that's interesting," she said noncommittally. "Would you like to join me in line?" She handed me her Ralph's bag full of *Spawn* comics and we chatted amiably about how long the line was and her continuing love affair with the character and how devoted his fans were. I didn't mention my many unreturned phone calls or my mission to find her, since she seemed preoccupied with getting her books signed and I felt it was important to make my sudden appearance seem less predatory than it felt.

After Amy got her five favorite *Spawns* signed and purchased the latest copy of her new passion, *Elf Quest*, we stood awkwardly in front of the Golden Apple. I'd made all the small talk I could. Now I was anxious. My proximity to her, after all my unreturned calls and lingering thoughts and the damn list, made me sweat like the lone brother in an all-white police lineup.

"Can we get together?"

"My number hasn't changed, Rodney. Not since we met. My number has not changed."

"I'm gonna call you tonight."

"Okay," she said cautiously. "If you like."

And then she took the Ralph's bag out of my hand and was gone. Amy strode away from me, her attitude wary yet curious, mine bewildered and excited.

12

said, "Well, you look the same," and my best friend replied, "Stop messing with me, Rod," with more irritation than anger. I was holding two Farmer John hot dogs and a Coke, and Tim had nachos in his lap and a beer in his hand as we sat watching the Lakers and Sonics run layup lines. Tim and Bernice had gotten back two weeks ago but between unpacking, shopping, and (I'm assuming) screwing like rabbits on Easter Sunday, I hadn't hung with him since the wedding.

"C'mon, man, if I can't mess with you, who can?"

"I know, Rod, but damn, nigga, you got to lighten up on this marriage thing. Now that the wedding's over I want to get back into my old rhythm."

"Get back?" I said sarcastically. "Tim, you can't get back. That's through, money. You need to find a new rhythm."

"Rod, when you get down to it, nothing's really changed but her name."

"Okay," I answered as the buzzer sounded, ending warm-ups, and the players returned to their benches for introductions. "Let's test it, then. How many games does she want?"

"What?"

"How many Laker games does she want to go to now?"

Though Tim and I had been going to Laker games for five years, moving down from the rafters through guile and bribes, the seats we shared at the Staples Center were actually in his name, since at the time we bought them he had a higher limit on his credit card. That fact hadn't been a big issue before, but now I anticipated trouble.

Trying to sound reassuring, Tim said, "It won't be a problem, Rod," and shook his head as if I was crazy to even bring it up.

"Oh, you mean you've already put your foot down on this."

"No, I didn't 'put my foot down.' We'll just work it out. You don't go to every game and I don't go to every game. Certain games you'll want more than me, and vice versa. Instead of making hard and fast rules, we'll be flexible and respond to the moment."

As the national anthem played and we stood at attention, I observed, "Money, you sound like a damn marriage counselor. What did you do on your vacation—read *Men Are from Mars, Women Are from Venus* one, two, and three?"

"No," he said as we sat down. "We just read the first book."

"Out loud no doubt."

"Well, yes."

"Oh."

Tim was my best friend and I loved him like the brother I never had. Still, it would be hard getting used to this sensitive version. I mean, reading a relationship book out loud? That was taking things to a whole 'nother level. He was clearly embarrassed by his admission, so I shifted back to common ground—basketball.

As the game progressed we traversed the easy terrain of sports—cataloguing Shaq's free-throw deficiencies, Kobe's ongoing development, and the Lakers' chances of building a dynasty under Phil Jackson's guidance. Tim was my old homie again—opinionated, funny, and carefree. I loved laughing with him again—married or not.

The Lakers collapsed in the last two minutes, with Shaq's legendarily poor free-throw shooting undermining the squad yet again. On the way out of the Staples Center we riffed on Shaq's millions—his record deals, his movies, his commercials—and how we lived in an age where no one was satisfied with who they were. "Being good at one thing," I remarked, "now allows you to be mediocre at everything else." Tim cosigned that observation and then got quiet. When I suggested we stop somewhere for a drink I saw Tim's eyes dart down to the clock in my car: 10:15 P.M.

I was gonna mess with him again but before I could apply the needle Tim suggested we stop at the Shark Bar. "We could get in there before last call."

"You know there'll be women there, Tim. I don't wanna endanger your vows."

"My eyes are still my own, Rod." Now that was my homie Tim talking.

The Shark Bar wasn't as hot as it used to be, but it always had its share of cuties scattered about, either having late dinner or conversing with gentlemen happy to spring for a Sex on the Beach. A reddish brown lady with lots of store-bought hair and her very own breasts stared at Tim from the moment we hit the door. Tim, as was his habit, had a martini. When I remarked on his chesty fan Tim shifted his body sideways, giving the lady shade in an impressive show of integrity in the face of temptation.

Perhaps provoked by some simmering sense of lust, Tim slid into an otherwise unexpected and aggressive celebration of marriage. "The great thing about being married is that you can be sentimental and it's not uncool. You can buy tons of flowers. Enough chocolates to get sick on. All kinds of cute, lovey-dovey shit and your cool card doesn't get revoked. In fact, the more people know you did all this, the higher your standing among friends and acquaintances."

"More like acquaintances than friends."

"True dat."

"But," I wondered, "don't you already miss being free, single, and fly?"

"So far, every damn day," he admitted, "but except for Miles Davis, no one stayed cool forever."

"And he whipped up on women," I volunteered. "But they kept coming back."

"True dat," he agreed again. "You know, Rod, and you can never for a minute let Bernice know I said this—"

"Come with it."

"There's something real masochistic about being married."

"How's that?"

"Well, sometimes—no, a lot of times—you have to just bow down and let yourself be dominated."

"You mean compromise, right?"

"No. I mean dominated, walked on, controlled. A lot of times you just have to give in if you love someone, and let them come out on top."

"Traditionally that comes under the heading of 'henpecked.' Meaner-spirited people might even say 'pussy whipped.'"

"Rod, you have never been in love, so you don't know what the fuck I'm talking about," he retorted. "It's about loving someone so much that their way becomes your way, that making them happy is more important than getting your way."

Out of the corner of my eye I noticed Tim's fan saunter slowly past us and Tim, bless his heart, trying to look without looking.

"What the fuck did Bernice do to you out on Bora Bora? If she can bottle it, you two could be millionaires."

"You really don't get it, do you, Rod?"

"Just explain to me how she became Wilson-Waters."

Tim sighed and explained. "We were laying up in the bridal suite and she was on top of me, her head on my chest.

She told me how happy she was. I told her how happy I was. We started talking about names and partnership and team-work. Next thing I knew I was suggesting we—"

"You were suggesting?"

"Well, she might have mentioned it first, but I'm the one who said let's do it."

"Damn, nigga, go no further."

"Why?"

"You keep talking like that and I'm gonna abandon my quest."

"Quest?"

"For a wife."

I kicked him the ballistics about the list and my mother's words and Amy Davis. I'd been so busy messing with him I hadn't really revealed how much I'd been affected by his mar-riage. Typical of our relationship, Tim had been a catalyst—he did something and I reacted. Still, nothing had been as big as his marriage, nor as weird as my quest.

By the time I'd finished, it was last call at the Shark Bar and Tim had swallowed his martini with unusual speed. "Well," I said finally, "what do you make of that?"

"Bernice expected something like this."

"Oh, did she? And what did the little woman say pre-cisely?"

"That you were likely to get engaged now, within the next year or so, as a reaction to our marriage."

"And why, my brother? I'm sure she had some insightful observations about that."

"She thinks you'll want to catch up. That by getting mar-ried I'm leaving you behind. You know, becoming an adult."

The lights in the Shark Bar were now on full blast. Time to go, yet we'd only begun to scratch the surface. In my head I was searching for a snappy reply, yet nothing came. I just laughed dismissively as if that comment hadn't irked me.

Outside on La Cienega Tim said, "Hey, Rod, I hope I didn't hurt your feelings."

"No, man, you didn't," I replied, half lying. "You just should have told me what you think. Not what she thinks."

"Oh, man, I think it's cool. Look, I'm a civilian now. You still in combat. I got to live through you now. To me it sounds like a plan. I don't know if you'll get a wife, but you might get some pussy, and who's against that? Look, man, I gotta jump. Call you tomorrow."

Shit, it sounded like no one was taking me seriously. Roberta treated me like a teenager. Bernice was expecting a knee-jerk reaction. Tim thought I just wanted some ass. But now I was just more determined.

13

Adele dropped a pink perfumed envelope on my desk. "What are those? X-rated photos?" The address said it was from Caron. You could feel the pictures inside.

"No," I answered. "They're probably wedding pictures."

"Doesn't mean they're not X-rated."

Inside the envelope were, as I expected, Polaroids from the wedding, of the bride and groom, various guests, and a cute shot of me and Caron walking arm in arm. Adele surveyed them all with an appraising eye and then held up the shot of Caron and me. "She looks like a keeper."

"We'll see," I said noncommittally. "Hadn't thought much about it. We'll see."

For lunch I walked down to the Pinot Hollywood on the corner of Gower and Sunset, where I ate broiled salmon and gazed at the photos, fascinated by one of Tim and Bernice cutting the cake. For some reason it reminded me of a morning that followed a frustrating night.

When Tim first started dating Bernice I figured her for just another woman. At best I thought she'd become another episode of *Serial Monogamy*, that prime-time program where Tim committed to a woman for a while until he wasn't committed anymore. That's how we'd lived since college. So I didn't care who Bernice saw me with, figuring she wouldn't stick. There was a period during their courtship when I was juggling like crazy. There were at least two weeks where Bernice must have seen me with four different women. Not long after that, Bernice, apparently starting to feel solid about her place in Tim's life, started messing with me.

One Sunday night Bernice, Tim, and I were waiting outside the theater for my date. Now that previous Friday she'd seen me having drinks with Shavon at the Shark Bar, and that Saturday afternoon, after Tim and I had played ball at the Hollywood Y, Bernice had seen me leaving with the aerobics instructor when she came to pick Tim up.

So first she makes one of those "So who's on the menu tonight?"–type comments, as if to suggest I'm a frivolous, shiftless, jive nigga. I take it in stride. My man Tim seems to like her, so there's no need for me to get salty and make him have to choose sides. At this point I was still confident it would be with me, but why push it?

So I laughed and made what I thought was some self-deprecating kiss-ass remark. "I'm just doing my best to try and find a woman like you, Bernice. I just haven't been as lucky as Tim." This apparently came off more cutting than I intended because my friend gave me a "Back off" look I took to heart.

When Aleshea showed up in front of the theater she kissed my cheek, shook Tim's and Bernice's hands, and quickly flowed into a riff on hair that I excerpt here: "I had to tell the woman at the beauty shop today that no one brushes my hair but me! I'm sorry if I hurt her feelings but it really had nothing to do with her, it's all about me and mine. You see, my mother never knew what to do with hair. She was Danish and my father was in the army. But that's some other drama."

Now my date was not stupid, nor was she goofy. Aleshea just tended to talk too much. To be frank, Aleshea's mouth was a river—an overflowing river. The only time you could dam it was when you kissed her or when she was on her Stair-Master, which she strode religiously every morning. Unfortunately, I did not come by this information some happy morning after. No, I knew about this ritual because Aleshea had, in meticulous detail, outlined her daily routine to me on our previous two dates.

"Anyway," Aleshea continued, "her hair was frizzy and blond. My hair was my hair, with lots of kinks. Now, she never did anything real weird to it. Sometimes it was real cute when she styled it. It just wasn't her hair—it was my hair, my black-girl hair. So I've always been particular how it was dealt with. So I'm sorry how I had to handle it, but that's just how I am. So that's why I was late. So, what movie are we seeing?"

Now, Aleshea's willful loquaciousness in itself was not enough to justify Bernice's contempt, but I believe my date's chief liability was her color. Aleshea had pale skin, reddish hair, and thick legs encased in a black dress. I'd never asked Aleshea if she was mixed but her place of birth—Washington State just this side of Canada—suggested one of her parents was white. Until her hair diatribe I didn't know her mother was from Europe. But for Bernice, Aleshea was just confirmation of her accusation that I just wanted "a red bone," though the truth was, beauty was way more important to me than color.

So the combination of Aleshea's mouth and her color had Bernice radiating enough attitude to turn the evening radioactive. After the movie we headed to dinner, where Bernice was catty and condescending to a talkative but basically nice woman. But I saw that as a sexual asset. It gave Aleshea and me a bond—one that I hoped would lead me into Aleshea's bed.

After dinner I went over to Aleshea's place—she had a condo in Park La Brea, a white-walled high-rise apartment complex that stood out in the midtown district like candles on a cake. We stood by her window sipping wine and looking at the Hollywood hills. I put down my glass, came up behind her, laid my groin against her backside and my lips against Aleshea's neck. When Aleshea let loose a satisfied sigh I just knew I was all in. Then she turned her head toward my ear. "Rodney," she said softly.

"Yeah, baby," I said with extreme kisses.

"Nothing's gonna happen tonight."

I said, "Are you sure?" and went back to my earnest nibbling.

"Yes, honey. I'm giving right now."

"Giving. I love to hear that."

She turned toward me and placed my face in her hands. "I'm giving," she explained, "to the blood doctor."

"Oh."

"So, let's cool down."

"You sure?"

"Let's go over to the sofa and talk."

"Talk? We talk a lot already."

"What? Don't you like talking to me?"

"Oh yeah, baby. Of course I do."

So we moved back to her sofa and she went into a talking jag about her mother that seemed to go on for hours. That's the thing about dating—so much of it is listening to stories, stories that you will often have absolutely no interest in. What did Chris Rock say on HBO? Two hours of therapy for twenty minutes of pussy? Well, there are many nights when feeling her tongue in your mouth is all the penetration you're gonna experience, but there'll be more talking than on an Oprah Winfrey special.

It was two-thirty or so when I got back to Adams Boulevard. It was quiet except for the breathy sound of Tim and Bernice. Talk about on and on to the break of dawn! The two of them just kept going at it—hungry like the wolf. Me, I had blue nuts and couldn't masturbate because of them shouting, "I love you!"—"No! I love you!"—on the other side of the wall. They were batting the word "love" back and forth like a tennis ball. It was kind of ridiculous to me the way they used the act of fornication as a forum for devotion.

But when I woke up red eyed at noon and watched as she poured pancake batter while Tim guided sizzling turkey bacon across a pan, I looked at how they moved and how they joked and realized that just maybe I was wrong about Bernice being just another girl.

The photo of them cutting the wedding cake reminded me of that morning. Food, love, sex, romance—when they all came together it could be sweet. My salmon at the Pinot Hollywood was tasty—well seasoned with a lemon nearby for me to squeeze—but the cake Tim and Bernice had cut seemed more nutritious.

14

Tameka," my sister instructed from the kitchen, "let your uncle win one!"

"No, Mommy," Tameka replied, "if I let him win, he'll never learn how to play."

I was in the middle of yet another pleasurable yet humbling Saturday afternoon at my sister's house. Thirteen-year-old Tameka, the oldest of my sister's clan, had once more defeated me in NBA Jams. This time the trashing came 109–87. Even worse, I lost with the 2000 Lakers versus Tameka's retrofuturistic, gender-bending crew of Hall of Fame old-timers (Kareem Abdul-Jabbar, James Worthy) mixed with current WNBA stars (Rebecca Lobo, Sheryl Swoopes, Lisa Leslie). Her retrofuturistic gender-bending squad gave Shaq and Kobe fits, though in all honesty I have to lay the blame on my shaky manipulation of the controls.

"You wanna play again, Uncle Rod?"

"No, Tameka," I said, rising up from the edge of her bed, "my shooting finger needs a break. Why don't you play someone more on your level?"

"You mean Tawana?"

"Yeah. What's she doing?"

"She's in there vegetating as usual," Tameka said with a smirk. "She's not athletic like me, Uncle Rod." I smiled in agreement—this girl was a star of her middle school's basketball team—though I really wanted to urge her to get away from the NBA Jams controls and go outside to gossip, learn new dances, get hickeys on her neck, and all the other things thirteen-year-old girls are so expert at. Tameka, however, was going nowhere but back to her video game—this time pitting her mixed doubles basketball team against the 1996 women's Olympic team.

In contrast to the interactive Tameka, her sister Tawana existed in a self-created state of catatonia. My eleven-year-old niece sat in the living room wearing CD Walkman earphones while staring at the *Jerry Springer Uncensored* tape through trendy yellow-tinted glasses. Talk about sensory overload— the sound of Tyrese's first album was leaking out of her earphones while yet another choreographed catfight broke out for the amusement of the owlish host as my sister's middle child took it all in behind artificially colored eyes.

I felt like tapping Tawana on her shoulder and giving her a stern talking-to about experiencing the world and not taking it in through the media. Then I caught myself because *(a)* I am part of an institution—publicity—that manufactures pop culture as shamelessly as Springer and *(b)* I'd given that lecture at least three times in the last six months and Tawana's eyes were beginning to glaze over when I stopped by. I know the signals of a woman's fading interest well and all Tawana's lights were flashing red.

So I left Tawana to her own devices and slipped into the kitchen, where Tanina, the last and littlest of my three nieces, teased piles of dough into fat pale rolls. It was her grandma's, my ma's, long-treasured recipe for butter rolls, which had been passed along through generations of our women. At four Tanina was too young to understand all the nuances of making Grandma's rolls. Still, if enthusiasm were the sole requirement for success, Tanina would one day be a butter roll master.

Often I thought Roberta a mess. Too many men. Too many babies. Too little contraception. Yet I had to admit she was a good mother. Outside her door were the deceptively neat homes of South Central L.A., where powerful seductions could be found behind the doors of gated homes and drop-top Caddys. Yet on this Saturday afternoon her daughters were in her home, comfortable and entertained and, at least on the surface, not on the verge of destructive behavior.

My sister supervised a contemporary home—everyone in their own space yet content, either using techno toys or, that oldest of children's pastimes, learning to cook. Yeah, sister was doing all right.

"So," the good mother said, "Tameka kicked your ass again."

"Something like that," I replied. "Of course, I don't play that hard. I mean, she's my niece."

"Uncle Rodney," Tanina interjected. "You said you should always do your best. You said when I do my homework I need to, to, to—"

"Focus," I said, completing the thought.

"Don't worry, baby," my sister offered in a soothing voice. "Your uncle always tries hard. Your sister just kicked his ass."

I took a seat at the table next to Tanina and kissed her small copper cheek. She playfully rubbed it off and then stuck her tongue out at me. I laughed at her and then asked her mother, "Roberta, do you think it's a good thing to curse in front of your baby girl?"

"Ass," she said, sauntering toward me, "is not a curse. It's another name for a donkey and the rear end of a human body. Ain't that right, Boo?" Tanina agreed with her mother and then smiled as Roberta stood behind her and put her hands over hers. She guided Tanina's fingers and together they kneaded the dough into triangles with lovely swirls, these triangles that, baked by a finely tuned oven and watched over by my sister's knowledgeable eyes, would in an hour or so be the highlight of my dinner.

As beautiful as this scene was, it also made me sad. This was how my mother taught my sister. Hands on hands, fingers atop fingers. My mother sadly would be doing no more teaching—at least not physically—and me, what was I contributing to the tradition? As if she was reading my mind—a frustrating ability Roberta actually seemed to possess—she said, "You should have learned how to make rolls, Rod-nee."

Being a glib sucka, I shot back, "So I wouldn't have to eat here?"

"So," my equally glib sister riffed back, "you could get you a wife."

"The way to a woman's heart is through her stomach? That's new."

"Rod-nee, you can't be a player forever. Even that fool Tim realized that. At some point you gonna have to make yourself useful."

I just laughed and watched as she, with Tanina's help, placed the tray in the oven.

"Why don't you teach me now?" I suggested.

"You borderline being a lost cause, Rod-nee," she answered and then closed the oven. Roberta sent Tanina to go wash her hands, leaving me and my sister to joust alone.

"'Cause I can't cook?"

"'Cause you wouldn't bend over backwards to do anything that would make you a better man but you'd crawl on your knees to stay a boy."

"What are you talking about?"

"You always have some excuse for getting rid of a woman. Too dumb. Too sassy. Too busy. Too too. But you're always ready for the next girl you can stay with long enough for the next 'too.' You act like all other triflin' brothers but you smarter than that."

"You mean your babies' fathers?" I spoke in a forceful whisper that I hoped she, but not her daughters, could hear.

"I tried to make a life for them, Rod-nee," she explained with a little edge in her voice. "That they couldn't face up to their responsibility is not my fault."

"But," I said quickly, "it's my fault that I rather exit a situation than give a woman a baby and split."

"It's your fault that you never took a motherfucking risk with a woman in your life. You so skittish, I'm sure not one of those girls knows what happened. You there, you gone. Bet you escape so quick they don't even miss you. You like a trivia question: 'Who was Rodney Hampton?' Answer: 'Some nigga I kinda liked but left so quick I didn't get a good look at.' Shit, if you weren't my brother I'd probably have forgotten you myself."

I was about to tell her to fuck herself when Tameka came into the kitchen to tell me the Lakers game was on. So I pulled back my poked-out lip, sucked back my anger, and went with my nieces to watch the game. It was seven-thirty in Philly, where Shaq, Nick, Eddie, and Kobe were about to confront Allen "the Answer" Iverson, the cockiest, crossover-dribbling, cornrowed-hair-wearing, biggest-Reebok-contract-having point guard in the league.

Despite the pleasure of having Tameka and Tanina up under me, making me feel important and protective, Roberta's words, as they had forever and would forever, gave voice to my self-doubt. I gave too little, I guess, and Roberta clearly gave more than she had to.

Yet in our dysfunctionality we were certainly brother and sister. We responded to the same stimulus—our father's death—with such diametrically opposite responses we formed a complete circle. Three hundred and sixty degrees of messed-up love. She had three babies, three men, and one busy, lonely present. I had 133 lovers (give or take), three lost loves, and one barren, active present. I hated Roberta so much. I loved Roberta so much. And I'm sure she felt the same damn way about me.

Thankfully the Lakers won and my sister cooked expertly, so that by that evening's end I felt more self-satisfied and stuffed than unworthy. After the girls had retired to their rooms and Roberta had wrapped me some leftovers, I told her how her words had semi-ruined my evening.

"What?" she replied. "I hurt your feelings?"

"Kinda."

"Well, just think about this: I love you, Rodney Hampton. But I know you too. I ain't trying to make you mad. I'm trying to make you think."

"I hear you."

Then Roberta threw me a bone, aka a compliment. "Besides, with all the uncle training you getting, you are bound to be a good father."

"Yeah," I agreed, "and look at all the prime baby-sitting talent you got here."

Back in my apartment I sat on my sofa watching *Sports-Center* and noticed how lifeless my place was. No little-kid toys. No art class drawings. No *Seventeen* magazines. No textbooks. No wide array of cereal. No butterfly barrettes. No crayons. No report cards. No smudges by the light switch. No children learning the lessons of their grandma.

Just me and replays of alley-oops and silly market-driven

nicknames and ham-fisted puns by announcers and a remote control I punch with the rapidity of a fourth-grader shaking his leg during a spelling bee. One woman short? Seemed like I was missing more women than that.

15

Timothy Waters Jr. had his office on the second floor of a pale white office building on Crenshaw not far from MLK Boulevard and Magic Theaters. I remember when it was just Tim and a secretary. Now he had a staff of six, had been profiled in a half-page piece in *Black Enterprise* magazine (courtesy of yours truly), and was a prized member of every small-business association east of La Brea.

Waters Real Estate had evolved from selling black working-class families their first middle-class homes to selling new immigrants the working-class homes of displaced African-Americans. Tim worked in a world where the transfer of property was conducted between people of color 90 percent of the time, using money from banks that were white owned 80 percent of the time. Because of the nature of Tim's clientele, his busiest hours were often 5 to 8 P.M., when workingmen who spoke various Spanish dialects sought homes outside the old Hispanic 'hoods like Boyle Heights.

This particular evening I listened to Tim's spiel through the partially opened door of his office. Like any good salesman, Tim sold dreams along with concrete and dirt. "There's not much more to life than a wife, a kid, and a home." He spoke as if each word were honey. "They form the triangle of life. They shape you. They give you definition and a sense of purpose." I was sitting at the desk of Tim's just departed assistant, trying not to chuckle as I eavesdropped.

"It may sound strange coming from me, but owning your own home is about manhood, about putting away childish things and accepting the responsibilities of being a man. Are you ready for it?"

"Yeah, sure," a small, clearly humble man replied in the singsong English of a working-class Chicano.

"I know you, Mr. Lopez. You have a lovely wife, a great son, and two sweet girls, so I know you know it's time to solidify your place in this city. The places we're gonna look at tomorrow are part of you telling the world, 'I'm ready and able.' *Sí,* Mr. Lopez."

"Yeah, sure," he replied again, and I now wondered if Mr. Lopez was more bewildered than impressed by Tim's game.

"Okay, we'll meet tomorrow at 823 West Street—just one block over from Crenshaw."

Mr. Lopez was a sturdy man with beefy arms, an unembarrassed beer belly, and skin the color of sandpaper. He wore khaki pants and a shirt with the words "Parks Dept. City of Inglewood" stenciled on the back. He nodded a greeting at me as he headed out the front door.

"That was one hell of a speech, Tim," I announced. "Maybe Bernice needs to burn your copy of *Glengarry Glen Ross*, money."

"Yeah, I guess I've been getting carried away lately."

"What's with all this manhood and responsibility stuff?"

"A lot of my customers respond to it, Rodney. Nowadays most of my buyers are Hispanic—Mexican, Salvadoran. Some from Equador. They are strong as hell on family and manhood issues. All I'm doing is letting them know I get it—that I'm not some jive black guy just trying to jack them, but that I feel for them. Besides, these days I mean it."

There was a big map of L.A. on the wall across from his desk. From below Culver Boulevard, on out to LAX, and then south through Inglewood, Lynwood, and Compton, Tim had little red, blue, and yellow tacks stuck to it. "The red tacks are properties for sale," he explained. "The blue ones are awaiting closing. The yellow ones are recent sales."

"Looks like black folks are selling cribs like crazy," I observed.

"Basically that's what's happening," he said and then moved over to the map, pointing as he spoke. "Our folks are getting old and retiring. A lot of them are heading back to Texas, Louisiana, wherever. Their kids don't want the spot and are heading out to the Valley if they got some paper and out to spots farther east like Pomona if they don't."

"Pomona? Shit, that's just three degrees from hell, isn't it?"

Tim shrugged. "I just sell it, I don't judge it. Within ten years there'll probably be as many black folk in South Central as there are on the Dodgers."

"You think?"

"Rodney, what do you think I do all day? I got demographic breakdowns. I got census figures. I'm out here trying to sell. Your family."

"Yeah."

"Your family is typical."

"I got it," I said, cutting in. "We sold the family homestead to some people from Guatemala."

"Word," he agreed. "It's people like you that are making sure my wife gets the mansion of her dreams in a gated community. Remember our bachelor pad on the fucked-up side of Adams?"

"Yeah."

"Now a family of eight is squeezed up in there."

"Damn, that place barely had room for two."

"These folks, Rodney," he said thoughtfully, "they live like they really believe whatever doesn't kill them makes them strong." He moved back behind his desk and scooped up his coat. "Okay, my man, this spot better be hittin'."

The Blaxican Cafe was a spot on La Cienega a few blocks south of Pico that I'd been approached about representing by the owner, Leroy Martinez. Leroy's father was Chicano and his mother black, so he grew up with a split personality in predominantly Hispanic East L.A. Part of Leroy was a low rider, part of him a soul brother. For most of his fifty years Leroy had toiled as a chef at traditional Mexican restaurants, while in his spare time developing a unique culinary blend of his mother's and father's heritages that he called "blaxican."

One of his cousins, a busty Latina named Flora who I'd dated a few years back (number eighty-seven on my scorecard), recommended me when Leroy started looking for hype. Blaxican food was a unique concept, perhaps too much so, but I figured that's what made it promotable. Before our formal meeting I decided to come in on the down low, check the place out, and eat as a customer, not an employee.

Tim and I were grooving on a tasty concoction called sweet potato guacamole when Circus strode into the restaurant in a cowboy hat, long vanilla-colored duster, and cowboy boots with pencil toes. "What kind of spic nigga place you got us at, Rodney?" was Circus's greeting. Tim laughed and I felt a headache coming on.

Circus was Tim's "other" best friend. They'd been on the USC football team together and shared many fun times nursing injuries and using medicinal amphetamines before games. Circus brought out Tim's jock instincts, while I played into Tim's more enterprising side. He'd go to strip clubs with Circus and act stupid. He'd go to clubs with me to act suave.

Circus and I were Tim's yin and yang, which generated a

love-hate tension between us. We both loved Tim and mostly hated each other, though we both tried not to let it go there. But that I'd been Tim's best man (and he hadn't) didn't make Circus like me one bit more.

Circus aka Theo Morris talked a lot but very rarely about himself. He was a man of opinions and observations but introspection was not his thing. I really had no idea what he did other than "work in sales," though he'd made it clear to me numerous times that he wasn't involved in drugs, other than steroids when no one was looking. Circus was a big showy man whose face didn't hide any idea that passed through his shallow mind.

Apparently he'd just come back from Japan 'cause he spent much of our dinner describing Tokyo nightlife and ordering (and drinking) Kirin beer like water. And as had always been my experience around Circus, he was hard on our waitress, even threatening to withhold a tip if she didn't "tighten up her game."

Tim winced at his ex-teammate's overbearing manner, but as usual he didn't say anything. So if he didn't, I couldn't. That's the way it worked with these two no matter how much Circus's behavior made my butt chafe. Finally, when Circus snapped at our waitress about his lukewarm fried chicken fajitas, Tim leaned over to his pal and whispered ever so gingerly, "Don't you think you're being a little rough on the lady?"

"Rough?" Circus looked at Tim, then at me, as if he couldn't believe the question. "I see you don't understand what we're dealing with here. You see how big that woman's chest is?" Our waitress was a size 36C or so, though otherwise she wasn't very remarkable. Knowing Circus, I couldn't wait to see where this was going. "Well, let me tell you that you can't trust a woman built like that. My women have big butts but little tits and I do that for a reason." I kicked Tim under the table as he tried desperately to keep a straight face.

"That's because girls be lying," he announced. "It could be plastic surgery. It could be a push-up bra. It could be a very hairy man with plastic stuck on his chest. But with a small-titted woman you know what you're getting. It means she's come to terms with her body and that she's comfortable with herself. A girl with a small chest is not lying with her body—she's telling you the truth."

If you lived in L.A., a city that profited by illusion, there was no more socially accepted illusion than fake titties. If movies were make-believe, breast implants were fantasies made concrete. It was technology turning flat flesh into bright headlights. It was a lie the town saluted and Circus, despite his bugged-out logic, made a certain kind of sense.

Perhaps the look of tacit agreement on my face emboldened Circus to include me in on his next rant. "You think our man has changed?" he asked me in reference to Tim. At first I resisted the bait, replying, "It's supposed to change you."

"But has it?" he continued.

"Why," Tim cut in, "are you talking like I'm not here?"

"Look, we're your best friends, right?"

Tim nodded affirmatively, though he looked worried about what he was really agreeing to.

"So who's gonna see the change better than me and your boy here? You living it, so you got no perspective."

What I added was, "The marriage didn't change him. It was the decision to commit that changed him. The ceremony and all that just confirmed what he'd already decided months before."

"I like that, Rodney." It was Tim. "I think that's how it's supposed to work. It's a gradual thing."

"Bullshit." This was Circus. "You ain't changed one damn bit. You dressing it up good. You making all the moves but you still a pussy hound, Tim, and sooner or later you'll start barking and wagging that tail of yours."

Very calmly Tim said, "I'm married, Circus."

"And what about the night before your bachelor party?" A leer passed Circus's face that would have scared a Sunset Boulevard hooker.

"You aren't my friend, you stupid motherfucker." Tim was red with embarrassment and glee, like he'd been caught by his father screwing his baby-sitter in the basement. My dinner companions laughed hard and giddy. There was a big joke happening at the table that I hadn't heard the setup for.

"The night before the bachelor party?" I said with the utmost curiosity. "I thought you had a business meeting."

"I did."

"I surprised him, Rodney. I knew he was meeting some home owners out at Aunt Kizzy's and met him there. I knew you'd keep the bachelor party pretty tame — not wanting to get in bad with Bernice and all that. But I wanted Tim to get his freak on before holy matrimony took control."

"Tim," I started, but Circus cut me off.

"Hey, I told him not to tell you or anyone else. It was our own little secret. A flashback to our days as Trojans, so to speak."

"So someone tell me what went down."

"You mean," Circus laughed, "what came up." Tim broke into another round of laughter as Circus began. "I took him out to this spot I know by LAX. In the front it's a strip club, but if you make an arrangement with the management, you can go into some rooms in the back."

"Circus," Tim informed me, "has become something of an expert on these joints."

"So," Circus continued, "we get in there and my man tells me he particularly likes two girls—a fly Latino girl and, you'll love this, a sister who looks like Bernice."

I had to chuckle at that. Even at the strip club he couldn't escape that woman. "The difference," Circus added, "was this Bernice had some lying-ass 38Ds. So when he went to the men's room I did some negotiating."

Tim picked up the thread now. "When I came out of the rest room they were there, waiting on me. They took me out in the back and gave me a twenty minutes I'll remember a long time."

"Told you." Circus sat with his arms folded with a satisfied grin. "Precommitment, postcommitment, it don't matter. Hound to the bone."

"No, Circus, it does matter." The leer fell from Tim's face and his newer look—the married man happily under wraps—reappeared. "That was then. I was still technically single. But I did feel guilty."

"Not when they were double-teaming that dick." That was, you probably guessed, Circus.

"I did feel guilty, Circus. And I felt bad at the bachelor party too. You know what, gentlemen? I am very content right now. Very."

"I believe you, Tim," I said supportively.

"All right, Tim," Circus said and then took a long drag on his latest beer. "So let's go to that strip club right now. Let's see how strong those vows are."

Tim said, "Fuck you!" He didn't say it mean, though. He spoke with a twinkle, as if the challenge of proving his fidelity appealed to him. There was a moment when the challenge was going to be taken up. I was sure of it. Then Circus pulled back.

"Nah," he said casually. "I shouldn't even be pushing it like this. I know married men who go to strip clubs all the time."

"Yeah," I volunteered, "old men who aren't getting any at home. I can testify as Tim's ex-roommate that he and Bernice are doing the nasty with gusto."

Tim raised his glass in a toast. "Amen," he said. I raised my wineglass and chimed in. "Amen."

We looked over at Circus. He looked back at us, shrugged, and then raised his bottle. "Amen." We clinked glasses and then motioned for the check. When our much-maligned waitress delivered the check, Circus grabbed it. "It's my pleasure, gents."

Out on La Cienega Boulevard it had dropped down to the fifties and I buttoned my leather jacket as Tim and I walked toward our cars. "Your ex-teammate is really on some shit, Tim."

"Yeah. No question. Hey, Rodney, sorry for not telling you about that night with Circus. It wasn't something I was proud of."

"It's cool." It wasn't really. But what's done is done. "So tell me something, Tim." We were standing by my Mustang. "What does Circus do for a living nowadays? He never talks about work. Yet he's always traveling and always has something ill on his mind."

"Well, you're not gonna believe this—he told me not to tell you, but what the hell—Circus makes porno flicks."

"Directs?"

"A little now and then. But mostly he stars in them."

"Circus is a porno star?"

" 'Star' may be pushing it, but he works. He's actually popular in Japan. Does films there all the time. Even ones where he doesn't have to screw. I think this porno biz is where all that breast stuff comes from."

"Damn, Tim, you got any more wild secrets I should know about?"

"Yeah, one. You may not still believe this, but you are my best friend."

"Word."

"To the motherfucking mother."

We hugged good night and then, as he walked away, I threw in, "Kiss the little woman good night for me."

"I'll tell her you said good night," he said as he started walking away, "but I'll kiss her for myself."

16

When I got home that night I tried Amy Davis's number again. Twice I'd called after that Sunday we'd met and twice she hadn't called back. Her answering machine message was "Thank you for calling. I'm not home right now but I can't wait to speak to you. So leave your name, number or numbers, and a brief message. God bless."

God bless. She kept a Bible by her toilet for quick reference when consumed by nature. I thought of her on the toilet, leafing through John or Luke, looking for the proper quotation to describe her feelings toward me as my voice floated into the bathroom.

In life, three was a charm or a curse—a trilogy or a strikeout. Three wasn't in balance like two or four could be. It was decisive. It was one thing or the other. It was one right or one wrong. Definitive and precise. So I called a third time, knowing this was it. I'd forced myself on her at the Golden Apple, but perhaps she wasn't gonna answer any of my calls just to prove how foolish I was.

The answering machine was on again. Her voice, full of God's love and inviting as hell, emanated from my receiver.

"Hey, it's Rodney. Maybe me calling wasn't a good idea. I don't know. I just want to see you. But maybe—I mean more than maybe—you don't want that. I—"

"Rodney."

"Hey."

"Rodney, I'm sorry. I've been busy."

"Sure. I understand. I mean, sure."

"So," she asked tentatively, "you still wanna get together?"

"Absolutely. I don't have an agenda. I mean, I just want to catch up. If that's cool with you?"

"What are you doing Friday evening?" she asked cautiously.

"I am totally free."

"Come over, then."

"For dinner?" My voice was mad excited. "You still cook good?"

"I haven't forgotten a thing, Rodney."

I ignored the potential implications of that response and replied, "So, how about seven-thirty? Eight?"

"Eight-thirty, okay? We'll talk then, Rodney. Lots has gone on."

"I hear you."

That Friday, I drove by Rich's supermarket on Wilshire and picked up a bottle of cranberry juice (Amy used to devour the stuff), then made a left onto La Brea, going from my hip, multiracial 'hood out toward Leimert Park, one of the nicest 'hoods in tan L.A.

Amy lived in a pink two-story stucco house with a porch, a palm tree, and white trim. The house was well maintained and looked like the owner had painted the trim since my last visit. I parked across the street, slipped on my rust-colored blazer, and acted casual as I strolled up the walkway, though my stomach was bubbling. I paused outside Amy's door, affixed my professional smile upon my tense, way too revealing frown, and then remembered I'd left the roses I'd purchased that afternoon on my office desk.

When Amy opened the door I took serious inventory of my ex. That smile of hers was unchanging—I imagine she'd popped out of the womb with it and the undertaker would be admiring it while administering the embalming fluid.

Her eyes were dark and hooded, like a sky covered with

clouds, and her body, thick and lovely in that cream dress a few years back, looked stouter and more matronly. "You look good," I announced with all due professional insincerity.

"You don't mean that," she replied after giving me a friendly hug.

"Yes, I do," I said, lying well. "You feel like a woman."

"Oh really," Amy said as she led me in. "So when we met you were mistaking me for a teenager?"

"No. You just look more mature now."

"Fat," Amy said flatly. "That's what you mean, Mr. PR Man. But that's okay. I always did enjoy hearing you talk."

And so I did. As Amy completed the meal—tossing together a salad as the lasagna warmed in the oven—I recounted my less than brilliant career, dropping in the current gossip about Bobby and Whitney, Will and Jada, Halle and Eric. It was light, it was fun, and best of all, it was all about no one we really knew. Whatever our own issues were, they were camouflaged, at least for a while, behind the celebrity gossip that binds us all into one big nosy community.

Amy's place had changed quite a bit since my last visit. A new picture of Jesus Christ was on the wall near her gold-framed black-and-white portrait of Martin Luther King Jr. The plastic she used to cover the furniture was gone. In its place were a hip-looking shabby-chic sofa and love seat. There was also a glass coffee table and a large mirror over the sofa. The big Bible was still by the stereo but it was in a red leather binder now and even her television looked newer and several inches wider.

When I commented on the new decor Amy replied, "I can't take all the credit," in a strange tone. I figured it was just referring to some girlfriend she'd fallen out with.

When she asked about my mother the evening took a melancholy turn and never got straight again.

"She doesn't sound good, Rodney."

"No," I agreed, "she doesn't. And if you saw her, well, it would just make you cry."

Amy brought the plates into the dining room and we sat at the table. "Sounds," she suggested, "like she's lost the will to live."

"Well, she's never been the same since the fire."

"It's like that house represented your father, Rodney."

"Yeah. You might be right."

"So maybe it was like he died all over again. God bless his soul. God bless hers too."

"The funny thing is, as distant as she can be, she's actually putting pressure on me to get married." This made Amy chuckle and say, "Poor thing," which was obviously my cue to apologize. My real face came through now. Guilt took center stage. "Amy, you've been so sweet to let me come by. You're even feeding me. But I believe I have some explaining to do."

"Don't," she said firmly. "Don't even go there. Don't apologize. Don't say you're sorry. Don't talk about hurting my feelings, because you don't know a thing about hurt feelings." Her riff over, Amy softened and offered me some wine.

"You're drinking now?"

"Just some wine. It's in the Bible, you know."

"Yes, it is."

"Well, then."

It was a tart red wine that went smoothly with the lasagna. Over our first glass I tried again. "So, we're gonna act like nothing happened?"

"Nothing did, Rodney. Not really. Whatever you think you did was just a little sumpthin' sumpthin'."

"It meant that little to you?"

Amy sighed, paused, and (I guess) figured she'd have to go there with me. "In retrospect, Rodney, our relationship was nice," she began. "But I wasn't giving you what you wanted, and me—I wanted a more devout man. You were a polite Christian, Rodney, and I wanted someone who had more passion for Christ."

"And you found him?"

"I guess you could say that, Rodney." She looked down at her plate and then at me. "I don't trust men very much anymore."

"I hope I had nothing to do with that."

"Well, Rodney, you certainly didn't help. But it really wasn't just you. In a way it was a lot of men. Disappointment builds up. Then you look at it. You figure out what it means."

"Amy, I can't believe you sound so cynical."

"Well, you know I wasn't always like this. I wouldn't have said any of this before. Now I can only look at what life has shown me."

"But Amy, you're a Christian."

"What? I'm supposed to ignore my life? Loving Jesus Christ hasn't made me a fool, Rod. If anything, it's helped me see men for what they are. If you haven't truly embraced Jesus Christ, if you are not living a righteous life, you are not to be trusted. And sometimes even then."

"What if in your heart you're a good person?"

"When was the last time you read the Bible I gave you?"

"Yesterday."

"And before that?"

"The day before that."

"And before that?"

"I don't remember."

"So you got in two days of Bible study. Two days of getting ready to see me again. Yet back when it might have meant something special to me you didn't crack the Bible."

"That's not true. I—"

"So you come back into my life, knowing who I am, with two days of Bible skimming in you, and I should trust you? You figure you can finally talk your way into my snatch?"

"You're playing with me, Amy, and that's cool. I can take it. And as always, the food's good. But something else is going on. Something worse than me dropping you off in front of the church. If you wanna tell me, I'm ready to hear."

She looked at me thoughtfully and then sighed. "George Davidson Jr.," she said. "He was the reason I never called you. When I walked into choir practice that night he was standing just inside the door. He was looking down at a program and then he looked up at me and he smiled and held out his hand. It was as if he was waiting for me. He joined the choir and what an addition he was. What a beautiful voice George Davidson Jr. had. Sounded like Andrae Crouch. I stood up there singing and all I was thinking was, right there in West Angeles Church, God had blessed me with the man I was supposed to marry."

I got very afraid now. There was no ring on Amy's left hand and no joy on her face. This tale was gonna end bad. No question about that, so I tried to back down. "Amy, you don't have to tell me any of this. You know it's really none of my business."

"I know it isn't. But you came back expecting to see me as I was before. I'm not that woman anymore, Rodney."

"I see."

Now Amy got real dreamy eyes. I was her guest but when she started telling her story, it wasn't just for me. "George Davidson Jr. had the most impeccable manners. He held the door. He pulled out the chair at the table. He never forgot a birthday or an anniversary."

"Anniversary? How long were you with this guy?"

"He remembered the date of the day we met. On that date every month he gave me a bouquet of flowers."

"So," I cut in, "how much did he steal from you?"

"From what I've said you know that?"

"I know a little about men, Amy, and the only man who's that attentive is a pimp, a gigolo, or a straight-up con man. So which was George Davidson Jr.?"

"Could I tell it, Rodney? I'll tell you what happened, but let me tell it how I feel comfortable, okay?"

"Okay, Amy. I'm sorry. Go ahead."

"George always used to say, 'God blesses those who plan.' I'd love it when he talked like that. When I was seeing you, Rodney, you were very sweet."

"Thank you."

"But you never had plans."

"What do you mean? When I was seeing you I started up my PR company. I was seeking out space. I was recruiting clients. You even helped me pick out the typeface for my stationery."

"Your plans were always for yourself, Rodney. Not once did you ever make plans for us."

"I disagree."

"For the long term, Rodney. You could plan a night, but I never felt you could plan a life. You understand me now?"

I felt like leaving now. I'd been insulted, dissed, ridiculed. But now I had to know—really had to know—what had happened to this woman. Suppressing my anger, I suggested, "So, this George Davidson Jr. was planning your life?"

"Yeah, he was. We talked about how many babies was the right number."

"And what number was that?"

"Three. A boy, a girl, and a boy. In that order."

"That's what you and George Davidson Jr. decided?"

"Yeah. That's what we did."

"Anything else, like where you wanted to live?"

"A condo in Marina Del Rey 'cause he loved to go boating."

"Okay. I've heard enough, Amy. Where is George Davidson Jr. now?"

"I don't know for sure. The police think—"

"The police?"

"The police think he's back in Vegas. Apparently that's where he's based."

"God blesses those with a plan."

Anger flashed across her face—she wasn't feeling me right there. "Do you want to know, or not?" I apologized and she resumed.

"He said we needed something of our own. Something we could plan together."

I was feeling jealous when I said, "Whatever he did later, he made you love him."

"Yes," she replied softly, "he did."

"So tell me the bad part now, Amy." I wasn't asking—I was pleading. "I want to hear it now."

It started about three or four months into their time together. George Davidson Jr. mentioned buying a boat and how much the water meant to him. They'd go out to Marina Del Rey to walk along the docks and gaze at boats with

97

George Davidson Jr. explaining the ups and downs, ins and outs, stems and sterns. "The ocean was the Lord's greatest creation," he told her. "It's where life comes from and where, in all its variety, it blossoms under his eye. We're made of water and most of the world is too. Water is our truest connection to God."

Anyway, his credit, due to circumstances Amy didn't really understand (and clearly wasn't intended to), was shot. Between his singing, Bible quoting, and boat talk Amy was dazzled, supportive, and willing to cosign a loan with an out-of-state finance company George Davidson Jr. found. All her numbers—credit cards, social security, bank accounts—were given with love. So was, if I read correctly between the lines, her closely guarded chastity. George Davidson Jr. got access to everything that wasn't nailed down and a thing or two that had been on lockdown.

"He got all your savings?"

"No. He left me something."

"Nice guy."

"Because it was fraud, my bank and the credit card companies have been understanding. They don't blame me. In fact I bought all this furniture right after it happened. Everything in here reminded me of him."

"What was George Davidson Jr.'s real name?"

"Yusef Huggins. And Lionel Hurt. And Ricardo Humes."

"Damn."

"He apparently lives in Vegas, travels to cities around California and Nevada, and then disappears back into that cesspool."

"Right out in the middle of the desert." I had to smile at the irony of the man who loved water running his game from out in Nevada. It was mad funny if it wasn't so foul. "And I thought I'd had an impact on your life." Amy was starting to look a little teary eyed but before I could say anything she suggested we go to the movies.

The rest of that night Amy was as fragile as a snowflake and I kept waiting for her to evaporate before my worried eyes. We drove over to the Magic Johnson Theaters off Crenshaw and saw some action movie with Bruce Willis and a couple of black folks in the cast. Amy appeared mildly entertained, as if venting to me had, at least for a moment, cleansed her mind.

Me, I was so sad. I felt bad for Amy and her big soft heart. Had my minor betrayal set Amy up for this bigger one? Perhaps I'd so weakened her that George Davidson Jr. smelled her blood in the water and moved in like a shark. But, no, that was my ego talking—that would be overestimating my impact on her life. I was just a blip on Amy's screen, a small disturbance overwhelmed by and vaguely remembered in contrast to the abuse visited upon her by her next man. After the movie I didn't know what to say, so we drove back to her apartment in silence. "Can I call you?" I asked when we'd parked in front of her place.

"I like you, Rodney, but you know I'm not really over all this."

I slid my professional face back into place and spoke with practiced optimism. "You are good people, Amy. You will be all right."

"All right, yeah." Her voice was as wan as mine was false. "But I'm not sure I'll ever believe in things like I used to."

Now I really went for the positive spin. "God," I said forcefully, "will always be there for you, Amy."

"Yeah," she agreed reluctantly, "but I'm worried I won't be there for him."

I kissed her with more sympathy than passion and then, as

I did years before, watched her exit my car and enter her house. A little wider. A little slower. Still strong and lovely. I savored this view of Amy Davis while slowly crossing her name off my list.

17

My sister's hands were magical to me. Now, don't get me wrong—her voice grated, her words stung, and her attitude toward me left a lot to be desired in the area of familial respect. Yet when she did her thing, it was something to behold. Back when Bo Derek put braids in the American imagination, Roberta was a girl, a child really, who had already mastered the twirls, turns, and above all, twists crucial to braiding black folks' hair. It seemed girls and guys would travel from all around South Central just to sit on our stoop and let Roberta manipulate their woolly heads. This was a gift not handed down from Ma, but one that sprung directly out of Roberta's soul.

Black hairstyles are fluid and dramatic, so for any given six months to a year, braids can take a backseat to other stuff, but my sister was always in demand. No matter the hot style of the moment—be it greasy curls or baldies—someone in the 'hood was always looking to get their hair braided. Roberta's natural dexterity led her to master a wide range of styles—from the casamas braid to the Senegalese twist and the silky dread. She could create the regal Angela Bassett look, the Janet Jackson of *Poetic Justice*, and the long straight trademark braids of Brandy. Whatever design you sought, Roberta Hampton could provide.

Despite her mastery at kneading hair, it wasn't until her third pregnancy that Roberta took weaving seriously as a cash cow. Before then it was just something to do for friends. Sure, they tipped her, and she'd often receive offers from various salons to join them, but unfortunately, my sister's main focus was men, not hair, and no amount of cajoling by Ma and me changed that. It was the reality of her pregnancy by Tanina's father—a married liquor store owner in Inglewood—that finally got Roberta to take stock of her life and appreciate her magic fingers.

So to add to her mix of public assistance and child support from two of the three babies' daddies (the liquor store owner acted like Roberta had Tanina by virginal conception), Roberta opened for business. Together we'd built a mini salon in her garage, but most of her work seemed to happen in the kitchen as butter rolls baked, kids studied, and Oprah charmed the masses.

When my business was slow and sometimes even when things were busy, I found myself sitting in Roberta's kitchen, scarfing down rolls as I watched my sister's fingers. I guess the truth was it reminded me of our mother. Not that Ma was a hair-twisting demon like Roberta. But there was something about my sister ministering to all these needy heads that comforted me. So even when Roberta got on my case it was hard to leave.

"Did I tell you what my brother was into now?" Roberta was threading a string of neon yellow hair into the dark roots of Destina Troutman, the heavyset wife of a local grocery store manager. Destina was chunky but funky. Despite the folds of flesh around her belly Destina carried herself with the confidence of a lady who had it going on. She was sexy enough that in my early, callow twenties, I might have given her a tumble, but thankfully I now had larger goals.

"No, girl," Destina replied, "but right now I got all the time in the world, so don't leave out a thing."

"Well, that man over there—"

"You mean me, your brother? Remember that as you tell it, so you don't get yourself in trouble."

"As I was saying, *that man* over there, well, he went and made a list of all the women he's slept with."

"How many is that?" Destina asked excitedly.

"One hundred fifty."

"What!"

"No," I corrected, "one hundred thirty-three."

"That's still a real round number there, Rod-nee," Roberta said, and Destina, eyes dead on my groin, said, "Amen." Then she followed up, wondering, "So what you gonna do with that list, Rodney?"

"He's gonna marry one of them women, right, Rod-nee?"

"Marry them?" Destina was surprised and a bit disappointed. "Oh, I thought you were planning on running through them all again."

"No," I replied firmly, "that's not my intention."

"Yeah, Destina, my brother is looking for true love."

"Shit," Destina interjected. "I'm just looking for a new love. Why you wanna get married anyway? Just have yourself a baby and be a baby daddy. That's what most people do now anyway. I'm one of the few fools out here who's married nowadays."

"But," I offered, "your husband's a good man. He manages a store. He stays home. He's a good father and all that good stuff."

"And I haven't had a good nut in ten years. Not one he helped me get anyway."

"Don't listen to her, Rod-nee. She loves that man to death."

"Uh-huh, tell another lie like that and the ceiling's gonna fall right on your lying head, and I need my hair braided, girl, so relax yourself and tell the truth."

We all laughed. Destina was a feisty lady but I knew she cared for Mr. Troutman as much as she loved joking about her sex life. She was sort of the Rodney Dangerfield of Roberta's braiding set—take my grocer, please!

"So," Destina inquired, "what's really up with this list, Rodney?"

"It's simple, I guess. There are three women on this list that, in retrospect, could have been my wife. So I've been trying to find them to see what's up with them now."

Roberta, sarcastic as hell, added, "You know this man isn't my brother, right? He was left on the porch when he was fresh out the oven and he's been undercooked ever since."

"You know he's about seventy percent crazy," Destina volunteered, "and thirty percent all right."

"You better explain that thirty percent to me, Des, 'cause I'm confident he's one hundred percent wrong."

"I gotta say I don't believe there's anything wrong with digging up an old lover. Like there was this guy Bilah. I was twenty-three and he was nineteen. I met him at a gas station over on Manchester. He offered to pump my gas. I really didn't need his help but he was Al B. Sure fine, and I loved me some Al B. Sure, so I let him help me. From that day on we were inseparable. It was like he was my right hand and I was his left. We were tight like that.

"I mean I loved him harder than I'd loved anything in my life, 'cept my mother and father. But he was younger than me and at that age a few years can feel like ten. He would do stupid stuff like bring me Kool-Aid on my birthday."

Destina smiled at that memory and Roberta did too. "I mean it was kinda cute, but my friends expected he'd pull out some wine or champagne or something like that. They treated me like a kid after that and began messing with me about him.

"After a while Bilah's being young began bothering me.

Not a lot, you know. Just enough so we'd have little arguments. Nothing real. Just stupid stuff. Then I met Mr. Troutman. I would go in his store and buy little shit. Bread. Milk. Tampons. He'd flirt a little. But when he asked me out, I was surprised. He wasn't bad to look at—I just hadn't looked at him like that before. So then, you know, I started looking at him that way. Now he's my husband."

Roberta and I were ready for more. What did you tell Bilah? for instance. Details like that. Destina stopped and looked at me, like she'd awakened from a brief trance. Finally, I guess since it was her shop, Roberta asked, "Well, what the fuck happened to Bilah?"

"What do you mean?" Destina was now playing it real dumb, which was neither convincing nor becoming.

Trying to goad her on I said, "You just dumped him and married the grocer?"

"Yeah, something like that," with false pride.

"Okay," I said, leading her on, "sometimes you must wonder what he's doing now."

"I know what Bilah's doing," Destina said. "After I told him I was going to marry my husband he went and joined the army."

"Do you keep in contact?" Roberta wondered.

"I got a P.O. box set up. He sends me letters sometimes. From Korea, Germany, Texas. He's been in the army ever since we broke up. He says he likes it." Then Destina looked at me and Roberta and it must have hit her that she'd truly said too much. Her next words were, "Hey, are there any more rolls left?"

I handed Destina a roll, which she began to eat slowly. Seemed like that was all we were gonna squeeze out of Destina this afternoon. My sister had a good three or four more hours to do on Destina's head, so maybe she'd get more of the blanks filled. Sensing the shift, I just stuffed two rolls in my backpack and headed for the door.

The rest of the day I answered the phone and wrote yet another letter to the Urban League about working on their Black History Month fund-raiser. Yet what I was really thinking about was Destina, Bilah, and the grocer.

Everybody has an unfinished love story—some tale of passion and loss, of devotion and distance. Even if you're married and content, there is still some part of you that yearns, usually quietly but with abiding intensity, for a past love. It's nostalgia. It's selective memory. It's the fear you made a mistake. I don't truly think Destina feels she should be traveling as an army wife with Bilah. Still, I'm sure the idea has passed her mind when things at home aren't good. It's a yearning that reminds Destina of her innocence and the freedom of choice that's a fleeting gift of youth.

Compared to Destina's yearning, my quest is far from deep. I'm not married. These women weren't lost to me by the life-changing ritual of marriage. I lost them just being a restless, noncommitting man. And perhaps in that is where my opportunity lies. This list is my chance to be special, to break away from my life as a typical male and do something special.

Yeah, Amy didn't work out, but I wasn't crazy to hope it would. This quest may be impractical but it is not crazy. Just ask Destina. Fine-ass Belinda. Tall, butter-soft Sabena. They were both still out there. All I needed was the will to find them.

18

But Tim, don't you think we need a new carpet?" Bernice was at the head of the dinner table looking at her husband for affirmation. Her husband responded with calculated sweetness. "Honey, it's not that we don't need one," he said earnestly. "It's just that with all the bills we have, between the wedding and the honeymoon and this condo, it's an expense we can hold off on. Next year, honey. Next year a new carpet makes sense." Satisfied by his logic, Bernice took a sip of wine. I looked down at my plate, carving my chicken and smiling to myself.

Upon returning from their honeymoon Tim and Bernice had moved into a two-bedroom Marina Del Rey condo. It wasn't that spacious but it had a lovely ocean view and good security. Bernice grew up in a Bloods territory out in Long Beach, so she was very particular about locks, bolts, and burglar alarms. Her dream house was one inside a gated community, which explained the brochures stacked on their living room table.

Tim wasn't enthused by this idea, but as was his practice in handling domestic issues, he was biting his lip for now. It seemed Tim's philosophy of husbanding was initially to be as accommodating as possible to Bernice's ideas. He'd nod, say, "That's a good idea, honey," and go with her to look at houses, cars, clothes, you name it. When the time was right he'd make some very practical argument regarding money that would, for the time being, delay the spending of cash.

In the Wilson-Waters household Bernice was the dreamer and Tim the pragmatist, a coming together of opposites that seemed to work. The reasons that romantic relationships and most marriages don't work are legion, but the ones that work all share one thing—the people involved find a way. Though clearly I have no real expertise on commitment, I do have a theory: it seems to me in successful couples there's an alchemy of love, understanding, and compromise that defies easy analysis, glib categories, and self-help psychobabble. It is a mystery unique to each couple. Just as no two people are the same, no two couples love the same. As much as Tim and Bernice's togetherness impressed me, I knew whatever worked for them wouldn't necessarily work for me. Still, it was intriguing to look across the table at Caron's beige beauty, slender lips, and open face and wonder, "What if?"

Bernice worked in business affairs at Warner Bros. television; Caron worked as a paralegal at a special-effects production house. Bernice volunteered at a South Central soup kitchen; Caron volunteered at the AIDS Walk every year. Both came from relatively stable working-class homes—Bernice's father divorced her mother after Bernice graduated college, while Caron's folks had been together thirty-plus years and rarely talked.

These were the superficial similarities. The true bonds were weirder than that. Bernice and Caron both had a deep affection for England. Not the contemporary England of Tony Blair, Seal, and pubs, but the regal kingdoms of Shakespearean verse. Years ago they'd fallen in love with Mel Gibson's *Hamlet* and afterward began religiously collecting the many cinematic adaptations of Shakespeare's plays, from *Much Ado About Nothing* (featuring a dashing Denzel Washington), *Othello* (featuring a brooding Larry Fishburne), and the MTV-influenced *Romeo and Juliet* (featuring skinny Leonardo DiCaprio).

Though neither woman had actually read much of the Bard—I'm sure they knew a verse here and there—they took pleasure in the passionate loves and betrayals that shaped his most popular works. The root of their fixation was Gibson's *Hamlet*, and away from the numbers that defined their work-days, Bernice and Caron saw themselves as princesses waiting for their vacillating princes to come to their collective senses.

The ladies also shared an affinity for the British actress Helena Bonham-Carter, whom they first spied as Ophelia in Gibson's *Hamlet* and whose career they then followed from *A Room with a View* to *Wings of the Dove*. Despite Bonham-Carter being as pale as a December moon, Bernice and Caron found in the actress—with her haunted eyes and feisty intonation—an Old World role model who battled convention and sexism while wearing great antique dresses. Don't get me wrong. Bernice and Caron liked *Soul Food* too—but there was a dreamy, Eurocentric, defiantly non-ghetto quality to their taste that explained the Elizabethan motif at Bernice and Tim's wedding.

I met Caron at a Halloween costume party at the Zeta Phi Beta sorority held to raise funds for a Watts homeless shelter. I came dressed as James Brown circa early seventies—leather pants and vest, no shirt, big Afro wig, and a custom-made belt that read SEX MACHINE. Tim came as a six-foot-four Eazy-E— dark locks, Dickies jacket and pants, Compton baseball cap, and a Jheri Curl wig.

Keeping with their Shakespearean obsession, Bernice and Caron came as nineteenth-century courtesans with white wigs, huge ornate dresses held up by wires, and pushed-up bosoms. I was quite taken by Caron's buoyant breasts and comely looks, but she had a boyfriend at the time—a dentist, as I recall—so I smiled but didn't bare my teeth.

As Bernice became the center of Tim's life, Caron and I were often thrown together socially and forged a playful alliance. We teased Tim and Bernice together. We helped plan surprise parties for them. Often Caron picked my brain for Bernice about Tim, enlisting me (usually reluctantly) in efforts to keep the home fires burning.

Caron and I developed a certain chemistry but it never felt combustible until after Tim and Bernice's engagement. From the day he proposed, during a weekend on Catalina Island, until she gave me her pager number at the wedding reception, I felt Caron appraising me, like a house that needed some remodeling. I could understand that. The marriage of your best friend makes you view your life differently. "Will I find love too?" you wonder.

Outwardly you are totally supportive and happy for them. But inside you find yourself mourning as well. There's a palpable loss of closeness. Many of the roles you filled for your friend—counselor, confessor, conscience—were now rightfully their mate's role.

And that's as it should be. There'll always be things you two share. But what's shared can never be too secret, never so intimate that it could threaten the marriage vows. So Caron and I shared the passing of our old friendships with Bernice and with Tim and the struggle to birth new ones. It was a bond, but not sturdy enough to support a love affair.

"So, Rodney," Caron asked playfully during dinner, "now that Tim's not running with you anymore, do you still hang out as much?" Translation: "Without Tim to attract women, are you still getting laid?"

"Of course not," I replied with my typical mock sincerity. "Right now my focus is on building my business. The only checks I receive are those I generate myself, so lately it's been all about the Benjamins."

"Come on, Rodney, I know that's not all you've been up to." It was Bernice. Was she alluding to my quest? Had my boy sold me out?

"What," I said innocently, "are you talking about, Bernice?"

"Rodney, I hear you've been looking up your old girlfriends. You have a list of some kind?" I glanced over at Tim, who, conveniently enough, was looking down at his plate. I knew then he'd surely told her every damn detail. She probably would have enjoyed a reluctant admission out of me, so I decided to just be brazen and spill it all out on the dinner table.

"Yeah, that's right. I have a list of names. Women from my past. Out of that list I'm hoping to go back and find my wife."

"No, he didn't say that." This was Caron.

"Yes, girl, he did." This was Bernice.

As the women's high-pitched laughter filled the dining room, I added, "I just wanna be happy as my man Tim." Tim's not the kind of person who rolls his eyes, but if he did, he would have right then. "Ladies," I continued, "I take it you think I'm a little crazy."

"How many names do you have on your list, Rodney?" Bernice was prompting me for her amusement.

"Well, I've actually only been looking for three women. That's all."

"But," Caron wondered, "what about that list? How many girlfriends have you had?"

"No more than Tim."

"Oh no," he said quickly. He stood up and picked up his

plate. "I'm not in this. You're on your own, my brother." He put his plate in the sink and slid off toward the bedroom. "You just talk amongst yourselves" was his parting line.

"So," Bernice said, "are you gonna answer Caron's question?"

"I think that's all I'm gonna say about that. The bottom line is I need to go back and clean up a mess or two I've made in the past and, you know, maybe rekindle something good."

"Caron," Bernice asked, "how would you react to some old boyfriend who tried to come back in your life?"

"I'd tell him to go get one." The ladies laughed again and gave themselves high fives. Deeply embarrassed, I just sat quietly until they calmed down. Finally Caron said to me, "Seriously, Rodney, do you really expect these women to welcome you back?"

"I don't know," I mumbled. "It just feels like something I have to do."

"That's all right." Bernice reached over and placed her hands on mine. "Get this out of your system. Maybe it'll cleanse you for your next woman."

"Are you a romantic, Rodney? It sure does sound like it," Caron said.

"I don't know, Caron. I never really thought about it."

"You know, Rodney, this list thing is kind of bugged, but there is something sweet about it too."

"He's looking for love, huh, Caron?" Bernice was half making fun, half making a point. "Rodney really wants to do the right thing."

"But," Caron said, flowing with her friend, "he just hasn't figured out what the right thing is."

I raised my right hand like a student. "Ladies, you think I would be correct in saying what I need is a good woman?"

"Don't be sarcastic, Rodney," Bernice scolded. "We like you. It's just that you need an attitude adjustment."

"Adjustment," Caron agreed.

"Adjustment?" I repeated.

"I remember when I first met Tim. You were there, Rodney."

"Yes, I was."

"What I thought was Tim wanted to do the right thing—he didn't know how. Sometimes men need a little guidance."

"Direction," Caron agreed.

"Yes, girl," Bernice chimed in. "Sometimes you gotta Spike Lee these men."

Suddenly my emotional state was a Ping-Pong ball being bounced back and forth across the table's plates and forks for Bernice's and Caron's amusement. Thankfully Tim rode in to save the day. "Hey, folks, *Soul Food* is coming on DirecTV in ten minutes."

With microwaved popcorn in a big bowl and black soap opera cinema on the big-screen television, we sprawled out in the living room. Bernice laid her head on Tim's considerable chest in the center of the floor, I sat on the floor with my head propped up against the sofa, and Caron spread herself across the sofa above me.

About ten minutes into the movie she reached down and rubbed my head playfully like I was a child being petted. By the time Vanessa Williams's husband got caught boning her cousin, Caron's hand had slid down to my neck in a soft, caressing way. I didn't encourage her. Nor did I tell her to stop. It was a very sensual feeling—Caron's pretty hands rolling slowly across my dome and shoulders. Neither of us spoke about what she was doing; neither of us acted on it.

By the time *Soul Food* had been consumed Tim had fallen

asleep and I, citing a visit to my mother the next morning, was heading for the door. Bernice gave me a sisterly kiss on the cheek and apologized for messing with me. I graciously accepted. Caron gave me a deep hug with her pelvis pressed up against my groin. It felt good, so I promised Caron I'd give her a call, though I still wasn't convinced it was a good idea.

Back home I was watching the late *SportsCenter* when Tim called. "What's up, dog?" I wondered.

Tim spoke in a whisper. "If you're my best man, you won't go out with, call, or—God forbid—lay up with Caron."

"No carnal knowledge?"

"Money, if you fuck her and she likes it—it's bad 'cause you'll dog her and I'll have to hear about it. If you fuck her and she hates it, I'll have to hear about it. If you fuck her and date awhile and break up, I'll hear all that too. In fact, doing anything but asking Caron to marry you after the first date would ruin much of my life. Rodney, it's like throwing a pass in football—two of the three things that could happen, an interception or incompletion, are bad."

"Damn, Tim, you are married."

"Word."

"To the motherfucking mother."

"Don't worry, Tim, I don't think it's a good idea either. But—"

"But if she keeps rubbing your head—"

"She might get to rub my head."

"Rod, man."

"I'm playing. I'm playing. Word. I repeat, word."

"Yeah. Word to the goddamn mother."

"Goodnight, Mr. Waters-Wilson."

"Yeah. So who won the Lakers-Sonics game?"

19

I'm sitting in my offices across from an eighteen-year-old rapper who looks like a young Denzel and his white manager from Bakersfield, California. Before taking this meeting I'd given Roberta a look at his decidedly crummy, barely in focus promo shot and she'd volunteered to knock his barely legal boots. This was encouraging since my sister's libido had long been a reliable guide in deciding what male clients to handle.

So I sat behind my desk and listened to Derrick Vincent, professional name D-Vince (as in "D-Vince from the Field"), articulate his plan for world domination. "I'm gonna turn Bakersfield into the new Compton, yo," he proclaimed. "I'm gonna immortalize it in rhyme, yo. I'm gonna make the Field part of national—no, international—slang and I'm gonna make videos with honeys in hot tubs." As Derrick talked his manager, Sam Neil, a man as white and pallid looking as any descendant of the Okies could be, sat beaming as if this was his first time hearing this rap.

And you know what? So far, so good. D-Vince had released two twelve-inches on Da Field Records, both financed by Mr. Neil. The first, "Jackie Brown's Revenge," was the bloody tale of the lead character in the Tarantino film about running drugs out of Bakersfield airport. This record flopped and deserved to. Thankfully D-Vince's second effort, "Fully Loaded," wasn't bloody, despite its title, but celebrated the beauty of lovely young women in a funky style reminscent of L. L. Cool J's "Around the Way Girl."

When the Beat, L.A.'s big urban station, played it during a

Friday-night mix show the phones lit up with requests for the artist's name. D-Vince was suddenly hot. Jive Records out of New York bought the national distribution rights, and just like that, D-Vince and his Mr. Neil were bordering on the big time.

Which is where I came in. I'd been recommended to them as a good publicist. Ordinarily I'd have passed. This could have been a one-hit-wonder situation and all this talk of "the Field" just felt old. Eazy-E and Snoop Doggy Dogg had worked that angle—obscure city spawns rap singer—when D-Vince was at home watching *Ren & Stimpy*.

But after meeting the kid I felt he had the potential to be a twenty-first-century sepia sex symbol, one ready-made for *Right On!*, *Black Beat*, *Sister to Sister,* and teen idol Web sites across the globe. D-Vince was a great visual package. No lying there. Even better, he could actually rap a bit. I mean, he wasn't B.I.G. but he wasn't Puffy either. My new client was a solidly mediocre talent with matinee idol looks—the kind of package an enterprising media maven such as yours truly could really run with.

"We'll have a lot of fun together, gentlemen," I said confidently, "as long as we understand each other."

"What do you mean, Mr. Hampton?" his manager asked.

"I mean that Derrick and you have had success with a love man record—a record that girls like and that has real pop potential. I'm not interested in handling any artist, no matter how lucrative it could be, who talks primarily about gatts and jackin'. I did that years ago."

"No need to worry, yo," D-Vince interrupted. "I know what you're about and I know what I'm about. I got on playing to the ladies and you want me to stick to that game plan. No problem, yo."

"We're gonna get along fine, Derrick."

"So, Mr. PR, what's on tonight? It's a long ride back to the Field, yo. So I was thinking you could take Sammy and me to a few clubs. Get us accustomed to the lifestyle we plan on living full-time in a minute. So what's up?"

As much as I was looking forward to working with D-Vince, this wining and dining stuff had gotten old a long time ago. And while Mr. Neil looked like he'd be happy with two beers at the hotel bar, Derrick was radiating that horny young man energy which meant a long night. I knew the vibe so well—it was the one Tim and I had back on Adams Boulevard before weddings and wives. So with some anticipation and considerable trepidation I made plans to hook up later with the men from the Field.

After they'd left my office an idea occurred to me—one that made me laugh. I'd been trying to figure out the best strategy for connecting with Belinda. She was too cynical and ironic for me to be too direct. I needed to be cooler, more off-hand in reaching this lady. D-Vince's desire to party seemed the perfect setup.

Before reconnecting with D-Vince and his manager I went home, showered, trimmed my beard, and slipped into my best black DKNY suit—a holdover from my days with Belinda—and a light gray silk shirt. While I was trying to look cool my anxiety about seeing Belinda started to create acid in my tummy. So, instead of heading out to Belinda's new Santa Monica club immediately, I decided we'd stop first at Bar Fly on Sunset for sushi and reckless eyeballing.

I introduced D-Vince to an amazon blond personal trainer right out of *Playboy* magazine named Bianca, who had my client's biceps swollen with glee. Bianca was just being polite while she waited on her Benz dealer boyfriend, but D-Vince was ready to declare devotion just because she chuckled at his jokes. I damn near had to leash him to get him out of Bar Fly. The kid was so amped he didn't notice when Bianca dropped his hotel room number under the table. When you're young (and handsome) opportunity seems to reign and you think any woman that smiles your way can be yours if you just show interest.

"She was loving me, dog," D-Vince exclaimed as the limo transported us toward Santa Monica. "She's gonna call and I'm gonna get my swerve on, Rodney. Believe dat."

"True dat," I said while fighting back my amusement.

Belinda had come a long way from downtown. Literally. She'd moved her party completely to the other side of the city, and while she had retained some underground cred, her new venture was very Westside and thus very much about status and money. With the backing of some of the Eurotrash who hung out at Sunset Plaza, Belinda opened Eden's Taste two blocks from the Third Avenue Promenade, where it immediately became the hottest spot in a town perpetually craving newness.

The club's ground floor was a big white-columned room with a high ceiling, wood floor, walls draped with Turkish rugs, shafts of amber light, and huge speakers designed to pulverize your ears and cave in your chest. On a good night the throbbing bass could make your toes quiver. As a result the dance was a wonderful orgy of whirling bodies, spilled drinks, and sweat drops.

Downstairs, where the VIPs congregated, there was a long, crowded bar at one end, and at the other a bandstand occupied by a pop combo. Between these two points were wooden, candlelit tables surrounded by old embroidered chairs. The most sought after seats were the booths on elevated platforms set back against the walls. It was quite an evolution from downtown lofts. I was truly proud of her.

As I glanced around the downstairs I saw arrows pointing from person to person, relationship to relationship, clique to clique. The lines created by these arrows then transformed into a spiderweb of interconnections that trapped everyone in the room. Everywhere I looked the web grew in strength and I was just one more strand. Anywhere there are movers and shakers there is also a healthy percentage of hustlers. They have as much, and often more, money as the civilians, and their excess cash is laundered through legal businesses, prime among them music and fashion. Sometimes separating the drug dealer from the record producer from the boutique owner was impossible, unless you wanted to split some very fine hairs.

Somehow in moving from upstairs to down I'd lost my two companions but it was too early in the evening to be stressed by that. Besides, I was after big game. And then I saw something that, like Marvin, made me wanna holler and throw up both my hands.

Squatting down next to a quartet of young women I saw Circus engaged in another monologue with his muse. That sight was sad enough but what made it horrifying was that Kenya—sweet, sweet Kenya—was a target of his salvo. I walked over, determined to be as intrusive as possible. Kenya and her friends acknowledged me but Circus, in his familiar overbearing way, just kept on rolling. "If you thought I was arrogant I wouldn't be mad 'cause I might be and it serves me well, you know. If you thought I was arrogant I'd say it's just a perception, a thought outside me that doesn't define me for me, which you know is the only view that really matters, which is probably the best evidence possible that I am, indeed, arrogant." This made Circus chuckle—beware of those entranced by their own circular reasoning.

"Arrogance is a weapon I use, a barrier I've built to block all the arrows aimed my way. Like so much in this world it's a front, a pose, a position calculated to keep the little boy in me from spilling out and embarrassing me with a lot of easy-to-mess-with vulnerability. If you thought I was arrogant you're right but it's the only way to protect myself from all those real bad people out there. People like this guy lingering over my shoulder."

"You mean," Kenya said with emphasis, "my friend Rodney?"

Circus doesn't take hints. Kenya's "my friend" was a signal for Circus to lighten up and stop sweating her. But no way was Mr. Morris gonna let my presence deter him. Now it was a matter of pride. Whatever charm Circus possessed was based on his arrogant insanity. There was a light in his eyes when the spirit hit. The bright glint of inspiration that translated itself into a dangerous energy that attracted women. "The force," Michael Jackson once said, "it's got a lot of power." Well, Circus possessed the force and used it indiscriminately.

"Kenya, do you need anything, Kenya?" This was my hint for her to exit.

"No," she said coolly. "I'll be all right." Now I was worried. Was my Kinko's cutie gonna accept his challenge? Would she fall for the force? In truth I had no right to be jealous. Yet I could still taste one of Kenya's cute little pecks on my lips and it messed with me to think Circus might too.

I felt a tap on my shoulder and turned to see Sam Neil looking as blissful as a man could. Wearing a wild grin I wouldn't have thought possible a few hours ago, Neil announced, "Man, this is a great place." Without a doubt someone had given this man a tab of high quality X, which presently had the moneyman from the Field quite giddy. When I asked for D-Vince's whereabouts Neil pointed behind him and reported dreamily, "He just made a great new friend."

In a booth was D-Vince with a woman with golden orange hair styled into ringlets. A gray ribbon of smoke flowed from a very thin cigarette she held in a pose of calculated elegance. Up close she was even more glamorous, with thin plucked eyebrows, vivid red lips, and a face that viewed me from a high, haughty distance. It was Belinda, my ex-lover and current quest, sitting cozily with my handsome, horny young client. This was a nightmare with my eyes wide open.

"Rod, come over, yo! This is Belinda. Can you believe it? This is her place, yo!"

I stared at her and said, "I know her."

"Do you?" She arched her eyebrow and spoke in a very grand forties-Hollywood-diva tone. "Please, refresh my memory."

"Rodney Hampton. Hampton Media. Breakfast at Duke's. Your place at dawn."

"Hmmm." Belinda squirreled up her face theatrically, as if trying to recall some obscure trivia. "I must have been high," she answered finally, "but if D-Vince says you're with him I guess you can sit down."

"Oh yeah, Rod's my man. He's gonna help me blow up."

"This is your publicist, huh?"

"Yes, I am."

"Well, from what I can remember, he's a good salesman."

"Don't you like her, Rodney!" D-Vince shouted across the table. "I am feeling her!"

It went in this vein much of the night. Belinda made little catty comments, D-Vince expressed his devotion, and I, third wheel on a motorcycle, just rolled with it.

Thankfully D-Vince's attention span was limited. As gorgeous as Belinda was she was just one of the many spectacular ladies on the set. By evening's end he'd befriended two "shorties" who were part of a new R&B vocal group, and his manager, the taciturn man from Bakersfield, was hugged up with a six-foot-plus Danish girl named Inga.

As for me, I spent a lot of time drinking wine and fruitlessly trying to get Bernice to give me a serious word, much less a sentence. Around one o'clock I snagged her arm by the DJ booth and refused to let go. "Are you gonna talk to me?"

"Isn't it clear," she began, "that I am not? What is there to say? How long has it been?"

"A while."

"And now that you've reappeared I'm supposed to get all warm and fuzzy. Forget that, Shaft."

"Can I call you?"

"Phone calls cost money and so does my time."

With that she snatched her arm away and disappeared into the crowd. My business for the evening unsatisfactorily completed, I brusquely escorted D-Vince and Neil, minus their female friends, back to the limo.

Before leaving I scouted the place for sights of Circus and Kenya, but no luck, which was as discouraging as if they'd been dancing seductively pelvis to groin. At least then my eyes would see something concrete and have some fixed image to mull. Not seeing them made my mind concoct images of the porn star and the starlet that made me wince.

In the limo my two charges from the Field babbled about the women they'd met and talked of extending their trip and about L.A. women, while I stared out the window remembering Belinda's voice and Circus's leer.

After depositing them at the Bel Age in West Hollywood I had the driver take me to Sunset and Gower, where I slept in my office until six-thirty and then made a couple of calls to New York, catching folks just as they were walking in their offices. New Yorkers were always impressed when an Angeleno called them at nine or ten Eastern Standard Time. Even if you had nothing to say it made them feel like you were on top of things.

Still, that sign of manufactured competence didn't make me feel any less defeated. Between Circus and Kenya, and Belinda and D-Vince, it had been a long damn night. So I waited around for Roscoe's to open, hoping to cover the nasty taste in my mouth with two huge waffles and four chicken wings.

20

Come see me, Rodney."

"I'm coming Sunday, Ma."

"Come see me tonight."

"Ma, are you all right?"

"Rodney, you know good and well I haven't been all right in some time."

"I meant, how are you feeling at the moment?"

"I feel I want my son to come see me. Right now."

Visiting hours ended at seven unless there was some medical emergency, so the staff at Saint Mary's was a little concerned when I showed up in a Lakers warm-up and sneakers at nine-thirty on a Thursday night. Physically Ma was fine. A quick checkup confirmed that. But as she herself had said on the phone, my mother hadn't been all right in quite some time.

"Clinical depression" was the cold and exact term. I thought of her as a woman who'd left her house one morning and, somewhere along her journey, lost her way back.

"I'm glad you're here." She'd said it a few times since I'd arrived and I'd given the same reply every time: "It's good to be here with you, Ma." The conversation had not progressed far from that point.

When Ma was living with Roberta, the girls used to complain Grandma would get all excited and demand their attention and then, as soon as they focused on her, she'd drift off. Pretty soon her granddaughters stopped responding to her, which enraged Roberta though it was understandable. Ma had lost their confidence and just a little bit of their love. It was the key reason we'd placed her at Saint Mary's. This night appeared to be my latest turn to be frustrated by the woman I loved more than anything I knew.

I must have been fidgeting 'cause she observed, "You have always been a restless child."

"Always?"

"You kicked a lot in the womb and you've been anxious ever since. Never could sit still."

"I think I'm better now, Ma."

"You're older. When you get older you slow down. That's no news. But that nervous energy is all up in you. You know, when I was pregnant with you I was angry at your father a lot of the time. He was so busy trying to make pennies he acted like he didn't have a diamond at home."

"Ma, what's your point?"

"Rodney, don't snap at me or I'll reach over there and pop you." My mother was never the kindly, earth-motherly matriarch of black family lore. Rebe was naturally tart and spicy, like red pepper on rice. Still, the thought of this depressed little lady springing up out of her sickbed to pimp-slap me made me laugh.

"Don't laugh at me, boy!"

"Only if you tell me why you called."

"I don't know. I was thinking about your father and I can't see that man's face and not see yours." This made me uncomfortable. If I was fidgeting before, I was squirming now. So in a guilty tone I suggested, "I know I don't call or come over enough."

"You get busy."

"Yeah. But that's no excuse."

"Well, I have to agree. Your father busied himself right into his grave."

"Ma, he was shot by a mugger."

"He was shot 'cause he was out there when he should have been home."

"Ma, you can't still be blaming Pa for his death."

"Rodney, you didn't really know your father. He was a good man but he wasn't a lot of fun. Given a choice between working or playing, he would work. He thought that was being a man. He wasn't all wrong but he wasn't always right for me. We never had enough quiet time together. I mean, I liked sitting up in bed and watching him breathe. It made me feel so good sometimes. But even then it was like he had one eye on the door. He was a damn good dancer—if you could just get him out on the floor.

"I mean, your father worked and I worked, so we were steady turning pennies into nickels. It was gonna happen but he was in a hurry. He'd be pulling on his pants telling me, 'This is for you, Rebe. One day we'll have more time.'" This memory seemed to exhaust her. Yet I pushed her, feeling that we'd somehow gotten to the real reason for her call.

"You trying to tell me something, Ma?"

Ma just rolled her eyes dismissively and told me, "I'm getting tired, so come give me a hug so I can go to sleep."

Ma's embrace was thin but loving. It was like she was mustering all her strength to hold me, while I was grasping her like a baby. I kissed her forehead, remembering how she used to kiss mine.

My favorite picture of Rebe Hampton was taken in the glory days of disco. My mother looks into the camera with her hair in a bushy brown Afro. She's dressed in a glittery see-through blouse that covers her bare shoulders and a black halter top. Red spandex pants are visible at the bottom of the frame. Hovering in the back of the picture, bouncing little rays of light around the room, is a disco ball.

My father took the snapshot, which is maybe why her smile is so long and beatific. No teeth are visible. Just her mouth, stretched out across her face in tangible satisfaction. As I left the room I saw a hint of that same smile as she closed her eyes. Feisty, willful party girl—that's my momma, for good and ill.

On the way home I took a familiar detour, turning left off Wilshire onto where Crenshaw Boulevard began, near the Wilshire Ebel Theater, and headed south. Back when L.A. was a white man's city the area I was driving toward was known as Darktown, a place where "coloreds" struggled to find peace and safety under the supervision of the most racist police force this side of Bull Connor.

Honestly, the LAPD isn't as bad as it used to be, though that's small comfort to the black or Chicano man spread-eagled on the ground for running a red light. Back when the Watts riots broke out in '65, then police chief Parker remarked (and I paraphrase), "One monkey threw a rock and then another monkey threw a rock."

Backroom beat-downs, backdoor payoffs, and the casual brutality visited upon black folk were done without conscience or fear of reprisal. A black-on-black murder was a nuisance, not a crime. As N.W.A. once rapped, "One less nigga I have to worry about."

I rolled down Crenshaw past Tim's office and the mall, past Maverick's Flats nightclub and the nondescript central office of the Los Angeles Urban League, and took a left about five blocks before I'd have crossed into Inglewood. Then with another right I was back on Victoria Avenue, a place of small, flat, dull one-story homes pushed back from the street and fronted by threadbare front yards. When I was a boy the residents here were working class and Southern and dreamed of sending their kids to USC. Now the avenue's residents spoke English as a second language and had their roots well south of the border. Its residents now worked all the crappy jobs black folks had abandoned, grown ashamed of, or, arrogantly, wanted the minimum wage for.

Right in the middle of one of Victoria Avenue's desultory blocks an immigrant family was making a life for itself in the rebuilt shell of my family's past. There were bars on the windows and the stucco walls had been painted an awful shade of green. But then, those weren't really our walls. The only part of the house that had anything to do with me were the foundations—the concrete walls of the basement, the front steps, the path that went from street to steps. Everything else had been rebuilt. My father was paying for the house when he died and my mother was struggling to keep up with taxes and leaks when it burnt brown like whole wheat toast.

A yearning romantic ballad sung in a thick languid baritone seeped out of the house. It was a nice song but it meant nothing to me 'cause this site made me think of other music—"Disco Inferno," "Heaven Must Be Missing an Angel," "Lady Marmalade"—the songs my mother played as she waited for my father to come back home until that night he didn't.

I wiped away a tear and drove off.

21

I feel the same way about mornings that Republicans do about the Clintons. Which is probably why my sister loves waking me up.

"Who dis?"

"Who dis? You better stop with that Master P mess and answer the phone like you got some sense."

"What do you want?"

"I need for you to baby-sit the girls tonight."

"What's up? Got a hot date with babies' father four?"

Roberta sucked her teeth like a pro and wondered, "Why you got to sound so foolish? Anyway, I'm taking a computer class. Learning PCs. The Internet. The whole nine."

"This your first class?"

"No. I've been going awhile."

"How come I didn't know about this?"

"Since when you got to know all my business?"

"I thought the hair thing was working."

"It's all right, but me making it a business was more your idea than mine. Besides, it'll give me arthritis if I keep doing it the way I am now."

"You know, in computers they got something called the carpal tunnel syndrome. It's high-tech arthritis."

"But unlike braiding, you sit down all damn day. I could get with that."

"What time you need me?"

"Six-thirty on the dot."

"All right."

Another day, another juggling act. Breakfast at the Four

Seasons with the head of Jive's national publicity office—a chubby blond named Nancy Bishop. D-Vince's album is about to drop and Jive thinks they can make him the new Fresh Prince. I was a little worried going in. If they're so high on the kid maybe they don't need me anymore. Might wanna handle everything in-house.

Over fruit, omelettes, and rich black coffee Bishop makes a cooler, quite complimentary pitch—join Jive. Senior director West Coast publicity, reporting to her. Because of my previous label experience and the fact that I'd have to close down my office, a nice low-six-figure offer comes from a company known to be tight with a dollar.

I counter: give me a fat retainer and farm out West Coast work to me. You'll pay me less than the salary, not be obligated to cover my insurance, et cetera, and yet guarantee the same diligence I've displayed on D-Vince. Without Jive's help I got him profiled in *Rap Pages*, the *Source*, all the black-teen-appeal rags; and the *L.A. Times* mentioned his underground rise from Bakersfield in its Sunday calendar "Pop Eye" column. All of which led to this breakfast. Bishop wasn't feeling my offer but was impressed by my initiative. She promised to take my proposal back to New York. Hers still stood.

As I turned out of the Four Seasons parking area onto Doheny, visions of a regular check danced in my head. Jive was a very solid company—R. Kelly, A Tribe Called Quest, KRS-One, and lots of sound tracks. Her offer was as tempting as the devil's con game. I'm glad I came back with a proposal of my own. Made it up on the spot. Gave her something to think about and prevented me from going "Yes" and leaping at that steady cash flow like a rabid dog.

At Wilshire I made a left and headed over to La Cienega and then made a right that would take me down past Pico, where I slowed down as I passed a nice Cuban restaurant called Versailles. About a block or two down on the right was the Blaxican Cafe, the world's first Mexican soul food restaurant. Leroy Martinez, the owner and chef, a chunky, handsome man with slicked-back hair, a thin mustache, and glowing brown skin, demanded, "You eat, then we talk."

So despite my Four Seasons breakfast I wolfed down a plate of fajitas and mashed potatoes, and then he took me into his kitchen ("How can you sell what you don't understand?") for a quick trip through his methods and philosophy. Leroy was a fervent man with a curious yet wonderful dream. Which left it to me to outline the challenges. "So, you want to attract an ethnically diverse crowd."

"Yeah, I want homeboys, *pachucos*, and whitey to all feel welcome. It's the reason I located it on the Westside. That, and the owner cut me a sweet deal."

"Where are you advertising?"

"The *Sentinel* and KDAY for black folk. Several of the Spanish-language stations. For the curious white dollar I've been doing business with the *Weekly*. Otherwise I've been hoping for reviews in all these papers and good word of mouth. As you know, I don't have a lot of cash."

"Okay, that's a good start. Now I have a plan B."

"Okay. How much will it cost me?"

"Nothing except one night of free food and we should be able to break you even on that."

"I like that, ese."

"One thing."

"Come with it, Rodney."

"You haven't opened yet."

"What do you mean? I've been open three months."

"No," I explained, "it's all been a run-through. The Blaxican Cafe doesn't officially open until the gala celebrity-studded event I'm gonna hook up."

"Is that so?"

"Oh, yeah, ese. I don't know about getting *Entertainment Tonight* in here, but I guarantee you some local TV, definitely local radio, and stars, writers, and other important freeloaders."

"So," he said through a big grin, "would you like some run-through food to go?"

I patted my protruding stomach and passed on his offer. I did, however, accept Leroy's $1,000 check and headed back to the office. After downing some Tums I sat and mapped out a plan to mix and match D-Vince and the Blaxican Cafe, using the rapper's listening party as the restaurant's official opening. I wrote up a plan for Jive. I wrote up a plan for Leroy Martinez. And then I giggled at the thought of billing both for the same gig.

Around four, I took Crescent Heights up to Laurel Canyon and went over the hill through some dicey late-afternoon traffic down to Ventura Boulevard and the sprawl of mass-manufactured fantasy factories known as Hollywood film/television studios. I took Barham past the Oakwood apartments, temporary housing for actors and musicians working in town, and over to Burbank, where I sought entry to bunny land.

The Warner Bros. lot is the sprawling site of Spanish-styled bungalows, huge soundstages, and fake streets seen on sundry television shows. Following the front gate guard's instructions I found the building I was seeking and looked for the offices of Chosen Peoples Productions. A homely but stylish black woman named Diana greeted me and did the good-assistant thing ("Coffee? Bottled water? Coke?") while I studied the framed posters on the wall. The most prominent poster was for

Stone Fine, the black women's hit sandwiched between *Waiting to Exhale* and *Soul Food* that made the writer-director Larry Jason Jones and producer Joey Stein players once more.

Both Stein and Jones were low-level legends of black cinema. Back in the eighties Larry Jason Jones was the only black director-writer getting any light in La La Land. He'd begun by acting in a couple of TV series before getting into directing episodic TV. Despite a couple of awards Jones couldn't get a feature until he made a low-budget black kung fu flick titled *Black Fist.* It was a B movie quickie that grossed $30 million in 1983. That break made Jones a hot property—he went on to write unproduced scripts for Richard Pryor, Billy Dee Williams, and Carl "Apollo Creed" Weathers.

Jones was about to hook up with Eddie Murphy when he nearly OD'd on bad coke, stumbling into a free fall that lasted five years. He did the odd lecture at a college here and there, and then kept sinking until he was directing low-budget music videos and soft-core porn under the pseudonym Bad Apple. When the black film wave hit in '91 and his name resurfaced as an influence on younger African-American filmmakers, producers began sniffing around again, including Joey Stein.

Stein had made his bones back in the seventies blaxploitation era, producing a couple of ghetto classics whose dialogue is still sampled by rappers. He segued into black sitcoms, made a grip in the *Good Times* era, and then tried to go mainstream, developing projects as white bread as the Mormon Church. Sadly it seemed that somewhere along the line Joey's white card had been revoked 'cause none of his shows made network schedules.

Around '92 Stein was sent the rough cut of a movie made by the Hu brothers (two Ivy League twins of black and Asian extraction from the Midwest) called *Menace in My House*, the comic tale of a dope-dealing father who discovers his son has been running a competing operation out of the family garage. Joey got them completion money, set it up with a studio, and raked in plenty of cash when *Menace* was a critical and commercial hit. That movie put Joey back in the game and led him to his union with Larry Jason Jones.

Of course, now it seems natural that the two hooked up, but for a long time personal problems intervened. Both men were married to one of the Callahan sisters—Larry to Nancy, Joey to Nikki—back in the days these two buxom brown bombshells did a calendar that became a fixture in black barbershops nationwide. Nancy and Nikki were, pardon the expression, model/actresses, which is how they met their future husbands. For reasons known only to the sisters the two Callahan women came to hate each other, a situation that made it impossible for Larry and Joey to talk, much less work together.

Following the inevitable divorces Joey and Larry finally broke bread. And one hell of a meal that must have been since it resulted in *Stone Fine*, a roman à clef about a family of crazy yet gorgeous black women, set in D.C. With Angela Bassett as the dominating matriarch and two gorgeous soap opera actresses as the battling sisters, *Stone Fine* made $60 million and resulted in an angry invasion-of-privacy lawsuit from the suddenly unified Callahans. After initially invoking the First Amendment, Larry and Joey settled out of court with their ex-wives, agreeing to have home video royalties applied to their alimony payments.

Some saw Larry and Joey as hacks. They saw themselves as content providers. I saw them as my next big check and kissed ass accordingly. "Hey, Rodney, come on in here."

Joey Stein, lanky, silver haired, and dressed in Tommy Hilfiger from head to Reebok sneakers, glad-handed me into his office. Lounging on a green leather sofa was Larry Jason Jones, a portly light-skinned man with the sad face of a child whose mother's been gone too long. "Larry and I have been talking about the Latino market and how the industry is selling itself short by not making more films for them."

Immediately I kicked into a spiel about the Blaxican Cafe and how it wedded these two communities together like movies should and how my party there would demonstrate this, blah, blah, blah.

"We have got to go there, Larry." Joey spoke in a rapid, high-pitched tone that would have been comical if I didn't need the business. "Cultural blending," Joey announced, "makes for great movies and long-running television shows." Joey looked to Larry for confirmation of this observation but the director just shrugged, clearly not impressed or particularly interested in Joey's sociological ramblings. Joey ignored the slight and continued on.

" '*Me llamo Joey Stein.*' That's as far as I've gotten but I don't need much more. If they ask me if I speak Spanish I say, '*Un poco, un poco,*' which means, 'A little,' and then I switch to English and I say, 'My English is better,' and since they all want to crack the English market anyway we go from there."

"But Joey," Jones said with a dismissive headshake, "you don't know a Cuban from a Chicano. So how are you gonna know a good Latino script from a bad one?"

"Same way I learned about you blacks," Joey retorted. "I listen. I learn. Hey, at least there are books you can read about Hispanics. It took me years to know when to say 'motherfucker' affectionately and when to say it as a threat. You got to think on your feet in the black game."

Jones looked at me and said, "Are you sure you wanna be seen around this guy? He's not exactly PC."

These two were quite a team—black cinema's answer to Laurel and Hardy. Not bad guys, though clearly not the brightest duo ever. If these two could make hit movies pulling in hundreds of thousands (if not millions), then anyone could succeed in this damn town.

Their new movie was titled *Night Shift* and centered around a lonely, overweight L.A. bus driver working the Sunset Boulevard route that runs from downtown to the sea from 11 to 4 A.M. One night as he's pulling away from the La Brea stop, a young woman bangs on his bus door just as he's pulling off. The girl is frantic and bloodied, like a young wounded deer. He wants to radio the police but she pleads with him not to. Instead she sits with him on the long ride out to the Pacific Coast Highway. Though scruffy and skinny, the girl is as beautiful as she is mysterious. For the rest of the night she sits near him, teasing info out of him.

At the end of his run the girl tells the driver she has nowhere to go, a fact that excites and frightens him. Lust overcomes reason and he takes her to his Ladera Heights apartment. She sleeps on the bed—he on the floor. An unlikely romance begins. The driver's friends all think she's using him. The driver, who now feels important because of her dependence, overcomes his suspicions and basks in her attention. Forest Whitaker was to play the driver. Jada Pinkett was slated to be the girl.

"So, gentlemen, when does the film start production?" It was time to get this party started, though I tried not to sound too impatient.

"Preproduction on *Night Shift* begins in a month with

some shooting in South Central, some in the Valley, and a bit on a soundstage here."

"You've done unit publicity before?" It was Larry.

"I haven't worked on films in production, but I've often worked with film companies on sound track and in hyping actors in tandem with film openings."

"That's all good," Larry agreed, "but there's only one priority on this film."

"And that's making Larry look good," Joey said with a sardonic laugh his partner didn't share.

Larry continued, "What I was going to say is that *Night Shift* is an important film that brings the life of the black working class into conflict with the criminal lifestyle homeless kids are forced into. Though the working class and homeless people are just one paycheck removed from each other, this will be the first time that relationship will be explored in a movie. Everything about the project must be done with respect for the poor and the love these two share." From a publicity viewpoint Jones was great—he spoke in perfect sound-bite paragraphs.

"All bullshit aside," Joey interrupted, "what Larry really means is that the stars have big butts, the extras have big butts, and the dancers have really big butts. And that's just the men." When the banter finally calmed down we got down to business details. They needed me to prepare the production notes, a packet of propaganda handed out to the media; arrange set visits for media; work on the EPK (electronic press kit), a compilation of video clips and on-set interviews from the production that local stations and cable entertainment shows aired for free. They didn't need me on set every day, but I had to be accessible on a moment's notice.

"Do the right thing," Joey said, "and we'll recommend you for more work."

Before leaving I sheepishly mentioned I had an actress friend who wanted to audition. "Sure," Joey chuckled, having heard this 2 million times. "You got a head shot?" He studied it a moment and his eyes got wide. "Larry, look at this." Joey slid the photo over.

"Shit," Larry said.

"What's up, gentlemen?"

"This girl looks a lot like the Callahan sisters," said Joey. "More Nancy than Nikki, right?"

"Maybe," Larry replied, still staring at the photo.

Joey added, "Like they did when we met them."

Larry looked up from the photo and stared at me. "Is this your girlfriend?"

"We're tight," I replied, "but, no, she's not my woman."

"She should be," he said with palpable lust.

On the way back over the hill I debated whether to tell Kenya about the reaction to her photo. Talk was the most easily dispensed commodity in Hollywood. Resembling someone's ex-wife (or wives) didn't guarantee work.

There was lust in their eyes but a sweet kind of wonderment too, as if Kenya made them remember a better, younger version of themselves. My quest for lost love made me feel a bit like that. Longing for something sweet from the past— hoping perhaps to marinate the present with the same flavor. Which is why I decided not to tell Kenya any of this. Let that scenario play itself out without Kenya thinking she's already got a job. Let her go in there and create with a clear mind.

22

Back at my office it was finally time to talk money with Adele. "I'll give you more money when we solidify all this new business," I told her. "It looks like a real busy period coming up. Plus I still have hopes for that Urban League bid."

"It's all good," she agreed.

"But that's not all," I added. "This additional money means additional responsibilities for you, Adele."

"Such as?"

"You'll go to the movie set on days I can't make it. You'll go to D-Vince's video and photo shoots when I'm elsewhere. And I'll hire someone who'll be anchored to the office, who you'll supervise. In other words you will no longer be my assistant, Adele. To the world you'll be an account executive for Hampton Media."

Adele folded her arms at that and smiled knowingly. "But," she said, "within these walls I'll remain your slave, right?"

"But with a tender young slave of your own to lord over. Sounds like fun, right?"

"Only if he's a very cute boy," Adele asserted.

"Okay, I'm willing to bend on gender."

"You are funny, Rodney Hampton." The phone rang. She picked up the line and announced, "Hampton Media," then she cut me a look as she added, "Adele Miller, account executive, speaking. Oh, hello, Merry. How have you been?"

Merry Spencer, an old friend, successful businesswoman, and number 47 on my list of 133. That was long ago—back when Michael Jackson was still brown. A lot of water under that bridge with Merry—a veritable flood, in fact. She and Adele were having a lovely old conversation about Adele's family when I wondered aloud, "You think she might wanna speak to your boss?"

Adele sighed and asked, "Merry, do you want to speak to Rodney?" She laughed heartily at whatever witty thing Merry said next and then handed me the phone. "I'm going to the rest room. Wouldn't wanna inhibit you, boss man."

I didn't even wait for Adele to leave the room before I hungrily picked up the phone. "Where you at, money?"

"In my convertible," she replied. "Wind blowing through my hair."

"Merry, you don't have any hair."

"Are you sure, Rodney? We black girls are tricky. You have no idea what I might have done with my hair."

"True dat, money. But you didn't answer my question. Where are you?"

"Are you listening, Rodney? In my convertible. I've been telling you for years you've got to be more sensitive to what women tell you."

With that as a clue I looked out the window. Merry was a trickster, a games player who loved surprises and lived for the shocked reaction of others. And sure enough, there were Adele and Merry, lounging next to Merry's black BMW convertible, both of them waving up at me.

"I see you."

"I would hope so," she answered. As usual Merry's black hair was cut close. Vintage Oliver Peoples frames rested across her pretty, light brown face and two sparkling diamond earrings decorated her earlobes. "I've invited your staff out to a late lunch, Rodney, but I guess you have to come too. Do you have some time, media mogul?"

Cravings is one of the Sunset Plaza sidewalk cafes that define that particular patch of the city. It anchors a strip of sidewalk eateries and boutiques that create a little community of see-and-be-seen establishments in the heart of West Hollywood. At a table to our left sat the *Green Acres* lady, Zsa Zsa Gabor. To our left was *Steve Harvey Show* costar Cedric the Entertainer. Whether old Hollywood or new-jack L.A., everyone at Cravings sat under big umbrellas wearing shades.

Merry looked wonderfully chic wearing black slacks, blouse, and sandals in gloriously sunny L.A. Homegirl had come a long way since we'd met years ago on the set of a McDonald's commercial featuring several R&B singers. Back then Merry was a junior executive at a black-owned advertising agency. Her style was radically different then—her hair was in a meticulously fried flip, light brown contact lenses covered her irises, and she wore boxy pants suits that camouflaged her beauty. Still she struck me as ambitious, young, bright, and very fuckable.

I was at the height of my ho-running record-business years, but Merry was more than a hit-and-run. She lived in New York. I was in L.A. So we arranged to play sex tag on our business trips. A cool weekend in my Manhattan suite. A hot one in her Beverly Hills Jacuzzi. It was all mop and glow for about a year until she pulled an engagement ring from under her pillow one night, leaned, and asked me to marry her.

My face must have shattered into a million pieces, judging by the way she burst out laughing. "It's a joke, Rodney! A joke!" She rolled over holding her stomach, she was laughing so hard. Me, I squeezed out a smile but I was not amused.

After we'd agreed we couldn't be lovers anymore I expected our communication would cease. Instead we ended up running into each other at the Grammys and hit parties all night long. I had planned on scooping some scantily clad nookie but ended up hanging with Merry, drinking champagne and cracking jokes. A friendship was born. Once the sex ended we actually became friends.

When Spike Lee started doing Nike spots in the mid-eighties the white agencies began paying attention to behind-the-scenes African-American talent. Merry was wooed by several white agencies, but instead of signing with one of the New York big boys, she joined one of those cutting-edge agencies based in the Northwest. Just as Seattle was becoming synonymous with cool, this little black girl from Queens was right up in the mix, writing national spots, commuting from East to West Coast on a weekly basis, and falling in love with one of the few brothers up in Bill Gates's Microsoft mix. It was a true Nubian fairy tale.

During her trips into town we would meet at Thai Dishes, a restaurant in Santa Monica where we'd sit back and analyze the culture together over *pad thai* and curried rice. Merry's lifeblood was in the intersection of African-American culture with white suburban dollars. As a result she listened to rap records, kept up with Terry McMillan, and religiously attended black hair shows. If it was black and commercial, Merry was on it.

Every time I dined with Merry I experienced deep pangs of jealousy whenever she pulled out pictures of her husband, Nicholas, and their home on an island in Puget Sound. So when her marriage of six years crumbled two years ago—apparently over his unwillingness to have children—I didn't come close to crying. I'd never met Nicholas (really I avoided a few opportunities), so I had no personal animosity toward the man. I probably gloated a bit too much when Merry told me of the split—something Adele noticed and still hasn't forgiven me for.

It's not like I benefited. Following her marriage's demise Merry went into a series of short monogamous relationships with (in order) an L.A. screenwriter, a Nigerian art dealer, and a New York doctor. "Merry's a one-man woman, Rodney," Adele once observed. "She likes being with one man at a time. She's not frivolous like you. You could have been that man."

I'm not convinced of that. Unlike with my special gang of three, I'd always felt like Merry and I had an ending. We'd moved naturally from lovers to friends. That was the end of the story.

"Ronnie's up to my shoulder now." Adele was describing how her eleven-year-old boy was growing, and Merry was eating it up.

"Yeah, Ronnie's something else," I added. "I like him so much I've already agreed to let him marry Tawana."

Merry told me, "Rodney, you better stop playing. You know there'll be no man good enough for those girls. How's Roberta doing anyway?"

"Braiding hair. Looking for love in all the wack places. The usual."

"So," Merry teased, "when are you going to become the ever popular baby Daddy?"

"You know I won't have a kid out of wedlock. The child Tameka, Tawana, and Tanina baby-sit will have a wife attached."

"I knew you were gonna say that," Merry replied, "but I like hearing it from you. It gives me hope, Rodney."

"But," Adele interjected, "Rodney hasn't told you his latest plan for finding love."

Honestly I wasn't going to tell Merry. Too many people knew already. It was getting embarrassing. That, however, didn't stop Adele from breathlessly relaying the story of my list.

"That," Merry decided, "is one foolish game you're playing, Rodney."

Adele was surprised that Merry didn't find it amusing. "I thought you'd think it was cute."

"No." Merry stared at me across the table with an intensity usually reserved for her clients' bad ideas. "Here it is the year two thousand, but Rodney here is chasing after his past. To me it shows the man is afraid of the future. Instead of being open to new things and people, he's going backwards. He doesn't wanna risk a thing and you only win in life by taking a risk."

"Why," I wondered aloud, "are you talking like I'm not here?"

"I'm sorry," she said coolly. "I just figured you're so obsessed with the past you must be a ghost."

Now I got a little sarcastic. "So, what kind of doctor are you seeing now? A brain surgeon? Plastic surgeon? What?" My tone was so hostile that Adele excused herself and headed swiftly to the ladies' room.

"I'm not seeing anyone, Rodney."

"That won't last."

She smiled shyly and replied, "I hope not."

With that my anger subsided. I found Merry so damn witty, I could never get but so mad at her. "How come," I wondered, "we stopped going out to Santa Monica for Thai food? How come you call at the last minute to let me know you're in town? How come you invited Adele to come eat with us?"

"A lot of questions, Mr. Hampton, but the answer is simple

and they go back to the same reason I think your list is foolish. We'd fallen into this weird rhythm. Ex-lovers. Friends. It all began feeling too vague to me. I've really grown to like things clear in my life. I've been married and divorced. All that real-life stuff. So I like things simple now."

"Am I hearing right? Do I get the feeling that you still have feelings for me?"

"Of course I do, Rodney. Why do you think after all these years we're still in touch?"

"For a woman who doesn't want things vague I'm now not sure what kind of feelings you have for me."

"I don't have to explain myself to you, Rodney." She sounded dismissive, like this was all she had to say. "I just have to do what I think is right for me." Adele came back to the table and we dropped that conversation, steering the talk back to Merry's latest ads for fast food and athletic shoes.

My mind drifted. I was in a suite at the Rhiga Royal in Manhattan. I was on the bottom. Somehow we'd fallen off the bed and my head was underneath the window. Our bodies were a good four feet from the edge of the mattress. I still don't know how we got there.

When Merry asked, "What's on your mind, Rodney?" I just smiled. Afterward she snatched up the check and I walked her, alone, to her car while Adele waited by mine. "How long are you here?"

"A couple of days. But I'll be shooting a spot."

"No Thai food?"

"Probably not. Besides, you'll be out hunting down the corpses of your dead relationships."

"Funny."

She grabbed my right hand and placed it against her cheek, as if I was slapping her. "Feel better now that you've slapped me, Rodney?" Her skin was butter soft, and for a few moments I rubbed it like a tailor fingering fine silk. Then she leaned over and kissed me ever so lightly on the lips. It was soft, it was sweet, and it was exquisitely brief. "See you around, ghost chaser," she said, and like a breeze, she was in her car and gone down Sunset Boulevard.

23

The haze outside the window was obscuring what certain days was probably a panoramic view of Beverly Hills. Every now and then I found myself glancing out at the hovering, tangible, full-bodied air as I spoke, trying to convince the atmosphere, along with everyone in the room, that I knew what I was talking about.

"So, Mr. Hampton, could you summarize for my colleagues why the L.A. Urban League should hold its annual fund-raiser on Valentine's Day?"

The speaker, Joseph Kwanza, owner of scores of strip malls and head of the local Urban League, was a man composed of circles. His face was round and brown as a mint treat left on your hotel room pillow. His soft, Pillsbury Doughboy stomach bespoke a hearty appetite for pies, cakes, and well-stuffed dinner plates. And his deep, resonant voice sounded as round as a whole note from a baritone horn.

At the oval conference table I looked in a clockwise circle at Kwanza and his two subordinates as I gave my answer. "February," I said, "is Black History Month, and Valentine's Day is in February, yet rarely, if ever, has the potential synergy of the two been explored. Black History Month is a time of reflection on the rich legacy of African-American women and men. Valentine's Day is a day when we stop all our other activities and focus on love, romance, and fidelity. I believe the two themes—black history and love—can be, pardon the pun, married in a fresh, exciting way."

After writing and calling Kwanza for months, trying to land a contract working with an organization full of nothing but respectable businessmen, it hit me I shouldn't simply be asking for a contract. To really make an impact I had to create some idea that made me indispensable to its execution. One night, after fantasizing that Tyra Banks had visited me in a Hooters uniform, this idea came to me.

"I propose that we celebrate the bonds between black women and men. On February fourteenth let us give thanks for each other and share our love of our mutual heritage and beautiful black selves. We'll have buttons that will say 'I Love the Black Woman' and 'I Love the Black Man.' People will give testimonials to their wives, husbands, lovers. All this can be framed as an argument for monogamy, safe sex, and abstinence. Our message will be romantic devotion is as much a part of our heritage as struggle. Next February the Urban League will celebrate a 'Romance with Righteousness.'"

Until then things had gone well. Mine was an original idea that could both excite and frighten the members of any old-line organization. So I'd been well prepared. At Kinko's the night before, with Kenya's help, I'd printed out a two-color proposal with a red, black, and green heart on the cover and the phrase "Romance with Righteousness" printed below it.

I'd anticipated being peppered with questions, including an outraged query or two about trivializing Black History Month and the Urban League. However, the only hard query I hadn't anticipated came from a poker-faced Kwanza: "What about our members married to whites or others outside the race?"

That threw me for a loop. I came up with some answer about brotherhood and multiculturalism as symbolic of the melting pot, but it wasn't smooth. I stumbled there—a stumble that became a fall when the receptionist later explained, yes, Joseph Kwanza had a white wife. Blond, to boot! After all those letters and calls I'd gotten to the seat of power and, in one unprepared moment, shot my ass in the foot—if such a feat was anatomically possible.

On the ride away from Kwanza's Century City offices and the crawl down Santa Monica Boulevard, I cursed my bad luck. I could see Kwanza dictating the letter now: "Your idea stimulated much discussion among our board members"—all of them undoubtedly living the multiculti life. "Unfortunately we feel the concept does not meet the institutional needs of the Los Angeles Urban League at this time. In the future if you have any endeavors the Urban League might wish to be involved with, feel free to contact us."

It would be a polite letter. No hard "Don't call us, we'll call you" vibe. More like a nice pat on the head and come back when you've thought up something more conventional. But I had gotten my meeting. I did get a chance to kick my ballistics, show my carefully shaved face, and for a half hour, escape the low-rent world of my usual clients.

Crossing Crescent Heights on Fountain I phoned Adele. "Two checks just came in, Rod. One from that jazz band from Inglewood."

"Those nonpaying motherfuckers."

"And one from that comic who writes jokes for Eddie Griffin."

"I thought we'd never hear from that fool. Well, that's good news."

"But there's bad news too."

"All right, hit me."

"The band owed us a G. They sent $650. The comedy writer owed $500 and sent $200."

I sighed. "Whatever. Cash in hand is better than air in your wallet. But please, Adele, deposit them before they turn to rubber."

This self-employed game wasn't for everyone and was barely for me. Despite the hardship, there was a certain satisfaction in being self-reliant that, in spite of slow (and no) paying clients, on most days made me feel important. When I worked at record companies, I knew I was a gear in a machine that would spew smoke whether I was well oiled or not.

The night my father was shot he was working the second of his two jobs. All my father's sweat poured out and evaporated off his skin to enrich other men. Sure, he got a house out of it. But the man my father worked for had homes (with an *s*), cars (with an *s*), and employees (with two *e*'s and an *s*). Why shouldn't I have that too?

The answer to that question was, well, maybe I wasn't good enough. I was persistent. I could juggle my ass off. Yet after three years in business, I was still scrambling. I'm looking for business stability, but the only thing I really control is my body. With everything else I need help.

So instead of heading back to the office, I took La Brea up to Sunset and then made a left on Shrader past the Hollywood Athletic Club on the corner, and then made another left into the Hollywood Y parking lot. It was about 11 A.M., so the unemployed actors, the comedians not on the road, the off-duty firemen, and the agile retirees would be gathering for some aggressive midday ball.

Using a Magic Marker I scrawled my name on the board in the old gym and then watched as three guys played H-O-R-S-E at one end, and at the other, a muscular elderly gent dropped in three-pointers with a set shot as ancient as canvas sneakers.

Overlooking the court was a grimy, tight weight room that had all the charm of a prison yard. Still, it was a good place to sweat.

I love working out. Working out hurts me. Either way I regularly put pressure on my body to respond to my mind's challenges. I work to make my muscles tighten, my shirt bulge, and the fatty tissues on my belly blow away like autumn leaves. That's what my mind wants. My body, however, is under no obligation to obey. My muscle mass doesn't expand easily. My stomach, after years of late-night meals and alcohol ingestion, defies sit-ups, stomach twists, and the almighty ab roller.

I suffered from that most acute of turn-of-the-century diseases—not AIDS, not herpes, not latex condom intolerance, but six-pack lack. In L.A. the most popular body part is not the butt, not the breast, or even the pecs, but the rigorous well-defined stomach. This unisex fixation is a unisex signifier. Aerobically fit, low-fat-eating, and disgustingly buff specimens of both sexes walk around with their bare midriffs displayed in cut-off shirts and tank tops, advertising the fruits of their labor for all the world to see and envy.

Recently, however, a more profound workout issue has overshadowed my six-pack lack—my bones are weaker than my will. My right wrist. My left shoulder. My left ankle. The arch on my right foot. They all betray me. They all collude in a stubborn conspiracy against my mandate. Often their plot renders me so sore that I move around afterward as gingerly as a newborn doe.

After my muscles were properly prepped I went down to the court, where a full was coming together. I greeted some guys I liked, nodded at those I didn't, and stretched my legs like a dancer. I remember when I could play all day on schoolyard concrete, breathing in that thick L.A. air with my only discomfort the stink of my perspiration on my skin. All that ended around twenty-seven when my ankles gave me my first intimation of mortality.

Now I try not to guard anybody too young or too quick. I don't mind checking a guy stronger than me. Give me a big slow guy and I'll lean on him, push him, and flick the ball away every time he tries to make a move.

Game time. I'm checking a fortyish, barrel-chested white guy, which usually means two things—I can beat him down the floor and he probably can stick a J. Of course, on the first play of the game he runs the baseline, cuts around a pick, and swishes a rainbow trey in my brown mug.

It's a bad omen. I can't make a layup while the guy I'm guarding lights me up for two more jumpers. While chasing him my right heel feels irritated. I start limping slightly. Despite my wackness, my five wins. I stretch my heel in between games and decide to get a little mean out there.

Next game I get a twenty-something black sitcom actor with a handle but no heart. I spend most of the game pushing, shoving, and otherwise moving him where I want him. I clean the glass for four offensive rebounds that result in two baskets for me and open J's for my teammates. A very pleasing game that leaves me feeling dominant, aggressive, and winning—a wonderful way to be at noon in the middle of the week.

A crew of high-flying new jacks have stacked the team coming on next. I see alley-oops and fast breaks in my immediate future. Due to my sore heel and my desire to maintain my cocoon of good feeling, I decide it's time to shower.

In the locker room I watch old men's bodies. Will my stomach jiggle like that one day? Will my ass look as pinched and pimply? It's scary to think that my private parts will dangle so low to the ground.

Maybe if my father was still alive, these old men wouldn't be so frightening. I'd just look at him and see myself in his flesh, in his folds, in his wrinkles, and know that it was part of nature, part of the natural cycle of life. I'd be comfortable with aging because I could look at it with love. While I was showering I imagined my father there with me, toweling off after we'd worked out together, joking with me that his was, after all these years, still bigger. I smiled to myself and then I cried a little. I don't think anyone noticed. Tried not to notice myself.

Back at the office there were faxes from Jive about D-Vince's album, a bill from Jackson Limousine re my night with Derrick and Mr. Neil, and about ten phone messages. I moved Tim's call to the top of the pile, hoping to torture my man about my midday ball playing while he labored in his white-collar uniform.

Tim's voice was as pale as his shirt when he answered the phone, so I told him, "You sound like a white man."

"Right now and up until six-thirty that's what I'm supposed to be."

"That's the gig, right?" I said.

"Word," he said.

"Word to the mother," said I. "Tim, guess what I did for lunch?"

"Judging by the gloating, fatigued, out-of-breath tone of your voice, I'd say you just finished laying bricks all across the Hollywood Y."

"That's the ticket, Mr. Waters-Wilson."

"You know, it's time we quit the Y and joined the L.A. Sports Club." The Sports Club was the town's trendiest gym, servicing a Tinseltown all-star team of movers, shakers, and six-pack show-offs.

"You got dough for that, newlywed?"

"I think I can squeeze it out of the household budget. Besides, it's way closer to Marina Del Rey than the Y, and if I'm serious about growing my business, which I am and I know you are, then we need to be elevating our range of contacts."

"I hear you," I agreed.

"I know you do. You've been making moves all this year. I've been watching and I've been impressed. I'm really feeling the same way."

"No more selling black homes to Central Americans?"

"I just want to sell, period. I'm for every color of the rainbow helping me build my company. At the Y we meet guys like us. At the Sports Club we'll meet the guys we want to be."

"Preach, brother Tim."

"Does the congregation say, 'Amen'?"

"Amen, Reverend Waters."

"So, what's my flock doing this weekend?"

Now I paused and my casual tone grew tight. We'd been having so much fun today I hadn't wanted to mention what I was about to mention, but then mentioning it was unavoidable. "Well," I began, "I'm taking out Caron Saturday night."

"Is this a date?"

"I guess it would fall in that category."

"Is this my wife's idea?"

"Come on. You know me better than that. Sure, Bernice has been an advocate, but there's real chemistry between me and Caron. I know it's not your idea of heaven, but for whatever reason, she seems real interested. Perhaps your wife told her I was a long-stroking daddy like her husband."

"Yo, man, leave me and my sex life out of it. You're a man, she's a woman, et cetera, et cetera. I just have this bad feeling you're gonna ruin my life. That's all that worries me. Otherwise you kids just go have a smashing time."

I laughed at that. Then we started talking about the Lakers and the difficulty they were having adjusting to Phil Jackson's triangle offense. It was inconsequential banter until Tim, with forced offhandedness, said, "You know the Utah game?"

"Yeah, it's next Thursday, right?"

"Bernice wants to go."

"Utah. As in Stockton, the Mailman, and the give-and-go?"

Tim took an exasperated breath before speaking. "I know you like them, Rodney. I know you enjoy all that fundamentally sound give-and-go mess, but—"

"No problem."

"Really?"

"No. No problem about the Utah game. You've given me plenty of notice, so I'm cool with it."

"Word."

"Word to the wife."

I tried to laugh at it. I mean, I'd predicted it. But I was still a little pissed, and maybe a little jealous.

24

The message I left for Caron was firm but not specific. "I'll be over around six-thirty. I want you to dress to impress. No evening gowns, but no reasonable flats either. We want sex appeal that'll make men jealous and elegance that'll make women envious. We're gonna make tonight real lush, like romantic lighting had been added to our personal movie. So that's the plan for tonight. Hope you're with it."

Around five forty-five I slipped on a beige linen suit, a chocolate silk shirt, a single gold chain, and brown Kenneth Cole sandals, splashed on some French cologne I couldn't pronounce, and used my trimmer to bring my mustache into shape. Figuring I was good to go, I slid into my Mustang and headed over toward Burbank.

Caron lived in a three-story condominium in Studio City not far from the Disney lot and a slightly longer drive from her job at Warner Bros. I rang on the car phone as I turned onto her street and spotted her up on her terrace in a low-cut black dress with her hair bobbed and bouncy. Up close in my car I admired her pedicured feet in open-toed mules and the depth of her dimples when she smiled.

"Is this what you had in mind?"

"Oh yeah," I said with the utmost admiration, and then we were off on our first date.

"Where are we going?" she asked.

"Why do you need to know?" I teased.

"Rodney, I didn't know you were so mysterious."

"I'm not normally," I admitted. "I'm usually a right-on-the-nose guy but tonight I feel inspired."

"Are you hyping me, Rodney?"

"The best I can," I replied and we both laughed.

Our destination was Santa Monica, specifically the Ivy at the Shore, an offshoot of the pricey Beverly Hills power bistro the Ivy. Through Bernice I knew it was one of Caron's favorite places, so trading on that information, I'd talked myself into one of its precious Saturday night reservations.

We sat in a glass-enclosed section that bordered the active sidewalk. Across from the restaurant was a boardwalk that overlooked the beach and the Pacific. Half a block away was the Santa Monica Pier, the place where I'd brooded over the list the day following the wedding. Now I was out with someone who wasn't on that fateful list and it felt liberating.

We had bantered about apartments and neighborhoods in the car. Now at the table things grew quiet. I'd been thinking about what we'd talk about all day. I came up with the following: "How about playing a game with me?"

"What, you gonna pull cards from out of that suit?"

"No, I don't have a deck with me. It's just that we've been together a lot of times. It's like we know each other but we really don't. So tell me something I don't know about you and I'll tell you something about me."

"Okay, I'll play." Caron considered a moment and then her face brightened. "Did you know that I am an expert on the work of Jean-Michel Basquiat?"

"No, I did not."

"Well, I'm not really an expert but I know a great deal about him and his paintings."

"Talk to me."

When Caron was attending Michigan University in the eighties she came across a *New York Times Magazine* cover story on Basquiat. On the magazine's cover the frizzy-haired black painter sat barefoot in a chair surrounded by paint, paintings, and the debris of his SoHo loft. Intrigued by both Basquiat's exotic Haitian bohemian looks and his garish, textured work, Caron, though a finance major, made learning more about Basquiat her hobby.

A few years back she'd even flown to New York for a retrospective of the late painter's career at the Whitney Museum. Caron spoke knowledgeably about Basquiat's world—his days as graffiti artist Samo, working with Andy Warhol, her problems with Julian Schnabel's film bio *Basquiat*. It was like Caron opened a door to another side of herself, and I was surprised, not at her interest in Basquiat but at how much I enjoyed exploring her.

"What about you, Rodney? What are you into that I don't know about?"

I'd debated telling her my secret life. I didn't share it with anyone, really. But tonight it felt right. "Me, I wanna write children's books," I said earnestly. "Maybe it's because I've loved to read since I was four. Maybe it's because of my three nieces, but I've been writing a story in my head for a couple of years now."

My tale was a simple one and, unfortunately, not complete. Sort of *Alice in Wonderland* meets a CD player in sepia. A black girl named Eboni can see music. When she hears music, colors appear before her eyes. The blues are an inky dark hue of its namesake color. Rock was various shades of crimson and scarlet. Hip-hop was the color of money. And so on across the spectrum of sound and the rainbow of hues.

But she can't make colors herself. Her piano lessons, taken under the demanding instruction of Abigail Stringfellow, gave her musical skills but still no colors emanated from her keyboard.

So one afternoon a frustrated Eboni repeatedly slammed her hands against the keys. Suddenly with a blare of sound the family's CD player flipped on with all six CDs inside spewing forth a cacophony of sound and color. Eboni pressed button after button as her ears and eyes were overwhelmed. The tray holding the CDs popped open and they started to glow. Eboni looked on in amazement until a swirling, loud rainbow rose up from the tray and sucked her in. Eboni fell through an ocean of blue before landing on the awning of a nightclub and then tumbled gracefully to the ground. Looking up she saw that the club's name was Kind of Blue, the same title as her father's favorite jazz album, which had been in the CD player before she fell in.

And then I stopped talking. "So," Caron wanted to know, "what happens next?"

I had to admit, "I'm really not sure. What I think is gonna happen is that Eboni embarks on an odyssey, going from CD to CD seeking a way home. Each CD has different music and represents a different color. The other thing is that Mrs. Stringfellow is sort of the Wicked Witch chasing Eboni."

"What are you waiting for? You should finish that story."

"I'd like to but I don't seem to have the time. You know how it is. I'm independently employed. Not a corporate girl like you."

"Rodney? Is it all right now if I act like I know you?" Her question made me laugh. "Sure you can," I answered.

"That story is so much you. I mean, when I've talked to you or seen you with Tim, I always got a feeling you were acting like you thought you were supposed to be—not who you really were."

This observation made me incredibly uncomfortable and I could feel my body heat up, not angry really, but embarrassed. Caron continued, "You can be very L.A.—fast talker, hypster, all that—but from what I've seen, you're always a little detached. Like you'd like to be somewhere else. I just never knew where else until you told me that story. Is this upsetting you?"

Of course, I lied when she asked, trying to smile and play off the way my brain flooded with blood and my toes wiggled inside my loafers. It was rare for anyone, except Roberta, to discuss me with me. Usually I was helping someone—professionally and personally—to get themselves together.

Caron was pressing a small hidden button and I chafed under the pressure. I turned the conversation around by inviting Caron to help me with scenes and conflicts for my little story. It chilled me out, lowered my blood pressure, and, in fact, helped develop a nice plot thread—that Eboni's parents were in conflict and her disappearance served to bond her mother and father.

Overall we had a fine dinner, good food, interesting talk. Yet her earlier comments about me still irritated, like a bit of dirt had lodged in my eye, a speck that made my iris red and with each rub got bigger and more bothersome.

After dessert I suggested we walk over to the Third Street Promenade and catch a movie. Instead Caron insisted we stroll over to the Santa Monica Pier. As always on a weekend night the pier was a carnival of youthful multiculti hormones. We were profoundly overdressed, which I pointed out to Caron, but she thought that made it more fun. Unlike other women I'd taken over to the pier, Caron wasn't interested in any of the rides. Instead she led me over to the arcade.

"Do you like Air Hockey?" she wondered.

"Sure."

"Good, I love Air Hockey. Go get some quarters and I'll grab a table." A Chicano couple were moving toward the last open table when Caron, displaying a rebounder's tenacity, slid herself between them and the table. I anticipated some beef but Caron just smiled and, with a quickness, slid two quarters into the game's slot and latched on to one of the two white plastic guides used to play.

Out of a slot next to where she deposited the money popped the yellow plastic puck that she casually flipped on the board. Then, with mounting aggression, Caron smacked her guide on the gray metallic playing surface. "Okay, Rodney, are you ready to rumble?"

Well, honestly, I wasn't. In Air Hockey aggression is everything. Once the yellow puck starts skimming across the board the game is won by him or her who can blast the puck fastest. Before I could really get going Caron had blitzed me in two games and was about to blast me a third time before I could bring the noise. After that I started bending my back and focusing on that frisky little puck, all of which Caron found incredibly amusing.

"You okay over there, Rodney?" she said teasingly. "We can stop if this is too difficult for you."

"No," I answered through gritted teeth, "I'm having a great time."

She chuckled at this and then slid the yellow puck off the right wall, across to the left, and then—bam!—right into my goal. I wiped my sweaty forehead as my elegantly dressed opponent smiled condescendingly at me.

Victory made her magnanimous because afterward Caron was quite affectionate. She clung to my arm like a vine. She patted my buns ("Nice," she noted approvingly). She stuck her tongue in my ear when we took a photo at one of those Japanese gadgets that place your face inside a colorful frame. It all felt very close and couplelike.

We walked away from the crowd over to the railing that overlooked the beach and the Pacific. We stood next to each other. Then I was behind her, my groin pressed up against her ass; my mouth was on her neck, her perfume was in my nose. I tasted her on my tongue. Slowly she turned and we were kissing in public just like all the other kids on Santa Monica Pier.

Back in my ride. Decision time. How hard to push up? Lay back, or bum rush? Riding back across Los Angeles, freeway to freeway, we were quiet, listening to Luther Vandross's *The Night I Fell in Love* and contemplating our desire. When we turned onto her block Caron's hand caressed the inside of my thigh, squeezing the muscle on the top of my leg, and then patted it. And that gesture spoke for us both—I want to, I'd like to, but not tonight, not so soon. "I had a good time," she said and I replied, "So did I." The goodnight kiss was fine— more affection than sensual. There was a suggestion of hidden intensity and the feeling one would be rewarded for patience.

25

Leroy Martinez outdid himself. There were fried chicken fajitas, sweet potato guacamole, macaroni and cheese with black beans, collard-green-and-string-bean burritos, and all manner of Negro-Spanish cuisine on display at the Blaxican Cafe the night of D-Vince's coming-out party.

Hundreds of people rolled down to the unfashionable part of La Cienega Boulevard to get free music, free food, and press their flesh up against brown people of various accents, Westside white folks of the liberal persuasion, and a sprinkling of expertly garbed Asians. To my delight the gathering looked like one of Belinda's parties back when she ran downtown.

My whole crew turned out—Tim, Bernice, Caron, Adele, Kenya, Roberta, and the girls (I love showing them life outside South Central)—as well as many wild cards, like Circus, Belinda, Joey Stein, and even Amy, who didn't stay long but did sheepishly get D-Vince's autograph and gave me a nice hug when she left. Seeing all the levels of my life in one room was like watching my favorite sitcoms morph into one hour-long drama.

Professionally I've never had a better night of wheeling and dealing. My Urban League contact, Joseph Kwanza, came with his wife, Millie, who was tan and quite chatty. Millie loved the food and spent so much time hovering around Leroy's kitchen I thought she was looking for work. Joseph was more reserved, eyeing the young multiculti crowd with amusing gravity. At one point he asked, "Is this ethnic mix typical of all your events?" So, wisely, I lied and answered in the affirmative, which got him nodding his head knowingly and no doubt making checks on my side of the ledger.

Clive Calder, Jive's president and founder, made an appearance since he was in town on some other business. Nancy Bishop made the introductions, and after Calder, D-Vince, and some local radio announcers posed for the obligatory trade shots, she told me the label had decided to accept my proposal for a three-month trial period. At the end of that time they'd reevaluate to see whether I wanted to come in-house or stay with the retainer situation, or whether they'd bring someone else in full-time. Three months of guaranteed money!

Joey Stein showed up with a new tan and a glad hand. He'd just come from one event and was on his way to another—I've noticed film folks don't linger at non-Hollywood parties. They flitter around like moths worried that landing in unfamiliar places puts them at social peril. Apparently Larry Jason Jones hadn't deemed my event worthy of his time, but Joey more than made up for his absence. I noticed that he catered to Kenya with a smooth deference.

When Joey Stein wasn't around, Circus stalked Kenya, gazing at her as the wolf does the lamb. To my dismay Kenya seemed to be inviting his lascivious looks. I was moving and shaking too much to pay close attention, yet I sensed her enjoying Circus's pursuit, which turned my stomach.

Similarly Belinda, who had managed to chip some of the ice off her tone when she spoke to me, didn't seem to mind the way D-Vince slid from embrace to embrace, apparently basking in even a sliver of the young stud's attention. I didn't press for more conversation, just happy to have established a beachhead, hoping she was as impressed with my party savvy as I had once been with hers.

Caron came with Tim and Bernice, wearing a red pants suit and a white blouse with red pumps. Bright and buttoned down, she stuck out at the Blaxican, as did Tim and Bernice, all three looking like representatives of buppiedom invited for politically correct balance. I noticed Bernice monitoring us for signs of chemistry.

Tim seemed unusually out of sorts, far removed from the food, music, and social mix of the event. I also didn't see him speaking to Circus, which I made a note to ask him about later. "Where's your head at, Tim?" I asked toward the party's end.

"I left it outside, my man. Sorry."

"Wanna talk later?"

"I'll call you. Soon."

And otherwise quite occupied, I left it at that.

26

Perhaps because business was picking up and I was feeling cocky, I woke up one morning determined to get Belinda to talk to me. I must have called five times in two hours, from nine to eleven, before I finally got Belinda on the phone. Apparently I awakened her, which made her curt and dismissive, but I decided to play to her anger and use it to tease a smile out of her.

"So," I said, "I'm a day late and several dollars short?"

"A day late?" she said with a chuckle.

"More like years, huh?"

"Why are you calling me now?"

"The reason is so silly, it's embarrassing," I admitted.

"Well," she said sharply, "you're already kind of a joke to me, so why stop now?"

So I told her about the wedding and what my mother told me and the idea that I might have missed out on my wife, et cetera, et cetera.

"Damn, are you sure you're a man?"

"Why you wanna ask that?"

"I just can't believe a man's mind would ever go there."

"And I can't believe you'd leave a man capable of such an idea hanging when he just wants to be in your presence again—even if it's just over dinner."

"Determined, huh?"

"And why not? I blew a good thing. I just wanna reconnect. There can be no strings attached, because you are the puppeteer, Belinda."

"All right with the metaphors, Shaft. I got you, okay? How about Thursday at Luna Park? Eight-thirty."

"I'll make the reservation," I said with satisfaction. "Can't wait to see you."

"We'll see." She laughed slyly and hung up.

Belinda lived on Rossmore a couple of blocks from Melrose in the direction of Hancock Park. When I called from the Mustang she wasn't ready, so she invited me up to her apartment, which was as warm as she could be chilly. The eggshell walls were adorned with all manner of small wood-framed paintings (mostly outdoor scenes), African masks, and plants that dangled from pots and somehow clung to the paintings and masks. By the door was an ancient upright piano and next to it a miniature Italian water fountain made of faux stone.

Belinda's personal space had an earthy, relaxing quality at odds with her superchic demeanor. No doubt she needed this rustic vibe to protect her spirit. In L.A. holding on to your soul required creativity. I'd worn a gray jacket, black shirt, and slacks and loafers just in case Belinda went uptown on me. But she came out casual chic in black pedal pushers and top, and an electric pink cashmere sweater that could illuminate a dungeon.

On the way over to West Hollywood we talked business—the politics of organizing and sustaining a nightclub in a city with so many things to do and so much distance between here and there; the politics of juggling several clients at once and trying to maintain some semblance of cash flow. Turned out her main objective for the evening was to cajole me into throwing my clients' parties at Eden's Taste. As I gave my Mustang to Luna Park's valet, Belinda was pitching hard. "You could have done D-Vince's party at Eden's Taste and fit in two hundred more people."

"Probably," I agreed, "but my goal there, quite frankly, was to make sure I did an event that benefited both my clients."

"What? Do I need to hire you to get your clients' business?"

I replied, "You kiss my neck, I'll suck your toes," to which she sucked her teeth in lieu of an answer.

Luna Park is an ultracool, ultrachic, multileveled restaurant-lounge-cabaret that drew from Hollywood hipsters, music lovers, and the surrounding gay scene on Santa Monica Boulevard. Bronze-beige walls, burgundy curtains, and subdued lighting bathed the sunglasses-at-night, tight-T-shirt, sleek-high-heeled-sandals clientele in a mellow gold atmosphere.

After we'd ordered our food and drink Belinda leaned over and arched those movie star eyebrows. "Now," she started, "that we're here I want you to walk me through your list again." I kicked more detail than I had over the phone. As Belinda listened her eyes glittered, looking amused and sympathetic.

"Tim's wedding really got to you, Shaft. I mean, a real extreme reaction. You must really be feeling your biological clock."

"Well, I hope it doesn't sound like that."

"But it does, Shaft, and you know, that's all right. Most people in the world are desperate for love or whatever they can get that seems close."

"So," I cut in, feeling it was time to turn the conversation around, "what about you? I remember your philosophy from before. Live and let's get busy. Have you evolved any?"

There was a short burst of laughter and then she said condescendingly, "I don't know if you're ready, Shaft. You were always the conventional type."

"Okay, then. Shock me." I folded my arms and sat straight up in my chair. The food arrived—seafood pasta for me, sushi for her—as did a big bottle of sparkling water. Belinda sat waiting for the waiter to leave, while I tried not to seem anxious. Some handsome white club kid with spiky hair came over to kiss Belinda's ring and ask to be on her guest list. I ate, sipped my wine, and tried to enjoy the spectacle that was Belinda. After her acolyte split she asked, "Are you ready now, Shaft?"

"Sure," I replied coolly. "Whatever you do or talk about is fine, baby."

"All right, then, Shaft. I am currently having a love affair with my vibrator." I laughed and smiled and said, "Go on."

"If I need a hug I call a woman; if I need a nut I turn on the vibrator. Either way I get what I need and nobody—least of all me—gets hurt."

"You can't tell me I didn't satisfy you."

"No?"

"Don't mess with me, Belinda."

"You right. You right. You could do a little somethin' somethin'."

"Thank you."

"But—"

"But what?"

"Ever notice how I'd immediately change the sheet after we made love?"

"And you'd wash my body too. I wasn't mad at that. I just thought you were the most seriously neat person I'd ever been with."

"It wasn't about neat, Shaft. It was about your sweat. I liked your dick but couldn't stand your sweat. All that foreign perspiration upon my person."

"You sweat too, you know."

"But my sweat wasn't like yours. Your sweat was heavy. I could feel it on top of my belly and my breast and on my neck when you used to drip down on me."

"I smelled that bad?"

"It's not you alone, Shaft. Everybody I've ever been with sweats too heavy for me. I sweat light. Right?"

"Yeah. I think I'm beginning to understand and it's a little scary. You've swore off having sex with any human being because this vibrator—"

"Beckford. His name is Beckford."

"Yeah, because Beckford handles all your business."

"Come on, Rodney, don't act so surprised. You remember when I had Denzel—"

"Denzel?"

"That brown vibrator I had before?"

"You kept it under the pillow, right."

"That's right. Kept it under my pillow. Sometimes your back hurt, remember?"

"Okay. I remember. But you never wanted to rely just on that before. Every now and then I'd use it to double-team you, but it was just an appetizer or a side dish. You talking like this new vibra—"

"Beckford."

"Yeah, right, Beckford has replaced all human contact."

"I said when I need a hug I call a woman."

"Come on, Belinda, I can't believe you've cut men all out of your life."

"I have for now unless they are the coolest motherfuckers in town. You bring me a man in L.A. or outlying regions who can do his business without turning my belly into a mop and that's a man I need to know."

"So what about D-Vince?"

She considered the question, twisting her face up thoughtfully while watching mine. "He strikes me as being cool under pressure." A pause. Then she smiled. "I'm not sure if I'm gonna fuck you. Is that what you wanted to know?" I grimaced but I didn't otherwise reply. "About that, Shaft, we'll just have to see."

Feeling stupid, I offered a weak "I guess it's none of my business."

"You used to be able to dance, Shaft. Let's see what you got left."

Upstairs a DJ was playing drum and bass from Britain—a music as anonymous, seductive, and late-nineties trendy as a fashion show. Belinda threw herself into the beats and I followed. The room was only half full so there was plenty of room on the dance floor, and Belinda, feeling extravagant and perhaps empowered by our conversation, sprung and moved as if no one existed but her. I was a satellite—at best a tall, brown moon—that rotated in her shadow. A muscular, energetic gay man in a Hawaiian shirt started to orbit and I found myself floating to the far reaches of Belinda's constellation.

Like a voyeur I studied Belinda's body, savoring it, remembering it, knowing full well it would never be mine again. I wanted to be jealous of D-Vince, of Beckford the vibrator, of the gay man in the loud shirt drawn over in admiration of her attitude.

I'd had my lively time with her and, of my own free will, ended it, so I had no kick coming. And that's the lesson I took from Belinda that night. With her, and with Amy, we'd had our time and it had passed. So be it. I sipped my last merlot of the evening, watched Belinda angle her loveliness near me, and I decided that night to end my quest. It was over. Sabena, I toasted, may you live long and never have to have dinner with me again.

27

They say her depression is acute and getting worse. They say she doesn't wanna eat. They say it's like slow suicide." The "they" who were suggesting all these horrible things about my mother was her therapist. The person who was speaking in a nerved-up tone about all this was my sister. Her car was rolling across Wilshire Boulevard after another sad Sunday at the nursing home. "Rod-nee, she's getting worse."

"Sounds like it." I was trying to act calm, but it probably sounded too casual.

"I wish we could do something."

"I know," I agreed, "but what?" I tried to change the subject by asking how come she hadn't been bringing the girls along.

"Tameka remembers how she used to be when she first moved in with us, so it makes her cry to see Ma now. Tanina never really knew her as she was, so she doesn't really know Ma enough to love her, which makes me real sad."

"And Tawana?"

"Funny thing. She's the only one who seems to have a grip on herself when I bring them. She'll sit with Ma all day. Wear her Walkman. Listening to her music the whole time. But soon as Ma asks for something or just moves, middle T's right there for her. That girl is so patient. I don't bring her just because her being so calm makes me look bad."

"That's weird, isn't it?" I said. "The media-overloaded one is the calmest person in our family. I guess that's a good thing."

"You know, Rod-nee, by bringing up the girls you're avoiding my damn question."

"Yeah, I know," I said sympathetically. "But what can I say? You've talked to the doctors and the therapist. It's not about medicine, it's about her will to live. What can I do about that?"

"When are you getting married?"

"How the fuck do I know?"

"Well, how's your list going? You reel in any old fish?"

"I'm not doing it anymore."

"What? You going celibate on me?"

"No. I'm through with my list, Roberta. It's been a mess."

"None of them wanna talk to you?"

"No," I said quickly, "they wanna tell me too much."

"Oh yeah."

"I found Amy and Belinda. Even had dinner with them. Both were bad mistakes. Really bad mistakes."

"So the list is over?"

"Didn't I just say that?"

"Okay." Roberta sat there a minute looking out the window while I drove. Between Ma's health and my sex life this was a very unpleasant conversation. I turned up the Beat as D-Vince's "Fully Loaded" came on. I'd planned on shifting the conversation to my successful promotional efforts, when my sister opened up my wounds. "So when you getting married, engaged, or just having a baby?"

"What is your problem today, Roberta?"

"My problem is that you're the only man in the family and it's time you started acting like one."

"If you weren't my sister, your ass would be out the goddamn window."

"But I am your sister and I'm putting it to you like this—I bet if you just acted like you were settling down, much less really goin' there, Ma would get a little bit better. I'm not sayin' it would save her life. I'm just sayin' it would be one more reason for her to get up every morning."

"You know, practically speaking, that my getting married would mean less money for you and the girls from me."

"Please, Rodney, money's not more important to me than Ma. Even you should know that."

One woman short. That's what Ma had said. I'd written down the list because of the wedding and all the emotions it dredged up. But I'd begun pursuing three women because of Ma's words. My quest was really begun to please her. Now Roberta was suggesting I just go out and find any old girl and front if I have to. I'm sure I could fool some unsuspecting woman to come with me to meet my ma as I played the role of devoted lover. That wouldn't be hard.

And it would be a lie. I've lied before. To women, to clients and magazine editors—all to get what I wanted or thought I needed. Yet even hype has a line that can't be crossed. I wasn't gonna lie to my ma about love. That was a line that couldn't be crossed.

When I told this to Roberta she sucked her teeth. But she knew I was right, and for the time being, that was the end of that discussion. Or so I thought.

"Did you ever call Bernice's friend? The bridesmaid? What's her name?"

"Caron."

"She was nice, right?"

"Yeah."

"Well?"

"Maybe."

"When did you get so reluctant in trying to chase pussy?"

"I'm trying to find a mate, Roberta, but I'm also not trying to front. I'm trying not to be a ho."

"Boy, you're a mess. I like you and all, like Ma said, but you are a mess."

Time to change the subject, I thought. "So you have a date tonight. What's this guy's hustle?"

"He doesn't have a hustle. He has a business. He's my computer trainer."

"What, you trying to tell me you're going out with a man who can both read and write?"

"And he can do both better than you."

"Okay, baby," I said, impressed. "You might be right. Hey, can I take the girls tonight?"

"I already hired a sitter."

"Come on now, I've been busy lately. Haven't seen them much lately. I'd feed them. You'll have leftovers and all that."

"Fine. But tomorrow's school. Get them home by nine. I'm just gonna go to the movies and come right back."

"Doesn't sound too romantic, Roberta."

"Hey, I know a lot more about handling men than you do. Believe that."

I dropped Roberta off at a grocery store near her house (the one owned by Destina's husband) and then went home. Before I picked up the girls I wanted to do some work on the production notes for that movie *Night Shift*. But after the phone rang I didn't get much done.

"My," a familiar voice teased, "your voice sounds sexy on Sundays."

"Where are you, Merry?"

"Shutters, out in Santa Monica. You remember it?" Back in the day it had been one of our spots. Great brunch. Great beds. Not necessarily in that order. "I've been shooting a spot the last two days along the PCH. Maybe I'm falling victim to nostalgia too but I was wondering if you wanted some Thai food."

"I'm baby-sitting tonight."

"Really? Bring them along. I haven't seen them since they were tadpoles."

"Thai food's a little too progressive for my crew, I think. But I have a better idea."

I rounded up my nieces, pulling them away from homework and video games, and shuffled them into my cramped Mustang. I muffled Tameka's and Tanina's complaints by blasting the Beat and playfully leaning my body when we took some of the deep curves on Sunset Boulevard in Brentwood and on out toward the Pacific. The journey out to the coastline on Sunset is one of my favorite drives, especially once you get past Westwood and the UCLA campus.

"We're going to Gladstone's, right?" It was Tawana, the middle child, who for all her video fixations didn't seem to miss much. Gladstone's was a family-oriented seafood restaurant located at the end of Sunset that had sawdust on the floor, fake nautical fixtures, and scads of celebrity photos on its front walls. When it was warm you could dine outside. When it was chilly, as it was this night, you slid into long wooden tables with your collected relatives.

We Hamptons were all settled in when Merry, in black stretch pants, shining black loafers, a white blouse, and a leather jacket, slid in. Tameka remembered her well and they hugged. Tawana and Tanina were intrigued by this elegant brown lady and watched closely how I acted toward her.

Merry was fantastic with the girls, talking fashion with Tameka and toys with Tanina (she'd done some spots for Hasbro). Tawana, as was her nature, seemed oblivious to everything, yet I knew she was observing it all. After I'd made a mess of my lobster and the ladies had devoured pieces of fried fish, Tawana, I guess feeling comfortable with Merry's presence, set the evening off.

"Merry, have you ever been married?"

"Yes, I have, honey. But I'm not now."

"Neither my mother nor Uncle Rodney have been married. Is that good?"

"Tawana," I said with fatherly sternness, "why are you being so nosy?"

"It's fine, Rodney. I can answer that. Being married isn't easy. It's harder than going to school or anything you can imagine. It scares people. But," she said, switching from melancholy to optimistic, "when it's good, it's great. I know each one of you will enjoy it."

"I'm not getting married," Tawana told the table. "Not until Uncle Rodney does."

"Oh," Merry laughed, "Tawana just put some real pressure on you."

I was knocked out by this one. "Why?" I asked Tawana.

"Because if you don't wanna do it, why should I, Uncle Rodney?" Tanina thought this comment was hysterical and she just started giggling like a fool. Tameka, older and wiser, just peeked sheepishly at me, knowing I was deeply embarrassed.

Merry was by now so charmed by my middle niece that she offered her a ride home in her convertible. So I had Tameka and Tanina in my Mustang, interrogating them about Tawana's comments, but both pleaded ignorance.

When we got them home Roberta was waiting anxiously in the living room. She vaguely remembered Merry and was cordial, but really was much more preoccupied with getting the girls to bed than with my love life.

On the way crosstown Merry and I stopped at the Shark Bar for drinks. Stevie Wonder and a party of five were dining at a front table. We retired to a comfy couch near the front door. Merry had a sidecar and I my usual wine. "Now what did you and Tawana talk about?"

"You, actually."

"Bring it, Merry."

"Nothing earth-shattering. She told me you had so many women it made her head dizzy."

"Oh no."

"That your mother and sister have almost given up on you. And, oh yes, how silly your list is. A smart little girl, Rodney. I think she has a future in advertising."

"Ha ha."

We bantered on about all three girls. Merry seemed fascinated about how Roberta and I handled them, balancing our work with being guardians and mentors. It went on awhile like this before Merry threw a curve.

"I've been reconsidering your list."

"And what conclusions have you come to?"

"Well, I was on a plane to Seattle the other day and I wrote down my own list."

"How many names?"

"None of your business."

"What number was I?"

"Oh, either three or fifteen. I forget."

"Sure. Like a woman would forget a lover. Not likely."

"I'll tell you this: making that list made me think. That was the best part of it. Looking at it makes you think about all your decisions. I don't know if it's a guide to the future but it says a lot about your journey to here and now."

"Do I hear a half compliment buried in all those words?"

"No, you don't."

"Okay. So tell me, who are you seeing now?"

She rubbed my nose with the tip of her finger. "That's for me to know and you to wonder about." I tried to pry it out of her but Merry was firm about holding on to this key bit of information. I got the idea she was single but Merry was enjoying her secret, so I let it go.

It was our first time alone in over a year, and happily, we flowed into our old conversational mode—movies (she was still Spike Lee's staunchest fan), books (she couldn't get into John Edgar Wideman, but she'd keep trying), and music (she finally admitted R. Kelly had talent, despite that Alliyyah situation). Time passed pleasantly. Her skin looked like satin. I felt myself smiling a lot. Before I knew it the drinks were taken off the end table and the lights were raised.

She'd parked her car across La Cienega Boulevard in front of a vintage instrument shop. We gazed at an ancient Marshal amp, the kind Jimi Hendrix used and abused, and we faced each other, and then she leaned toward me and kissed me lightly on the lips.

"Is that an appetizer?"

"No, Rodney, that's the whole meal."

"So," I said as I slipped my arms around her waist, "what are we doing for breakfast?"

"A bagel and OJ at LAX. Gate forty-seven. Meet you there at seven A.M."

I let her go and stepped back. "Do me a favor. Don't kiss me like that anymore. I'm an excitable boy. I can't take it."

"Which is why I do it."

She pressed a button on her key chain and her convertible

unlocked. She moved away. I watched her and I said, with more anger than I wished, "I'm just a game to you now. Is that it, Merry?"

"No." She slipped into the driver's seat and turned on the motor. "I just can't figure out what to do with you, Rodney." She didn't even wave.

28

was working late at the office one night when the phone rang and a female voice barked, "You weren't lying. You really don't love me."

"Hello, Kenya."

"Don't 'hello' me," she announced. "If you don't come tonight, don't stop by Kinko's ever again."

"Look, I've been busy."

"Do you have a copy of the L.A. *Weekly*, Mr. Media Man?"

"Yeah."

"Page fifty-eight. Theater section." On that page was a striking picture of Kenya looking mean and commanding, and under it a review that raved about her performance.

"Damn, Kenya, you blew the fuck up!"

"Thank you," she said, sounding pleased. Then she put a little bass in her voice. "I'm leaving one ticket at the box office tonight. One ticket."

"Kenya—" Click went the phone. Okay, little miss. Four hours, some good *pad thai*, and a stroll through the Virgin megastore later, I was watching Kenya's dark brown body stalk a small Hollywood stage like a panther. She had taut little-boy muscles in her arms and back; on her shoulders two black strings held up a clingy tubular navy blue dress that somehow made her look more delicate than she was.

Yet her character was neither dainty nor shy as she toyed with a beefy white woman tied to a chair as a small computer glowed menacingly on a card table stage left. It was the first time I'd seen Kenya act and it was more than impressive—it was arousing.

Kenya spoke with an air of cocky command that I didn't realize she possessed. There was this one monologue she did early in the play that got me open. "As an individual—which you most certainly are—you want to exist outside of community," she said authoritatively. Then she started to break her captive down.

"The thing is, what defines you as different from me and different from everyone else is only apparent in contrast to the larger community. In other words you exist as an individual only because there is a larger group." By now she stood menacingly behind the woman, speaking in a sneering stage whisper. "If we don't exist or, in this particularly pressing circumstance, survive, who are you then?" She strutted to face her prisoner, putting a hard brown hand around the lady's throat.

"Let me tell you—you are a definition without meaning, a symbol with no context, an individual with no collective to rail against!" Kenya snatched her hand away and crossed her arms, all the while burning a harsh gaze into the other actress's face. "In short you are nothing. So you better sign this paper before you disappear."

The audience, a sellout following the rave reviews, was vibing Kenya as strongly as I did, following her character's evolution from captive to conqueror with the intensity of a cat clocking a mouse. At the play's end Kenya stood center stage, bowing and smiling while I joined the rest of the audience in enthusiastic applause. As I looked around, feeling quite special about my connection to Kenya, filled with pride that she had desired me and perhaps still did, I spotted Circus in the back, standing and clapping too.

Afterward we stood by the dressing room awaiting the star.

"Yo, man," he said sarcastically, "your friend Kenya is all right. Her body doesn't boom like I like, but she's got flavor."

"Yeah," I agreed, "she does."

"We're gonna have dinner. You wanna join us?" My heart was evaporating like dreams in a dying man's mind and I'm sure it showed on my face. I glanced at my watch, then acted surprised at the time.

"No, Circus. It's later than I thought. I gotta finish a press release tonight. Just tell Kenya I loved it and I'll give her a shout-out later."

"No problem, my man," he said smugly as I turned to make my escape. As I moved through the theater's glass doors I heard Kenya's voice call my name. But the noise from outside—the cars and the theatergoers and the low hum of a busy night—muffled her words (at least that was my excuse) and I moved swiftly, quickly, away from the theater and Circus and my dark brown Kinko's cutie turned star.

29

The Universal CityWalk is a carefully fabricated slice of urban landscape. Upscale fast food abounds, like the huge Hard Rock Cafe at its far end. The many knick-knack shops are filled with souvenir T-shirts from UCLA, images of cartoon characters, and profoundly worthless trinkets like key rings and stuffed animals. Well-sanitized street performers sang, danced, and manipulated puppets for the amusement of Angelenos who otherwise never strolled.

In the CityWalk's central plaza water periodically spouted out of a submerged fountain perfect for children to prance in and for naughty boyfriends to pull their girlfriends toward. Back when Tim and Bernice were dating, it was a ritual for that dynamic duo to visit CityWalk for movies and a bit of old-fashioned hand holding. On the few occasions Caron and I tagged along, Tim and Bernice couldn't pass the water hole without wrestling over who would push who into it. Surprisingly often it was Bernice, pretty quick on her feet for an accountant, who tripped her much bigger boyfriend — splash! — into the spout's line of fire.

But on this Saturday evening, just half a year into their marriage, they walked past the spouting water without a nudge, much less a word. They did hold hands but it was more a clutch than a caress, as if each was afraid the other would escape.

Caron and I were just a few feet behind them, not holding hands but walking close together. "Do you think they seem a little tense tonight?"

"No," she lied. "They look like they always do. Why would you say something negative like that?"

Our little quartet was moving toward CityWalk's mammoth Cineplex Odeon after dining at Gladstone's, a barnlike, quite inferior version of the original out by the Pacific. The dinner itself had been a chilly affair. Tim and Bernice didn't say much to each other. It was mere couple cross talk—Tim and I talked about the Lakers, Bernice and Caron discussed the Royal Shakespeare Company's production of *Hamlet* coming to the Mark Taper Forum. I was vibing on trouble in paradise, though Tim hadn't said anything to me about any unusual stress. I guess when you're married you're not nearly as quick to tell tales out of school.

As for Caron and me, things had been progressing slowly. I mean we were kissing and conversing. That was all good. Yet the lady had the disquieting tendency to talk too much about Tim and Bernice. What they were buying. What they were planning. How nice they were to each other. It was beginning to occur to me that Caron saw us refracted through the prism of Tim and Bernice, like we were just sidebars to the main story, not worthy of our own headline.

I was starting to think our relationship was as prefab as the streets we walked through. No foundation. Just stuck atop the ground. A strong wind could blow us clean away. Even how we were walking—several strides behind Tim and Bernice— made it feel like we were keeping a respectful distance from royalty.

Feuding royalty at that. Outside the theater a marital spat ensued over which movie to see. Bernice wanted to see Meg Ryan's latest chick flick, while Tim was down for a thriller starring Harrison Ford. Caron, not surprisingly, sided with Bernice, while I really didn't give a fuck.

In an attempt to resolve this stalemate Tim proposed he go see the Harrison Ford flick with me and the ladies go weep with Meg. "You never wanna do what I wanna do," was Bernice's measured reply.

He charged back: "That's crazy. I always do what you want."

An exchange along these lines went on for about five minutes as people peeped and stared and continued buying tickets. Caron, quite unwisely in my opinion, put her two cents in by telling Tim, "You should listen to her, Tim. Really listen to her," which only made him madder. I took a step back and watched the three of them wrangling and knew right then, as sweet as Caron was, I didn't need to be dating her. It was all too incestuous.

While my friends were debating, Meg sold out, which I alone found funny. The Harrison Ford flick was actually pretty good, which the women admitted later. By the time the couples parted company everyone had mellowed out.

Caron didn't live too far from Universal so we were at her house in fifteen or so minutes. So I know she was real surprised when I turned down her invitation to come up. "Rodney," she said, "it's still early."

"No," I told her, "I have to get out early to see my mother," which was always true on weekends, and was also something I didn't always do.

"Is something wrong, Rodney?"

Initially I wasn't gonna get into it. I was gonna collect my thoughts and speak on my concerns with my usual professional smoothness at a later date. Instead I just blurted out, "I'm worried that we're all too close. It's like me and you and Tim and Bernice all seem like we're locked in the same tight box sometimes. Too much personal info is being jammed together. You know what I mean?"

"Are you saying we shouldn't go out anymore?"

"Look, I like you. Always have. You're sexy and you're smart. It's just that tonight worried me."

"Why? 'Cause they were fighting? What's that got to do with us?"

"The way it went down seemed ill to me."

"Ill? The only thing ill thing tonight was your attitude."

"Okay. What does that mean?"

"It means, Rodney, you don't understand the work involved in making a relationship work. Sure Bernice and Tim fight. They're having a rough time right now. The honeymoon's over and that. But they're gonna work through it. But then, you wouldn't know anything about that. It's just like Bernice said."

"What?" Now it was my turn to be irritated and defensive. "She probably said something like 'Rodney can't handle a real relationship. He'll find some silly way to sabotage everything.'"

"Not in those exact words."

"But I'm damn sure close. That woman is Tim's wife but she's just too damn deep into other people's business. First she urges me to go out with you and then she stabs my back."

"Well, it sounds like she was right. Just a couple of days ago she was talking about Tim and you, and how you might stop seeing me to rebel against Tim settling down. By hurting me you'd also be putting Tim down too. She'd seen a show about that on *Oprah*."

After she said the O-word I reached over and opened her door. "Caron, I used to fantasize that we'd make love together on a bed of rose petals. I really did dream that. Twice, in fact. But you and Bernice are too much for me. I don't think she's right about me but if she wants to be a prophet I don't wanna disappoint her." Caron shouted something insulting and then exited my car, though not before giving my Mustang door a serious slam.

Well, that felt right. Not good, but right. I was disappointed that Caron would likely not speak to me again for a very long time. And it disgusted me that the phone lines between Caron's and the Wilson-Waters house would soon burn up with denunciations of my weak character. But I'd said what I felt and if she couldn't hang, well, we probably shouldn't have been dating anyway.

The only thing that pissed me was anticipating Tim's call—tonight, tomorrow, the day after—to scold me, tease me, and boom out the loudest laughter he could muster.

30

Stewart Powell was not a handsome man if you define handsome, as most do, by a square jaw, strong eyes, and an engaging wide smile. No, Stewart possessed none of that. His chin was round and soft, his eyes small and elusive behind tortoiseshells, and his smile looked forced even when Stewart was having a wonderful time.

Back at Dorsey High, Stewart edited the school newspaper, which made him part of everything and central to nothing. I did a few pieces for the paper back then and remember him as a pleasant though unimpressive geek.

That was fifteen or sixteen years ago. We all worked desperately hard at growing up and Stewart Powell had succeeded more than most. He ran a computer preparatory school out of a storefront near the USC campus. At this establishment Stewart trained children and adults in the use of Macs, PCs, and the Internet. He also had a contract with the city of Inglewood as a consultant to their computer training initiative program. Yeah, Stewart had carved out a nice little niche for himself in the world.

He had grown a bushy goatee that disguised that weak jaw, and weight training had transformed him from a gawky teen into a musclebound cybernerd. Yet despite this transformation, it was still quite shocking to see Stewart sitting on my sister's sofa, having apple juice and one of my family's butter rolls with Tawana attentively by his side. The last time I saw a gainfully employed man in my sister's living room he was married to someone else.

So, as I relaxed and watched Roberta and my prickly niece

suck up to him, I kept wondering how in the world she'd wooed this South Central catch. "Your sister is so impressive," he said after his third or fourth butter roll.

"Really," I said, hoping I didn't sound too surprised.

"She's a true mother, you know." He spoke with a respect that bordered on awe. "The way she speaks about her girls, the way she handles them." His voice trailed off as he searched for adjectives.

"Yeah," I cut in, trying to help my man out. "She's always been great with the girls." Tawana sat next to Stewart, quiet as usual, observing our interaction with keen young eyes.

"You know," Stewart began again, "a lot of people treat having kids like a burden, like it's some problem. That's how I feel my ex-wife does it. But Roberta isn't like that."

Roberta stuck her head in from the kitchen. "Stewart, Rodnee, why don't you come in and get a plate now?"

Yet another Saturday at my sister's, but this was different. A new man was eating at the Hamptons'—one who appeared absolutely silly with respect for my wayward sibling. This was, to me, a weird, damn near surreal experience. Unlike a lot of dudes who try to force intimacy with a woman and her kids, working hard to be more charming than real, Stewart had a courtly quality to him I liked. I mean, if Stewart Powell had a game, it was a real low-energy hustle.

What was most striking was how he handled the girls. He appeared very content to sit with them and talk about school. Unlike a lot of adults (myself included), he didn't fade in and out with "Uh-huh" and "Really?" but listened with intensity to their scholastic stories.

After dinner the girls were in the back, messing with a computer game Stewart had given them, and we adults were still in the kitchen. Roberta sat at the head of the table sipping Japanese beer while Stewart and I sat across from each other devouring her sweet potato pie.

I knew Stewart the teen but was sketchy on the adult details. I was thinking of a cool way to get into it when Stewart turned to Roberta and wondered, "You think you and the girls would like to go to Disneyland?"

Now this was a loaded question in the Hampton household. Tawana's father, Tarik, had worked at Disneyland as a security guard/herb dealer, so Roberta had spent a lot of time traveling to and from Anaheim to see him. In fact, Tawana was likely conceived at a Disneyland hotel. Considering Tarik's failures as a father and a man I'd always suggested that the act must have occurred in the Mickey Mouse suite, a bit of humor my sister never found funny.

Testimony to how much Roberta liked Stewart was that she didn't make a face or reveal her distaste for the Mouse house. Instead she told Stewart, "Well, the girls have been there a lot in the past. They much prefer the Universal theme park."

"Okay," he said with some disappointment. "It's just that I'm taking my daughter down there in two weeks and I thought you and the girls could join us."

"That's sweet," I offered. Now I had an easy opening. "She hasn't been there before?"

"I don't believe so." He looked embarrassed by his answer. "I don't get to see her as much as I'd like. Her mother and I don't get along, you know."

"She keeps his daughter from him," Roberta said with contempt. "If a man wants to see his daughter these days, that's a damn blessing." Coming from Roberta I knew that wasn't just ass kissing. The lack of paternal interest displayed by her babies' fathers was a disgrace, one I did my best to camouflage for my nieces.

This idea that a child is, in any way, denied access to a willing father was evil to Roberta and I could see right then why the corny, earnest Mr. Powell was now eating the slices of sweet potato pie I usually take home with me.

"I'm trying to get custody," he explained. "I know it's hard raising a child by yourself, but I look at your sister and, you know, it gives me hope."

I cut Roberta an "Is this guy for real?" look but Roberta ignored me and grinned beatifically at Stewart, like this guy was the new messiah. Talk about saying the right thing! Maybe this brother had more game than I imagined. When I left, Stewart was still there, watching *X-Files* reruns with Roberta, who had never paid much attention to the show before. It was all very cozy.

31

Movie sets are a weird amalgam of army base, construction site, and theater workshop. Trucks, trailers, generators, and scores (sometimes hundreds) of people pitch camp on streets, in apartment buildings, and in deserts with military precision to record minutes, often seconds, of human interaction. Once on location, carpenters and electricians hammer and wire to make concrete the dreams of screenwriters, directors, and those unsung heroes, production designers.

Once the army has established a base camp and the builders have constructed a fleeting reality, the members of the theater workshop appear. Under the eyes of Teamsters and electricians, the director and a troupe of thespians playact for pay. It's a world within a world within a world that I always found fun and bewildering whenever life took me into it. That feeling alone would have been enough to make my first stint as a unit publicist memorable.

But there was an unexpected element: Kenya was becoming a star. After going gaga over her head shot, Messrs. Stein and Jones had their casting director read with Kenya. Coming off that play, Kenya's skills were sharp and she so impressed the casting director that the lady was recommending Kenya read for the lead.

There was no way that gig would go to a total unknown, but subsequent readings with Stein and Jones led them to offer her a prominent supporting part as the bus driver's sister, a character who works diligently to sabotage his relationship with the homeless girl. Though the homeless girl had much more screen time, the part of the sister was showy and sympathetically villainous in that you understood that love for her brother motivated her destructive actions. It was Sam Jackson in *Jungle Fever*. It was Kevin Spacey in *Seven*. It was Kenya Murray in *Night Shift*.

Every time I came to the set somebody was raving about "that Kenya girl" and how she was stealing the movie from its stars, Jada Pinkett and Forest Whitaker. Joey Stein was always patting me on the back and on occasion treated me to a sweet Cuban cigar as if we were proud fathers in the maternity ward.

Kenya, not surprisingly, became increasingly preoccupied. No gloating. No sanctimony. Not a lot of smiling either. I'd visit her tiny honey wagon and she'd be curled up studying her lines like a scholar. She was always pleased to see me, but sometimes it felt like I was one step removed from her new reality. The character she'd been in the play—strong, dominating, self-involved—was now a daily projection of Kenya the artist.

That side of Kenya had to have always been there. It was what brought her west in the first place. I just hadn't noticed it before. Sometimes you look at people but don't always see them. It's a lesson I should have known instinctively from my own work, yet I was always finding myself surprised by the depth of people I took for granted.

Often I tried to ask her about Circus, though in truth the questions never really passed my lips. And happily, she never mentioned him. Whether she was just sparing my feelings or was just too busy to even be thinking about him, I didn't know. Perhaps it was just a shrewd bit of politics since it was obvious to everyone around the film that the director was smitten. Crew members murmured about how Larry Jason Jones hugged Kenya after good takes—something that visibly grated on the leading lady. And they whispered about how he always sat with her at lunch and was seen happily coming out of Kenya's honey wagon after private rehearsals.

When I asked her about her relationship with Jason Jones, Kenya looked up from her script, said, "We are not boning!" and put her head back down dismissively. When I sat there, creating a silence rich with my disbelief, she looked up again and, with a sigh, explained, "He's helping me big time and I appreciate it. I mean, I need the help but there's nothing sexual going on. Tell everyone that, okay?" Then, with a wicked smile, she added, "Besides, I'm saving myself for you. Unless, of course, the search for the lost lovers is working out."

"No, it's over."

"So you found all three and they all rekicked you to the curb?"

I told Kenya a rather sanitized version of my quest that ended, "So I've stopped my quest. There will be no girl number three."

She shook her head negatively. "You are not through, Mr. Hampton. You put that energy out in the air, it hit the smog cover, and now it's bouncing around the city of dirty angels. Girl three is feeling you. You found the first two all detective-like, right?"

"It wasn't that hard, Kenya."

"So it won't be hard to get to you. She'll find you. One day soon you'll get smacked on those tight buns and it'll be her hand doing the squeezing."

There was a knock on the door and a PA stuck her head in. Kenya was needed on the set. She told me, "If I mess up this scene I'm blaming you and your crazy love life."

"Just be charming tomorrow 'cause I'm bringing MTV by for a set visit and I'm trying to get you in there."

"You're trying to get with Ananda, aren't you? Just remember, Rodney, that your ass is mine and I just lend it to your car seat." Then she pecked me on the lips and walked seductively away.

My little friend was clearly about one step removed from full-scale divadom, which was both endearing and real scary. Circus and Jones had already fallen for her feisty cuteness. Was I next? Or was I already on the ground, rolling over excited in the dirt, and didn't know it?

32

My whole life I'd been going to basketball games where it was all about male self-expression. Brothers dunking on each other and shouting. Referees blowing their whistles and assigning blame. Coaches in their best neo-Riley suits barked instructions and baited referees. The crowd, a mass of beer-saturated, popcorn-ingesting, hot-dog-munching ticket buyers, was largely composed of men letting off after-work steam.

But on this day basketball sounded feline. On the floor there was no macho strutting after slam dunks because the play was defiantly below the rim. The voices of authority—the refs and coaches—were higher pitched, though still intense. This being a Saturday afternoon, there was no let's-drink-beer 9 P.M. urgency. This was a Sprite-and-cotton-candy crowd, one in which baritones were rarely heard and for whom Lady Foot Locker sponsored the halftime entertainment.

My companion at this WNBA contest between the Los Angeles Sparks and the New York Liberty wasn't Tim or some other testosterone-driven creature. Surrounding me were my three nieces garbed in basketball jerseys, shorts, and gaudy overpriced athletic sneakers. They were with me to celebrate the height of nineties feminism—women as athletic bra goddesses.

Tanina, the baby, enjoyed bouncing her white-and-orange miniature WNBA ball off her bedroom wall. Tawana, connoisseur of all things watchable, regularly visited the Sparks' Web site for updated scores and stats. Tameka, who in another generation would have been ridiculed for her long bony arms, was en route to being the greatest shot blocker in her middle school's history—boy or girl—and had a chance at an athletic scholarship somewhere.

Since Tim, and thus Bernice, had no interest in the WNBA, I used his Lakers season-ticket-holder discount to grab seats for the Sparks' Saturday and Sunday matinees. It had become a lovely ritual actually, with the three T's and me hanging at the game, leaving Roberta to do hair, study her laptop, shop, or simply sleep. Though the bickering and battling endemic to siblings flared with regularity and Tawana too often inquired, "Why couldn't we watch the game on cable?" I genuinely loved these outings.

It was actually one of the few parts of my life that felt entirely, wonderfully responsible and adult. I loved it when they asked me for advice about school or, with sly indirection, questioned me about boys' behavior even as they denied their interest.

My excursions had another, much less benign purpose. There were lots and lots of attractive women in the stands. Sure, a great many were lesbians. But many more were like me—single adults with kids. Aside from talking to the girls, I loved scouting the Sparks crowd for comely single mothers.

On this Saturday the arena abounded with good prospects—women without men, women with fidgety little kids, women without rings, women who would find my squiring of the three T's extremely attractive. As the first half unfolded and Lisa Leslie led the Sparks to a 38–35 advantage, I spent most of my time eyeing women fans, making mental notes of which exit what single mother and her brood were situated near.

I was having a lot of fun when a familiar figure appeared

before my lenses. Sabena sat holding a soda in one hand and wiping the mouth of a bright-eyed little yellow girl with the other. She'd lightened her hair to a tasty-looking amber, but otherwise she was delightfully the same—her mouth, the athletic lines of her shoulders, the way she moved gracefully even when just clapping.

Sabena.

Her little companion was not more than four or five. On the ends of her hair were little purple ribbons that she toyed with when not spilling popcorn in her lap. Did Sabena have a niece? Yeah, but wasn't all her family in Houston? Still, it was summer and she could have been visiting Aunt Sabena. Or she could have been born after my time with Sabena, which, admittedly, was some years ago. Was she Sabena's daughter? Was Sabena married?

"Uncle Rodney, could I get the binoculars?" Tanina asked and, "One minute," I replied and, "Please," she pleaded and I, realizing I'd probably sounded unnecessarily mean, gave in. While I anxiously awaited the binoculars Tawana requested a large popcorn, obscuring my vision of Sabena and child as she ordered from the vendor and got her change. By the time the soda was being sipped and the binoculars had been returned, my subjects had left their seats, the halftime buzzer sounded, and little girls and their minders filled the aisles.

As was my policy, I sent Tameka off with her sisters to the extremely crowded ladies' room while I went looking for food and single women. Of course, my curiosity was killing me. In my heart I wanted to rush across the court, charge up the stairs, and search out my former love.

But in tribute to my recently rediscovered better judgment, I fought off the impulse and, instead, got on line for sodas and candy. Despite Sabena's abiding beauty I was sure now that chasing old girlfriends was a fool's quest and I was to be a fool no more.

With that settled, the rest of the afternoon went smoothly. The game was exciting, though the Sparks lost as the Liberty's point guard, Teresa Weatherspoon, hit a runner at the buzzer. The girls didn't argue too much, especially after Tanina fell asleep.

Afterward I planned to take them home but Tameka and Tawana wanted to go to the movies, and being a weak-willed uncle, I caved in. We rolled over to Crenshaw and Magic Johnson Theaters, where the girls lobbied for Wesley Snipes's latest grim-faced action hero. My choice was the latest animated Disney movie—an unpopular decision smoothed over by my purchase of enough Gummi Bears to fund any dentist's retirement.

I knew my sister would scold me, so I didn't call her, figuring I'd delay her eventual wrath until I gave back the three T's. It was all gonna be fine until Sabena and her little girl emerged from the ladies' room and walked right toward us. I wanted to duck, disappear, rearrange my molecules into their smallest possible measure of reality imaginable, and evaporate into air.

"Rod," she said, "is that you?"

"Yeah, Sabena. It's me. You look good, girl."

I leaned my body forward to receive whatever benediction she deemed appropriate. I expected a chaste kiss on the cheek; I received a friendly hug. "It's been so long, Rod," she said.

"Too long," I answered with an earnestness that embarrassed me. No wedding ring. Cool.

"This is my daughter, Ronelle." She was a small, shy beauty who shook my hand with surprising firmness.

"These are my nieces—Tameka, Tawana, and Tanina."

"I haven't seen them in years." That's right. "Tameka was a little girl then and Tanina was a baby." Half-forgotten, now intensely felt memories flashed on. A day at the circus with Sabena, the first two T's, and myself before I fled. So long ago—not so long ago.

"Uncle Rodney."

"Yes, Tanina."

"We're gonna miss the movie."

Inside the theater my family and hers filled half a row, with my heart pounding and my eyes glancing, looking, peering, seeking Sabena's face—my desire illuminated by the light projected from Disney's singing animals. When I wasn't watching her, I sometimes felt Sabena watching me too.

Ronelle was very solid evidence that Sabena's life had not stood still since our last encounter. If I had any lingering illusions about my importance to Sabena's life story, her daughter had eliminated them with a quickness. The question now was, what next? Ask for her number? Suggest we exchange numbers, thus splitting the burden of more intimate communication? What about just walking away? Isn't that what I understood now to be wise? Experience, the cliché goes, is the best teacher. A fool no more, I'd vowed just hours before with the self-satisfaction of a wise man. Now I was weak again. My goofy quest, born of jealousy, loneliness, and nostalgia, now pulled me back in like Pacino in *Godfather III*.

After the movie we marched our loved ones out into the parking lot with my grip on Tanina's hand so tight I was afraid I'd pull it off. Before I could ask for her number Sabena asked for mine. I pulled a business card out of my wallet and handed it to her slowly, as if I feared she wouldn't take it.

"So," she said, "you've started your own company."

"It's been going a couple of years now. I'm not rich yet, but it feels good to be your own boss."

"That's great," she said with genuine feeling. "We should talk." She requested another business card and then scribbled her number on the back. We hugged chastely. We bid good-bye to each other's little girls and we drove away. In the car the three T's peppered me with questions about Sabena: Had I dated her? Did I still like her? Was I the baby's father? To which I answered, "Yes," "Yes," and "Do you all want to walk home?"

Instead of going inside with them, where the three T's were sure to tell their mother about Sabena and raise all manner of new questions, I dropped them at Roberta's door and then sped off like I'd just committed a drive-by.

33

It was to be a weekend like most others. I was gonna hang with the three T's—a movie, maybe a ride along the PCH, and food somewhere exotic like Taco Bell or Fatburger. Then tomorrow a visit with Ma to get my weekly dose of guilt. Somewhere I'd squeeze in a date, though recently pickings have been slim.

But that all got rearranged on Saturday morning. Life had a new rhythm in mind.

"We can't make it, Rod-nee." It was 9:30 A.M. and my sister had awakened me from a very sound sleep.

"What's going on?" I asked as my eyes battled the slivers of Cali sun sliding around my window shades.

"Stewart and I are taking the girls away for the weekend."

"What?" I said. "It's like that now? So you and my three loving nieces are blowing me off to go hang with the computer programmer?"

"Don't make it sound so mean, Rod-nee. His daughter's coming along and we thought it would be a great way for everyone to get to know each other."

Then it hit me. "You aren't going to Disneyland, are you?"

"There's more to Anaheim than Disneyland. There's Knott's Berry Farm."

"Wow." Now I was wide awake. "For you to go back down to the scene of that crime, you must really like this guy."

"Yes." Roberta spoke with a giddy pride. "You act like that's impossible."

"No, I'm just surprised, that's all."

"When I first started feeling this way, I was too. Stewart's not what I was used to, but then what I was used to was shit, Rod-nee. You know that."

"Indeed."

"You know, what you're used to can be the worst thing for you."

In the background I could hear her doorbell. "Oh, that's Stewart. I gotta go. We're trying to get there by eleven-thirty. You'll have to go to see Ma tomorrow without me, okay?"

"Cool. Just enjoy yourself. And tell the girls not to forget me."

Welcome to a new century—my sister was falling in love with a man I wouldn't have to threaten, sue, or otherwise coerce into doing the right thing. So I lay there awhile waiting for the earthquake I was sure was about to destroy the L.A. basin. Nothing happened. Neither God nor nature intervened.

Now I had a free day I didn't want. I didn't wanna go to work, though I probably would. Tim and Bernice had gone up to the Napa Valley wine country for a guilty weekend. Caron was, of course, out of the question. Kenya, because of the buzz generated by *Night Shift,* had landed a week's work on some low-budget flick shooting in Texas. Merry? I could feel her in the air, hovering somewhere around in her trademark convertible, awaiting the right moment to toy with my heart. But that was me projecting. She was home in Seattle.

I turned on my Mac with the idea of doing some work on *The Girl Who Could See Music* when my eye was drawn to the "List" file. I opened it and there were all those names. Woodrina. Charlotte. Yim. And so forth. And there were the ones with stars next to them—Amy, Belinda, and Sabena. I stared at Sabena's name. I saw the way she looked then. I saw the way she looked now. I closed my eyes. I smiled. Then I dug out her number.

Without premeditation or forethought, I punched in Sabena's digits. The phone was ringing before I realized I wasn't supposed to be doing this.

"Hello."

"Sabena. It's Rodney Hampton."

A pause. A breath. A thought. "How are you, Rodney? I didn't think you were gonna call."

On my end, a pause. A breath. A thought. "But," I said with a publicist's sincerity, "you see, I did. So, Sabena, what are you doing today?"

"I was taking Ronelle over to La Cienega Park. She wanted a kite. Now we'll see if she can fly it."

"And after that?"

"We were gonna go have lunch somewhere."

"How about having a picnic with me?"

"Okay, if you provide the food, we'll provide the appetites."

"See you at the park."

An hour later I was stacking tuna and turkey sandwiches, bottles of water, juice, and chips into the back of my car and then cruising down Wilshire Boulevard thinking more about Sabena's face.

La Cienega Park is down a block from Wilshire, only five minutes from the Blaxican Cafe and right across from the Museum of Motion Picture Arts and Sciences. It is an extremely well cared for public park with baseball diamonds, a playground, and working rest rooms. Once the exclusive province of aging Jews and Westside Anglos, it now accommodates a significant community of Latinos, who dominate the ball fields.

But those sociological concerns were lost on Ronelle, who

was making feeble attempts at getting her sunflower yellow kite to rise. She was running in circles trying to get her party started. I doubted she'd remember me, so I was reluctant to approach, when I heard someone call my name.

Sitting on a bench waving at me was Sabena. Her hair was now in a soft, woolly Afro and her body garbed in an orange wrap dress, and her lovely feet were supported by black clogs. I came over and kissed her cheek.

"Here's lunch," I said, holding up my bag.

"I didn't think you were serious." She inspected the bag and seemed satisfied.

"Oh, yes. It's not every day I get to have lunch with Sabena, nurse/dancer extraordinaire."

"And my beautiful daughter."

"Ma, my kite won't fly." Ronelle had a disappointed, slightly petulant scowl on her face.

"Ronelle, this is Rodney Hampton. Remember we met him and his nieces at the movies?"

Ronelle smiled in recognition and asked, "Where are they?"

"On their way to Disneyland."

This idea excited her. "Can we go too?"

"Not today," her mother advised. "But look at all Rodney has brought us."

So we sat there eating—with Ronelle going back and forth between us and the kite—as the Saturday sun washed over us. I did most of the yapping, telling Sabena about my business, my clients, my family. Sabena accused me of being jealous of Stewart, which I denied though I knew she was right. We talked about Cedars-Sinai and the politics of such a huge institution. Somehow we got on the topic of AIDS and she related how hectic the hospital was during Eazy-E's last days, with rappers, gangstas, and anxious groupies everywhere.

By three o'clock Ronelle was so exhausted she'd fallen asleep with her head in Sabena's lap. It was a beautiful sight, one that gave me the motivation to ask, "What are you doing tonight? I'd love to take you to a movie or dinner."

"I appreciate the offer," she replied, "but there's no way I'd get a baby-sitter on such notice. What about tomorrow?" We agreed I'd call the next afternoon. When we parted she kissed me—firm, hard, and sexy—and I almost swooned. No matter how sweet a woman's skin is, even if it feels like rose petals dipped in honey, it rarely matches the taste of her lips, and Sabena's lips were juicy. I couldn't wait for the sun to go down and come on up again.

34

Ma looked like she had in the past. Her eyes were bright and alert. The lingering dullness my family now accepted as normal was gone. Back was the glow of the woman who used to turn the Slauson swap meet into her personal private runway.

"It's beautiful today, isn't it, Rodney?"

"Yeah, Ma, it is."

We sat on a balcony with a remarkably haze-free view of the Hollywood sign. The staff had been sounding cautiously optimistic that they'd found the right combination of drugs to lift Ma's depression. I had no reason to doubt them since this was certainly the most upbeat she'd been in months—maybe years. We even did something I remembered from happy times—we played twenty-one, one of Ma's favorite card games.

Back in the day, she'd have friends over after work at a bar, and at 2 or 3 A.M. they'd settle in for card games that lasted until morning. They'd drink piña coladas, eat pigs' feet, and play hand after hand of spades or, for a change of pace, bid whist. Many a morning Ma got up from a card game, took us to school, and then sat in for another hand or two before turning in to sleep.

I'd never really been much of a cardplayer. I lacked the patience to be a tool of chance that cards required. But it was quite calming to share something with Ma aside from memories. "What do you think of Roberta's new boyfriend?" she asked midway through our fifth hand.

"He's all right. A nice guy. Got his own business."

She pulled a bottle of Mylanta out of her pants, said, "So do plenty of trifling men," and then took a sip out of the aqua bottle.

"Yeah, but Stewart is different. He's calm and it seems like that's rubbing off on her."

She looked at me with a sly, teasing smile, slipped the bottle back in her pants, and said, "Roberta feels you're jealous."

"Nah, I just miss getting the extra pieces of sweet potato pie."

"You'll survive. So how's your love life, son?"

This was unusually direct for today's Rebe Hampton. When I was a kid Ma would as soon embarrass you as look at you. Since her depression kicked in she'd become wan and only sporadically assertive. This was an unexpected return to form.

I'd never really told her the whole story of how Tim's marriage and her "one woman short" wisdom had affected me. So, over our sixth game of spades, and in the diffused glow of the encroaching haze, I finally told her of Amy and Belinda. But mostly I lingered over my good fortune in running into Sabena. This, I told her, "must be fate, Ma. I'd given up, you know? Then, boom, she was delivered to me. I expect tonight to be very special."

Ma had nodded a lot. Interjected an "And what happened then?" a few times. But up until then she'd still been playing cards and listening. Now she put the cards down. "Boy, what is your problem?"

"You think this is all a bad idea, huh?"

She screwed up her face. "If your sister had went back over her own lengthy list of ex-boyfriends to try to salvage one from that junk pile you'd be screaming. You'd just talk about how crazy she was."

"Roberta likes what I'm doing, Ma."

"She probably likes the idea that you're making a real effort to find someone. I agree with her on that, Rodney, too. Obviously you've been doing some thinking. But if you don't remember why these relationships ended it's probably because it was so bad you blacked it out or something psychological like that."

"But look, with Sabena, I didn't chase her. I didn't interrupt her life. She didn't have to give her number. She didn't have to agree to see me yesterday. She doesn't have to see me today. It's all been her option, you know? This feels right, Ma."

"Okay. Don't let it be said I was negative about you trying to find happiness. I didn't pop you out into this world just to take up space. I want you to make a good life for yourself. If this Sabena woman helps you do that, then I'll be satisfied."

"Thank you for saying that, Ma."

"I meant it, son." Then out of the blue she asked me, "You ever hear from that girl Merry?"

"Yeah. When she's in town on business she calls me sometimes and we have dinner. What makes you ask about her?"

"She had a funny name but a good head on her shoulders. Knowing you, you probably thought she was too independent."

"Well, Ma, she married another man."

"Oh," she said with some disappointment.

So I felt obligated to tell her, "She did get divorced, though."

"Oh," she said brightly, "that's good."

"I thought you just said don't go back."

"Rodney, you picking people out of some list you made

when you were half awake and drunk. That's no way to guide your future. If Merry's kept in contact and you didn't chase her and it happened natural that you kept in contact, then it sounds like you and her have some kind of bond."

I left the home that afternoon wondering if I didn't like Ma better when she was listless and weird, 'cause this newly revived mother had gotten on my nerves. Merry was not in my plans. She was just an old school tease. In fact, I was gonna flick her from my mind like lint on one of her jet black suits.

Instead of going directly home I kept on Wilshire past Detroit and went on up to La Cienega, where I made a right and drove up to the Beverly Center, which was brimming with shoppers, mostly female, and people cruising, mostly male. In a city of millions the Beverly Center was one of the few sites of playful pedestrian traffic where eye contact, significant stares, and calculated flirting could occur on every escalator.

For me the Beverly Center had always been a site of urban romance. Back in the day, Tim and I found it a fruitful hunting ground, particularly the areas outside women's clothing stores like Victoria's Secret or Max Studio, where women flush from purchasing that sexy item of fantasy are filled with their own dreams of conquest.

This afternoon, however, I was a shopper, not a hunter, and headed straight for the Aveda shop, a place of the exotic oils, calming candles, and bath gels that have comforted me for years. After scooping up a small bag full of goodies, I headed home to my bathroom, putting a lit Aveda candle by the tub and using a generous helping of similarly scented bath oil, labeled "Calming," to turn harsh L.A. water into a caressing liquid.

After thirty minutes I was as chilled out as an ice tray. I picked up the cordless phone by the tub and called Sabena. "You still coming out to play?"

"Yes," she replied, "but I will be on call. I might have to go in and sub for a friend."

I heard that escape hatch open but I told her, "No problem," and said I'd be over at seven.

"Excuse me, Rodney, but are you high?"

"No," I answered with a chuckle. "I'm just taking a nice bath in Aveda oils. You wanna join me?"

"One step at a time, Rodney. I mean, we haven't talked in a long time."

"True. But yesterday was a good start."

"Don't get too romantic, Rodney."

"Don't worry, I'll act appropriately. Have you eaten at the Blaxican Cafe?"

"That place on La Cienega? Once. It was interesting but it's too close to my house. I'd like to get out of the area."

"Done deal. I got the perfect spot. See you in three hours."

Sabena looked real Erykah Badu these days—hair bound up in a white wrap, her torso in a white sleeveless top, a sky blue wrap skirt. "You look great," I said as we headed up toward Sunset.

"And you smell good, Rodney." She leaned over and put her face next to my neck. "Nice," she said.

Joss was a Chinese restaurant right at the spot on Sunset where the shops and restaurants of West Hollywood ended and the wide green expanse of Beverly Hills began. The food was artfully arranged on the plate and quite filling.

I was very relaxed—much more than when I met with Amy and Belinda. Maybe this was how I should have started my quest. With a warm bath and Sabena. After we ordered I sat back and looked at her, this stylish Afrocentric woman, and felt confident that nothing she could say could upset me as Amy and Belinda had.

For some reason being so comfortable made me forget my plans for easing into her business. So instead of laying back I observed, "I know it's hard raising a child without a father."

"Oh, Ronelle has a father. I just don't have a husband. That makes it difficult, sure, but a lot of people don't even have that and get the job done."

"Absolutely. My sister does it every day."

"You wanna know the story, Rodney?"

"If you wanna tell me, yes."

"Well, you always were nosy."

"You don't have to tell me."

"No, I'll tell you, Rodney."

After I slid out of Sabena's life, Ron, the white actor she'd been with that night I'd met her, had slid right back in, a sign of devotion that she took to heart. He wasn't pleased by her six-month sojourn with me, but I faded from importance, especially after Ron asked Sabena to marry him. She'd never been happier. To her "a devoted man was a rare thing" and she'd felt blessed to have reconnected with him.

Now I felt a familiar sense of anticipation. After all the love she had for this fool he had to have fucked up big time. From the moment we'd traded looks at Sushi on Sunset that white boy and me had been rivals. I was gonna relish hearing of his downfall.

"Ron had been very involved in planning the wedding," she began. "Unlike a lot of men he wanted the ceremony to be a reflection of our partnership, not just something he showed up at." That observation actually made me smile, as I thought of Tim's passive role in his nuptials. "That's why he was so special. He even came with me to pick out the wedding dress."

I was praying this didn't turn into one of those old white-men-treat-you-better riffs. Thankfully Sabena rolled back into the story. "It was one of those amazing clear January days, when the rain and the wind blow away the smog, and from the hills you can see from downtown all the way out to the ocean.

"We were in a shop off Beverly Drive with this cute old blue-haired lady waiting on us. Ron was sitting in a chair out in the shop and I was walking out of the back so he could see me in this white Dutch satin dress I loved. As I'm walking toward him his cell phone rang. He was looking at me. He was smiling. Then he flipped it open and said, 'Hello.' I knew it was a woman just the way his face changed when he heard the voice. And I knew it was one of his old women.

"He kept smiling. Ron is a good actor, but I knew this smile was a fake smile. I was standing up on this little platform right in front of him, looking like a black princess in a white Dutch satin wedding dress, when all the blood rushed out of his face and Ron was already pretty pale. I asked him, 'What's wrong, baby?' and he said into the phone, 'This can't be true!' and then he got red and angry, and nothing I could say calmed him. He stormed out of the shop, as mad as I'd ever seen him."

"Would you like some more wine?" The waitress hovered over us and all I wished was that she would go away so Sabena could get to what happened next. For her part Sabena looked as comfortable as a well-fluffed pillow. So it was she who agreeably ordered more wine as I remained in the tense, anticipatory state a well-told tale can leave you in. The waitress split and I watched Sabena like a child waiting on his allowance.

"So," I said.

She replied, "I really need that wine."

Thankfully the wine came swiftly and the story continued. "The first day," Sabena went on, "I don't hear from him. I call. I page. I sit in front of his house, even though his car isn't there. His mother doesn't know where he is. His brother doesn't know where he is. His agent says he doesn't know, but I know that sucka's lying.

"On the second day I get a call from my gynecologist—I'm pregnant." My head is swimming—this is deeper than *Melrose Place*. "And he tells me I'm HIV negative."

I say, "Okay," to that.

"Which turns out to be important."

"Why?"

"Because on the third day Ron shows up at Cedars-Sinai. He looks like he hasn't slept in days and his hair smells bad in that way white hair does when it hasn't been washed. We go into the cafeteria and sit in a corner. He drinks coffee. I drink tea. But my heart, it was like I could taste my heart in my mouth."

"Okay," I said now. "So he's HIV positive."

"Well, at that point he doesn't know. What he tells me is some stunt named Che called him in the shop that day, who he's been fucking while he's seeing me—"

"And not using a condom."

"—and he's supposed to be in love with me, but she's tested positive."

This was a lot of awful information to consume at one sitting. Betrayal, tragedy, and sex. Yeah, deeper than *Melrose Place*. This was Ricki Lake–level drama.

"So," I inquired, "was Che white, or black?"

"Why does that matter?" she snapped.

"Okay," I replied. "It doesn't really matter."

"The bitch was some hoochie momma from the Wood. He played a corrupt white cop in a rap video and she was a pop-your-coochie dancer. She might have screwed Eazy-E for all he knew."

"He boned a hip-hop video dancer without a condom? Baby, you were about to marry one dumb white mother-fucker."

Now Sabena teared up, the drops rolling down her shallow cheeks, the front of composure going, going, gone. I glanced around the restaurant, hoping no one thought I was the cause of this flood. But it was dark, the wine was flowing, and every-one was too into their own dramas to notice ours. So I took Sabena into my arms and she let her head find a place on my shoulder. Her cries shook my body and it made me feel good, like I was the protector of a lady in distress.

Then she stopped shaking and my calmness flowed into her and we were bonded and in that moment I became deeply infatuated with Sabena again. As silly as it was I couldn't help the feeling and I didn't want to.

"I'm sorry." She spoke softly, wiping her eyes and slightly pulling away from me.

"You got nothing to feel sorry for," I said. "In fact, I liked you in my arms." She gazed at me doe eyed and I kissed her hard with a boyish enthusiasm that was real. I left three twen-ties on the table and we split.

"Where are we going?" she asked as I took Crescent Heights and went left on Wilshire.

"Hey, aren't you a dancer? I mean, aren't you a very good dancer?"

"I haven't had much time for that since Ronelle was born.

Nowadays I work, I play with Ronelle, and I sleep. So we're going to a club?"

I didn't tell her where we were going but when we cruised past Fairfax she turned and said, "The Conga Room, huh? I heard that Jennifer Lopez owns a piece of it. I've been wanting to go there. So have you learned to dance salsa?"

"Things change," I said with casual cockiness. "You'll see." Unlike my night out with Belinda, I wasn't fading to black but stayed in focus, sweating step by step with her lean, beautiful self. In between dances we drank tequila shots and got goofy.

Sabena may have given up on her dreams of dancing in the New Year's Day parade but she still moved with a wonderful grace. Moreover, I believed her that she hadn't been out much lately. The way she swung her legs and wound up her pelvis, I'd have thought homegirl had just been released from County.

So it was with the utmost joy that I answered, "Yes," to the following question: "Don't you live somewhere around here?"

"About five blocks away, over on Detroit."

"Let's go see how you're living."

"What are we gonna do there?"

"Hang out," she said, looking me dead in the eye.

"Hang out," I repeated.

"Hang out." My face was now extremely close to hers.

"Hang out," I said again, after which Sabena giggled. "You are funny," she said. "I forgot that about you, Rodney."

About fifteen minutes later Sabena was sitting on my sofa surveying the surroundings and, with a wry smile, noting, "You certainly don't live with a woman."

"You can tell, huh?"

"Oh yes. That's good, though. It means you're not cheating on a woman you live with by bringing me here."

"I'm not seeing anyone, Sabena."

She flipped her hand dismissively and replied, "That's what they all say." A dark streak of melancholy crossed her face. Just a few hours before she'd told me a truly horrible story of love and loss. Despite the wine and the tequila and the dancing, all those emotions were just a sentence or two away.

So I didn't say anything else. Not a word. I just kissed her as I had in the restaurant—only softer, slower, deeper—tasting alcohol and lip gloss and her red, agile tongue. Sabena's skin tasted like it was lightly seasoned, like a tart, lively sauce that made the buds in the back of my mouth dance as I sucked on the base of her neck and scooted my tongue across the rim of her shoulders. There was nutritional value in this woman's body, the kind that built strength in a man and made her a movable feast.

I dined on Sabena and this wasn't a fast food meal. Eating Sabena required several courses, from appetizer to entree to dessert, and every nibble took me deeper into her until my belly was full and she lay there, long and brown and tart, and I was beaming and lazy, the way a good meal can make you. Sabena was the chef. I was the diner. For a long time no one wanted to clean up the dishes.

Eventually she got up and started rewrapping herself as I watched. I knew she couldn't stay but asked anyway, just trying to communicate my desire for a bigger meal.

"Yeah," she said agreeably. "That would be nice, but my baby-sitter's waiting."

"Hey, wasn't that thing about being on call just an escape hatch in case you wanted to ditch me?"

"My, my, my, you have a devious mind, Rodney," she replied. I noted this was not a denial. When her head wrap was in place Sabena tossed me my pants. "Gotta go, gotta go."

On the way to Cashio Street, where she lived, just off La Cienega, I was feeling crazy lovey-dovey and kept trying to find out when we'd reconnect. She just talked about her daughter's school schedule and said a lot of nurses were going on vacation soon. I listened but I didn't hear.

In front of her rental on Cashio I told her, "I'm glad I ran into you." I held one of Sabena's hands in mine and spoke in a prayerful tone. In reply her voice wasn't reverent but kind. Sabena's body was still with me, but her spirit had already moved into the house.

"And I'm glad you called yesterday. Hope my story didn't freak you out."

"Obviously it didn't."

She kissed me, told me, "See you soon," and then was on her way up the walkway before I'd even opened my eyes.

Autumn was creeping up on L.A. and the temperature had dipped into the fifties. Back in the spring no one thought my list meant anything. To Tim, Roberta, Bernice, it was a joke. A good-hearted one, sure, but a joke no doubt. I hadn't known what to make of it myself. Then Ma's words put me on track. Maybe all those 132 other names were just there to lead me to this night, this woman. Forget those that condescended to me. My list had come through. I didn't feel one woman short.

35

A week or so after my Sunday with Sabena, I was still sniffing the fumes, still gassed up by her return to my life. I was watching videos on BET, vibing on all the overlit sensuous videos black folks make, when a cell phone call led me to a definition of love.

"Hey, Rodney! I'm almost at your house."

I glanced over at my clock, which read 10:45 P.M. It was Tuesday. "And why, dear friend," I asked, "are you over here?"

"I'll explain when I get there. I'm turning off Wilshire onto Detroit now."

"Okay, I'll leave the door open."

About ten minutes later Tim walked through my door with the remnants of a Fatburger in his left hand. He was still in one of his business suits, but it look rumpled, even a bit gamey. "This isn't one of those wife-husband things, is it?" I wondered out loud.

Tim ignored my question and went into my kitchen, emerging with my newly purchased bottle of Ocean Spray cranberry juice. "What do you say we go over to the Conga Room tonight?"

"How about putting down my cranberry juice, sitting your ass down, and telling me what's up?"

He plopped down on my sofa and began chugging my Ocean Spray right out of the bottle. "You heard of a glass? I don't know where your mouth has been."

Tim sadly nodded his head in agreement. "You right about that."

Suddenly that Master P track where he raps, "Everybody say 'Uungh!'" rang in my head like a nasty bell. "Did you look Circus up on his challenge?" I asked accusingly.

"It's not that simple, Rodney."

"Okay, Tim, talk to me."

"It's been a tense couple of months. Bernice really wants to do the gated community thing. She brings it up all the time. I told her the Valley was too far away from my business. So she goes and sets up a meeting with the broker at that development at Rossmore and Wilshire. Like I needed her to do that."

"Yo," I interrupted, "don't spit in my cranberry juice."

"Oh, sorry, man. Anyway, so that happens. Then she's spending dollars out of our joint account without consulting me."

"On?"

"What did you ask me?"

"On. On what did she spend the money?"

"On mess like a new carpet. Stuff we don't need to do if we were actually moving within the year. So on one hand she wants me to become a slave to a big house behind a security gate. Then she goes and spends the money we'd need to make that move."

"Pissed you off."

"Big time."

"So in response you went out with Circus to that same strip club and had sex with two strippers."

"No!" he shouted at me. "I did not."

"You're sure now?"

"I was there, motherfucker!" He was getting heated and way defensive. I just sat there, acting as neutral as possible now, 'cause I knew there was something else coming. We were quiet there for a while. Him drinking more of my cranberry juice—me sitting there acting as blank as computer paper.

Tim began speaking softly, the way I imagine people do in the confession box. "But I didn't do anything, Rodney. It's just I felt guilty that I even let Circus put me in that situation. I had this big-titted Mexican girl all in my grill. And we weren't in the main room. Somehow Circus had got me in the back in one of those little rooms where you can do lap dances with the pants off. Circus was standing there holding up fifties and saying, 'It's on me, cuz.' That's how close I came. It's been bothering me ever since. I mean, I haven't been married that long and I almost went out like a damn roach."

"But Tim," I said as comfortingly as I could, "the key is you didn't. That's why you're a better man than Circus. That's why you're a better man than me. Your relationship with Bernice gives me something to aspire to. It's so good that Circus is jealous of it, so he tries to mess it up."

I moved closer to him now 'cause I really wanted him to feel me. "Listen, man, you're always gonna see different women and say, 'Man, I'd like to knock those boots.' That's just the animal in all of us barking. But the thought is not the deed. Right now you have not disappointed your wife—not really. Now you have disappointed yourself, but that's good. Remember this feeling. Hold on to it. You don't ever wanna feel this way again."

Tim slumped down into the folds of the sofa and swallowed more of my cranberry juice. His sigh seemed to fill my apartment. "Damn, Rodney, I know you're right, but the guilt is eating at me. I've been feeling so stupid and dirty I haven't even wanted to have sex lately. That's how fucked up I feel."

"It'll pass, Tim. You just got to relax and let that mess go."

We sat up for another hour hashing out Tim's feelings. The whole time my respect for him was growing. Just the fact that he put himself in a position to cheat had my man all tangled up, and that got to me. He was so committed to his wife that this weakness—which in the big scheme of life wasn't shit—depressed him. Tim was displaying some depths I hadn't often seen.

But after a while my awe wore off and I just got raw with him: "Tim, you got to stop acting like a bitch and go with her to look at Rossmore or wherever else she wants. It can't hurt. Actually, first you need to go home, do about fifty push-ups, make love to her like a champ, and then go look at Rossmore or whatever. And finally you need to buy me a fresh bottle of Ocean Spray."

"You haven't told me anything I haven't thought of, Rodney," he replied petulantly.

"Well," I said back, "that's the beauty of good advice. You know it before it's said. By the way, the next time you're in the mood to see a stripper, remember I'm always available."

"To go with me?"

"No, fool, to dance for you."

36

The Hollywood Palladium is on Sunset, one long block from my office on Gower. In the old days the Palladium was a big-band dance palace. At one point in the eighties it was hip-hop central, with local rap stars like Ice Cube playing there regularly. Now mostly it was used by Latin promoters for salsa, merengue, and other Hispanic bands. Its high ceilings and wide dance area also attracted commercial directors, who used it to create faux concert spots.

So on an October Saturday morning four hundred high school and college students, mostly girls, were being served Kentucky Fried Chicken and Sprite and given white T-shirts bearing the Sprite logo as assistant directors with bullhorns instructed them to act as if "D-Vince was the biggest rap star in the world" when he hit the stage for the ten to twenty times he'd be rapping in praise of Sprite.

The pop-oriented, sex-symbol image I'd encouraged D-Vince and his manager to exploit back in our first meeting had not only sold records but had caught the attention of several ad agencies, including the one Merry toiled for. I hadn't pitched her directly but Merry, with her usual pop-culture diligence, had followed D-Vince's progression from *Black Beat* to *Vibe* to *Sixteen* with interest. Sprite was always looking for cool, hip, unthreatening hip-hop flava to attach itself to and D-Vince filled that slot.

"So I must be good at my job," I boasted to Merry as we stood in the Palladium's balcony, looking down at the girls being wrangled into an excited mob. I continued, "I got you interested in my client just through publicity skills. Didn't even have to sell you directly. It was all subliminal."

"I'll admit you have skills, Mr. Hampton," she replied in a seductive tone. "You've become a good salesman."

"Thank you."

"We should work together more often."

"You have any ideas?"

By now we'd both turned from the teeming mob below us and were looking quite intensely at each other. It was a deliciously brief moment of unexpected and sudden lust—the latest addition to my growing list of flirtatious encounters with Merry Spencer.

Then a most unpleasant sentence descended from her brain to her mouth. "So," she wondered, "how's the ghost busting going?"

"Ghost busting? Oh, the list?" Oh well. Guess it was time to end the flirting and just be honest. I'd found Sabena and she'd turned me out and I was as open as McDonald's front door two blocks from a high school. I was gonna tell Merry all that. I truly was.

"Excuse me, Miss Spencer." It was a production assistant weighted down with a walkie-talkie and the anguished expression of someone being yelled at through that same walkie. "The representatives from Sprite want to speak with you downstairs," said the PA.

"Sorry, Rodney. Time for me to earn my outrageously high salary."

"Please don't apologize. Go earn our children's college tuition."

"You're funny."

No kiss good-bye. Just a smile.

I hung in the balcony awhile watching as the director

guided the crowd through its antics and D-Vince, media savvy after just two videos, played to the camera like a champ. During a new lighting setup I made my way downstairs and was about to head backstage when a security guard in a black tank top grabbed my arm. "Where are you going?" I looked close at the guard's face and realized his mocking smile belonged to Circus.

"Circus? I didn't know you did security."

"Rodney," he said cocky as hell, "I got muscles for every occasion. So what brings you around?"

I explained my relationship with D-Vince and Circus appeared vaguely impressed. "You got a winner there, part-ner. He's got young panties wet all over the room. Reminds me of myself—only not as smooth."

"So what's up with you and Kenya?" I asked impulsively, knowing it was quite possible he'd say something so foul I'd have to clock him.

To my surprise his face softened and became boyish, almost innocent. "We're just hanging, you know. Getting to know each other." This was uncharacteristically subdued. Almost, dare I say, respectful.

"She's good people," I noted and he agreed and began looking rather uncomfortable about discussing her with me.

To the rescue of Circus's rep came two comely girls—six-teen, seventeen, black and white—in Sprite T-shirts and hip-hop hair who wanted to get backstage to meet D-Vince. The leer on Circus's face suggested that fundamental showbiz equation: you add youth, the desire to meet a celebrity, and a gatekeeper's access to celebrity and you find that it equals an opportunity for exploitation.

"You know, this is D-Vince's publicist," he began. Then he

winked at me and I suddenly felt dirty. "He's the man who gets D-Vince in magazines and on TV."

This was a classic hustler's move. Pimp my access to boost your prestige—blow yourself up by being the man next to the man next to the man. I quickly bowed out, leaving those two girls to their own devices and their hopefully good home training. Circus was definitely garbage but it appeared even he had had his hardened heart cracked by Kenya. This girl was definitely gonna be a star.

Slipping backstage I saw love everywhere and in strange and funny forms. In the dressing room D-Vince's manager, Sam Neil, was holding hands with Inga, the model he'd met back at Belinda's party. Success had been good to him. Neil had replaced his wan, pale look with a reddish tan and some pricey, well-tailored gear. D-Vince sat with three extremely fine women attending to him. One of them was Belinda, who greeted me with the standard backstage courtesy hug.

To my continued relief (and surprise) the rapper was still as open and outgoing as the day we'd met. I hadn't yet detected that jaded sense of entitlement that infects most celebrities and is almost never totally cured. Lately I'd taken to crossing my fingers when we shook or embraced, a precaution against my professional cynicism contaminating his fun-loving soul.

In the hallway, not very far from D-Vince's dressing room, I could see Merry suavely negotiating her way through a web of white men in suits. Unlike some black folks who never quite get comfortable with white people, Merry displayed a wondrous ease in dealing with them. She had the gift of never appearing intimidated, contemptuous, or for that matter, too loving in getting what she wanted.

It was clear to me by the body language of several of these

gentlemen that some would be, had been, or were even at that moment desirous of private time with her. And perhaps, on those long days on the set, on plane trips to exotic locales, she, the beautiful divorcée, flirted with them as she did with me. Yet I wasn't jealous. I always admired her and would flash back on us years ago, two young, horny rookies. Cute then. Polished now. Not my woman, but a fine-ass one nonetheless.

37

After my busy summer and early fall, my business took a terrible turn in October. First of all Leroy Martinez told me he was closing the Blaxican Cafe.

"People just aren't getting it," he told me one afternoon after he'd met with an appraiser about selling off the chairs and tables. "People came in, checked me out, but it was too radical. People in this town would rather eat food from some foreign country they couldn't find on a map than deal with the fact that my cuisine is what L.A. is really about. I mean, I caught some people calling it the NiggaSpic Cafeteria. That was too much, Rodney."

Leroy already had a job lined up at an upscale Mexican restaurant in Zuma Beach. The man could truly grease, so he wouldn't be without work. Moreover, his hookup with Millie Kwanza had yielded a deal to write a cookbook and he'd been assured that, cafe or not, the book would still come out. Still, it pissed me off that it wasn't working and I wondered if I could have done more to help.

D-Vince's album had gone platinum and our work with Jive had, I thought, been excellent. Yet the label decided to hire someone else in-house. Nancy Bishop broke it to me over the phone from New York. "While it's admittedly been a productive relationship, it's clear to me we need someone in L.A. for whom Jive is a day-to-day priority, and not one job of many."

I took this well. I mean, the retainer thing had been my idea. I knew it could be short lived—the deal was for only a three-month trial. And as Bishop pointed out, "You really don't wanna work for anybody," which I didn't. Still, Hampton Media would miss the wonderful stability of major-record checks.

In response Adele and myself worked the phones, talking with the managers of a few of the Jive groups we'd handled about half committing to keep us on retainer or to hire us for their next album. Factoring in the flakiness endemic to the entertainment business, I figured maybe a third of those commitments were real. Still, if they did come through, that would mean more income than I'd had before I'd met D-Vince. Despite the fact I'd wanted to shift the business away from the music biz, at this point it was still what I was known for. I wasn't yet prepared to rely on nonmusic income.

Certainly the movie business wasn't looking promising. Since the end of *Night Shift*'s principal photography and since I turned in my production notes, neither Stein, Jones, nor anyone over there returned my calls or gave a satisfactory answer if we got them on the phone. My concern here wasn't money—the Steinvision checks had cleared quite nicely. Stein had promised to hook me up with other film producers and he hadn't even talked to me, much less given me leads for more work. I knew they were in postproduction, but my ego was bruised. Moreover Adele, who'd spent a lot of time on the *Night Shift* set when I was elsewhere, took the lack of response personally. "After all the times I listened to Joey talk," she said bitterly. "His wife problems, his problems with Larry, his studio problems—I can't believe he would dis us like this."

Following the film's wrap she'd had to come back to the office, and while we still had another assistant answering the phone now, she was getting cabin fever back full-time in the Gower office. The *Night Shift* gig had really shown her

the possibilities of the job and now she seemed more dedicated to the company. But without another big account she
was morose and I had no way to cheer her up.

Meanwhile the ex–Kinko's cutie had not just acquired a
smitten director but an agent, a manager, and a rep as a comer
around town. This was all good. Even the flirtation with Jones
made sense—directors and actresses are like engines and
wheels; they rolled well together. Adele confirmed that Jones
had fallen head over goofy heels for Kenya and that she'd led
him on to the degree her part had grown. Apparently he'd purchased her a bracelet the last week of shooting. Whether that
closed the deal or not Adele didn't know or simply wouldn't
tell.

Still, that master of the flying mattress, Circus Morris, was
still hovering about, and as much as I tried to put it out of my
mind, the image of Kenya and Circus furiously fornicating
occasionally creeped up on me. The last time we'd spoken
Kenya toyed with me on the phone, saying, "You never ask
me about my love life, Rodney. I mean, I know all about your
list but you don't seem to care about how life treats me."

"It's because I'm afraid to know."

"Jealousy is a big part of your personality. You know that,
don't you, Rodney?"

"No, I didn't, but thanks for pointing that out. Makes me
feel much better about myself."

"Me, I think it's cute. I like it when you get upset like this."

"You're not seeing Circus just to mess with me, 'cause if
that was the case you've already succeeded."

"Rodney," she said with all seriousness, "this isn't high
school. Circus has some very attractive qualities." Then she
paused and added, "That he makes your blood boil is only
one of them."

While Jive's decision disappointed, and Steinvision's lack of communication frustrated, and Kenya's bull bothered, nothing wore on me more than the Urban League's inability to say yes or no to my Valentine's Day idea. Joseph Kwanza and I spoke at least once a week to receive updates on the league's internal politics.

"There are so many vested interests," he explained, "so many people committed to old, safe ways of thinking, that an idea like yours that forces them to see the world differently is a threat. Not consciously but subconsciously."

It all sounded like another reason why my generation was uninterested in the established civil rights groups. The old boomers in this group seemed obsessed with ancient attitudes while the rest of us were dealing with the twenty-first century. I didn't see my proposal as revolutionary. It was fun, sexy, and very accessible while still respectful of their civil rights legacy.

"Be patient, Rodney," Kwanza counseled me. "We should have a decision by Thanksgiving."

This holding action made me feel helpless, something I ran my own business to avoid, yet here I was again at someone else's mercy. I know this was really the way of the world—no one has total control of their world; everyone has to wait on someone else's decision. Still, all this delay irked me.

Thankfully Sabena's presence in my life made all this bearable. We talked nightly on the phone. Sometimes she'd call me from Cedars-Sinai at eleven or twelve and talk for a half hour about what the L.A. night dragged in. We didn't always talk long—sometimes it was just "Thinking of you" or "How was your day?"

Actually I'd seen Sabena only a handful of times since our night of dinner and dancing. A couple of times we'd dined late at Jerry's Deli just across Beverly from Cedars-Sinai.

Once we'd held a kissfest in the corridors of Cedars-Sinai before a shift. She'd even spent the night with me, one blissful Sunday before leaving at the break of dawn to pick up Ronelle at her mother's. Mostly our encounters were brief, though not so short as to make them feel like quickies. As she'd predicted, the needs of her daughter, her job, and my schedule made it hard to connect.

Yes, there was a voice in the back of my head that worried about her inaccessibility, concerned that that might be a signal of second thoughts on her part. Yet whenever we talked Sabena seemed with it and that's all I could truly go on. Moreover, we were making plans. We talked of spending time in Cancún over the holidays or maybe going up north to the wine country. Actually, both were my ideas but she cosigned them and I even had Adele researching hotels. So that voice never rose in volume or intensity, because having Sabena in my life felt like I was bathing in Aveda bath oils all day long.

38

Tim was sitting at a table slurping a fruit drink when I walked up to the front desk of the L.A. Sports Club. A comely Asian lass with a cute cut, wearing a crisp white shirt, welcomed me. I pointed out my friend and told her I was his guest. "Oh Tim," she said with a big old smile. "Yeah, he told me to look out for you. He said you'd be the cute single guy."

"As opposed to the cute married guy, right?"

Tim was observing us from the table, a delighted leer upon his face.

"You like?" he asked, gesturing at the restaurant, high ceilings, marble floors, and general upscale opulence of the joint. Not to mention the lean, athletic bodies of the women strutting about.

"I got eyes, money."

The locker room was clean and carpeted. There were all kinds of machines as far as the eye could see. The weight room had every damn barbell you could imagine and some I didn't know existed. On the second floor, past the legion of tan, muscular bodies, was the Magic Johnson basketball court, which was NBA long and had a big scoreboard at its west end.

Guys were gathering together when we walked up. To our delight Magic himself and another NBA type were at the far end, joking and shooting hook shots. "Well," Tim turned and said, "are you gonna join, or you gonna stay at the weak end of the gene pool?"

Wish I could report that Magic immediately recognized

me as the second coming of James Worthy, but no, I fumbled away not one but two passes from the greatest point guard in history, and didn't receive a look from him the rest of the afternoon. Still, with Magic on my side we won a lot, and I was thrilled by the whole experience.

"Change, Rodney. It's all about change." Now we were both sipping fruit drinks fortified with Metrix, a protein-packed additive Tim turned me on to. I sat back, gazing at the grand surroundings, watching as the Asian receptionist strolled by and waved.

"Well," he said to me, "this is not the Y."

"Word."

"I got news for you, Rodney."

"News? I got news too."

"Mine's big."

"So is mine. But then you know that."

"Okay, big man, go first."

"I've been hanging with Sabena."

"A girl from the list, right?"

"The third one."

"Had sex."

"Oh yeah."

"Glad something good came out of it."

"But it's not just that. I think she might be the one."

"The 'one'?"

"Yeah. I haven't been this open in years."

"Tell me," he said dubiously, "the story."

I kicked the digits to him—almost like this was the old days and every sexual encounter was fodder for storytelling and laughter. But this was not the old days.

"So wait—you think, based on what happened, that this HIV-negative woman is your wife?"

"Well, maybe."

"She told you a sob story and then laid you, right?"

"That's cold, Tim. She doesn't deserve that."

"But unless you left out some crucial damn detail, that's what I hear, Rodney."

"And?"

"And be happy you wore your jimmy tight. Sex is always a good thing for a single man."

"Don't patronize me, motherfucker."

"Rodney." He spoke to me like I was a kid. "You know and I know how transitory this can all be. Sometimes you just want a nut—sometimes she just wants a hug. The real thing is built over time. It has ebbs and peaks and leaves water spilling everywhere."

"You telling me things are cool again at home?"

"No, money, they are hot. 'Smoking,' as Jim Carrey would say."

"Okay. Is that your news?"

"No, this is—Bernice is pregnant."

"Word!"

"Word to my wife and future mother."

Bernice was four months gone, with the baby due next March. She already knew its sex but Tim wanted to wait awhile. For some reason he found that old mystery, "Is it a boy, or a girl?" enticing. For the rest of that afternoon we talked of fatherhood—of our fathers, fathers of women we'd dated, fathers of male friends, and of being a father and how that would change us.

Though I was joyful about this truly blessed news, there was an itching deep inside, an intimation of that awful green monster growing ugly inside me again. Tim was moving ahead again—moving further and further away from the man he'd been on Adams Boulevard and evolving into a man with all the burdens and strengths the attainment of maturity entails.

Even his recent struggles with fidelity felt right since commitment comes with pressure; and dealing with that pressure, identifying its source, and then fighting it off were integral to the process.

As for me, well, maybe, I was making a two-night stand into something it wasn't.

39

Somehow one of the most beloved black restaurants in town ended up in Marina Del Rey. For nearly twenty years the African-American community had been making a right off the 90 freeway onto Medano Way and a left into a strip mall anchored by a Von's supermarket and a multiplex. Nestled in a corner and squeezed in amongst a bunch of other eateries was Aunt Kizzy's, a soul food institution whose walls are decked with framed photos of celebrities (and semi-celebs) past and present who have dined on the spot's rich, thick Southern specialties.

On a Sunday afternoon Aunt Kizzy's is always packed with churchgoers fresh from their weekly religious ritual and sinners just awakening from a Saturday night function. Most of the crowd was styled in suits and dresses worn to services. I stood out a bit in my short sleeves and khaki pants while Tim and Bernice, just back from Reverend Cecil Moore's African Methodist church in South Central, were looking appropriately dignified. Tim had even broken out a straw hat for the occasion.

Today they were having brunch with Sabena and me, making it the first time we'd all be dining together since our reconnection. Bernice wasn't feeling me as we waited outside Kizzy's. The break with Caron hadn't pleased her at all. Nor was she pleased with my sudden embrace of a woman from my list. Her attitude toward me on this Sunday was a throwback to the days when she saw me as a roadblock to Tim's "maturation."

"So," she said with obvious irritation, "where's the nurse?" At that point we'd been waiting a half hour for Sabena to show up.

"Sabena," I said, pronouncing her name slowly, "might have gotten held up at work. You know, saving lives is not a nine-to-five job." Tim, as was his manner in these situations, stood quietly by his wife's side, judging everything and saying nothing.

I'd paged Sabena twice. I did it again. But no calls came in on my cell. At Kizzy's they won't seat you on Sunday unless your entire party has arrived. Because Bernice was cranky, I suggested they go ahead and sit down as two. "But," Bernice pointed out, "doesn't that defeat the purpose?" She may not have been liking me at that moment but her curiosity about Sabena was stronger than her hunger.

An hour after the appointed time I spotted Sabena exiting her Volvo and striding hurriedly toward Kizzy's. From a distance Sabena, dressed in black leggings, a white blouse tied at the waist, and a baseball cap, looked as lean and sporty as her dancer's pedigree would suggest. Up close Sabena's face appeared drawn, like perhaps she'd been crying. She smiled for us but it wasn't deep or enthused. Tim, being Tim, was immediately captivated by Sabena's beauty, while Bernice surveyed her with a hawk's aggressive eye.

Brunch was awkward. Tim was eyeing Sabena and smirking at me, Bernice was studying me, and I was trying unsuccessfully to read my date's mood. Sabena was tight lipped and gave short answers to light queries. Question: "How you like Cedars-Sinai?" Answer: "It's all good."

Normally you could have explained it away under the guise of nervousness. My close friends. She was way late. All that. Then just after we'd devoured the corn bread and ordered the entrées, Bernice, trying hard to be sociable, said, "I understand you have a daughter. What's her name?"

"Her name's Ronelle." Usually between women, child talk is the ultimate icebreaker, like men and sports at a bar. I expected Sabena to pull out her wallet and begin displaying photos like a proud momma. Instead Sabena turned toward me. "Rodney, I need to speak to you."

"You mean in private?"

"Yes. If that's all right."

"Sure. No problem. Let's step outside."

I gave Tim and Bernice an "I don't know what's up" look as we got up. Sabena walked out of Kizzy's past the line of people waiting to enter and walked over to a bench. As I approached, Sabena looked at the ground.

"What's the matter, Sabena?"

"I'm sorry about acting strange in front of your friends."

"Don't worry about that. Please just tell me what's up. Maybe I can help."

"You have been very, very understanding. A lot of men I've told my story to have jetted like I was made of fire. I appreciate that about you, Rodney." I just nodded and tried to take her hands in mine, but she shifted them away. "But I have to tell you we can't see each other romantically anymore."

I said, "Okay," my all-purpose "I don't know what to say" word, and waited for more.

"Ron came by this morning and we worked it all out."

"Worked it all out with Ron? The man who ran away from you. Ron. The man who might have ruined your life by making you HIV positive. Ron. The—"

"That's enough, Rodney!"

"That's enough! Shit!" I sat there fuming as Sabena leaned over toward me.

"My daughter needs her father. She loves him, and for as long as she can have him, she should."

"But what about you? Do you still love him?"

"I don't know."

"You don't know?"

"Oh, I might. I think I might. Don't be mad, Rodney."

I just got up and walked away. I didn't say good-bye to Sabena. I didn't go back into Kizzy's. I just got in my Mustang and blasted out of that mall like it was a launching pad. Next thing I knew I was on the 90 pushing the pedal that drove me toward Hollywood.

I sat in my office clicking on my computer and then searching for the "List" file. There once more appeared my 133 names, all in the order I remembered them, from Woodrina to Pam to Merry and the holy trilogy of Amy, Belinda, and Sabena. I pressed the delete button and they went back to where they belonged—my memory.

Back home the adjectives "awful," "depressed," and "lousy" were a few I'd employ to define my mood. There were two messages on my machine. "Rodney, what happened? You didn't come back, money. What did she say to you? Bernice says she could see in her eyes that woman was gonna drop a bomb on you. When you're ready, you know where I'm at."

The other message was from Merry. "I'm in town for a week. Got something I want to talk to you about. Thai food, anyone?"

Didn't wanna talk to him and his growing family. Didn't wanna see her and her flirty self. I wanted nothing. So I just slumped into my sofa and that's what I thought about. Nothing.

40

I was damn near submerged in my tub with Aveda bath gel and candles throwing scents in the air as I tried to forget my horrible day. My body was mad tense and even this patented relaxation routine wasn't cutting through the huge knots in my neck and shoulders.

I tried to think optimistically. I figured my personal El Niño had finally peaked. The storm had been wicked — making the foundations of my business shaky and blowing my personal life away like leaves. This had to be it. The worst was over. All downhill from here. Unfortunately for me and mine the storm had a second wind.

"Rod-nee!"

"What's up, Ro-ber-ta?"

"It's Ma. She's sick."

"I know that."

"No. She's physically sick. They took her to Cedars-Sinai."

"What?"

"Her ulcer. She has a bleeding ulcer. She's been hiding it from the staff at the home. They didn't know until she coughed up blood at lunch. Please get here."

Dizzy as a child running in circles, I dried, dressed, and drove with my head pounding. The day my father died I felt like this. The night our house burned down I felt like this. That rainy Saturday we placed Ma in the home I felt like this. On every truly ugly day in my life, blood filled my head and it felt like it would leak out of every damn hole I had until there wasn't one drop left in me.

Despite being overwhelmed by this blood rush I somehow

made it to the wing where my sister, Stewart, and the girls were huddled together. We had a big communal hug, cemented by tears and sobs. I pulled Roberta aside and she directed me to a Pakistani doctor named Habibi who talked of Ma's inflamed ulcer, of removing it that night, and the insurance papers that had to be signed before he could proceed.

Dr. Habibi surely spoke calmly but it all sounded fast and barely decipherable. All I knew was that Ma was in trouble, they needed to cut her to correct it, and that, as the man of the Hampton clan, it was essential I stay calm and not panic, though my armpits were moist as a sauna.

Ma was asleep, looking deceptively peaceful in a room that contained two other equally sedated women about her age. There were other children there—adults like me reduced to scared kids. I stood by her bed watching my connection to all that had come before me lie quietly linked up to tubes and machines that monitored her remaining life force.

Roberta and Stewart were about to take the girls home when Tawana announced, "I'm staying with Grandma." It wasn't a request or a whining plea. It was a fact. That little girl was not budging.

Tawana and I sat together in the hospital corridor, me staring into space, remembering bits and pieces of my childhood, while Tawana played with one of those handheld video games. I watched her, realizing that this would be one of those memories she wouldn't truly understand until years later. Somehow this event would shape her and we wouldn't know how for years.

"Uncle Rodney?" I expected some question about Ma's condition, one of those tough questions children ask that adults fumble at the risk of the child's respect.

"You know, Grandma's gonna be all right."

"I know that, Uncle Rodney." She paused. "Uncle Rodney."

"Yeah, baby."

"Are you ever gonna get married?"

"I hope so. What makes you ask that?"

"I was thinking that you need to learn to be more laid-back—like Ma."

"Like your mother?" That made me smile. "You think your mother's laid-back?"

"She wasn't always. But when she met Stewart she wasn't trying to meet him. She just wanted to learn computers. She wasn't looking and he found her. That could work for you too. I know when I'm ready to have a boyfriend, I'm not gonna chase no one."

"You won't have to, fine as you are, baby."

"So are you gonna take my advice?"

"If you're gonna do it that way, then I better follow your lead."

"You wanna learn my game?"

Hours later Tawana was still with me, her game off, her head on my shoulder. Roberta and Stewart were sitting on the other end of the sofa, playing spades on his laptop computer. Dr. Habibi came over wearing a tired smile and his green operating room uniform. He reported, "It went well. Your mother is strong and is going to be fine. We got all the troubled areas."

Roberta wondered, "When can we see her?" and Habibi told her the next morning. We thanked him and huddled again. Tawana wanted to stay until Ma woke up but Roberta put her foot down and they all left, vowing to be back right after school tomorrow. Me, I was staying. No one was looking for me. No one was waiting at home. There was no other place for me to be.

My khakis were wrinkled and my shirt a sweaty mess, but I didn't care. I just laid my body down on that sofa and stretched out. Around 5 A.M. I woke up and wandered down toward Ma's room, drawn there on wobbly feet like a puppet on a string.

Ma was lying there with her eyes half open, the tubes and machines still hooked up, still monitoring her life force. I took one of her hands in mine and she stirred. That face that I shared with her opened and observed my love just as I observed her beauty. I said, "Hi," but she didn't speak. She just squeezed me back and closed her eyes. I sat there just like that, her hand in mine, feeling a childlike security in my mother's presence.

A nurse politely asked me to leave and I retired to the sofa in the corridor. I had a disturbing thought—if Ma died I would be two women short. Then I fell back asleep.

Not surprisingly I had a nightmare/dream. An old church. Long, unending pews. Dark, *X-Files*-style lighting. I stood naked at the altar. It felt like warm water was pouring down upon my head, making me feel strong and righteous. Then the church disappeared and a wondrous inky blackness engulfed me, like I was back in the womb, floating in that life fluid as blissful as my crowded mind would allow.

Sleep ended slowly, like the sun cutting through the clouds early on an L.A. morning. Even when I was surely awake, the warmth from the dream remained, like I was being cradled. Finally I parted my eyelids. My head was in a woman's lap. She had on a skirt. Brown legs slightly parted welcomed me to the day. Not until I turned my head and looked up did I know my benefactor.

"Good morning," I said. "Nice of you to come."

41

Thai Dishes is on the 1900 block of Wilshire Boulevard, not close enough to the ocean that you can smell the water, but far enough from West Hollywood that it can seem a hike from my part of town. That was one of the reasons we'd fallen in love with it. We never saw anyone we knew there. Few entertainment-business types—few advertising types. Just locals from the area and the odd Thai food junkies like ourselves.

We always tried to sit in the same booth. It was in the corner in front of the window, me facing the window and her facing the restaurant. A flaming pot of seafood soup. Vegetable curry. *Pad thai.* They were the backbones of our meals, though we'd try something new sometimes so we didn't fall into a rut.

I knew I looked terrible and surely smelled bad. But Merry gazed at me like I was gold. "So, you slept out there all night?"

"Most of it, I think. I went in and saw her early in the morning. I held her hand. Now she's awake and back to being herself."

"I saw. She's quite a lady."

"Yeah. So are you. What made you come?"

"Adele told me what happened." Then she paused. "I care about you, Rodney. You know that, don't you?"

"You've said so before, but now I know you really mean it."

"And how does that information strike you?"

"It strikes me good."

Now I got tense. Not tense with fear as I'd been on the way

246

to the hospital. Not tense the way I got going through the Hampton Media accounts receivable. Tense with anticipation, like Merry was gonna tell me something I really needed to hear. When she just looked at her food and didn't say anything else, I said, "Merry, you all right?"

"Well," she started and then stopped. Eyes looked everywhere but back at mine. It was a gesture similar to what Sabena had done the day before. I reached across the table and took her hand, and like my mother, she squeezed back.

"You know, I did my own list."

"You told me that. But you wouldn't tell me how many names are on it."

"Well, I'll tell you now."

"Okay. How many names on your list, Merry? No, let me guess. How about ten?"

She giggled. "How'd you know?"

"I just know you."

"Well, maybe you do 'cause making up my own list made me see you differently."

"Okay." Now I couldn't hear anything but her voice. Other people talking. Music in the background. The swish of traffic outside. Nothing. It was like when you play ball or make love and you're concentrating so hard you hear nothing but what you need to. That's how intense the moment felt.

"Of the ten men on it I keep in touch with only one. And that's you, Rodney Hampton."

I didn't say shit. I just held on to her hand and tried to continue breathing.

"I mean, I don't even keep in touch with my ex-husband, who I actually still care for. I don't talk to my high school sweetheart, that fool who popped my cherry in college, or the guy who offered to buy me a Beemer when I turned twenty-two."

"Not even him?"

"Not even him."

"Only you, Rodney. I only keep talking to you."

We sat there holding hands across the table. She waited for me to speak. I waited for me to speak too. Finally I said, "This is a wild time for you to talk to me this way."

"Yeah," she admitted. "I know. But you know, I've been one man short awhile." I closed my eyes when she said that. It was like she'd spoken some prayer that I'd forgotten from childhood, and like a true blessing, she'd spoken so truthfully that only by shutting out the light could I find the strength to accept it.

When I opened my eyes Merry was flustered. She didn't understand how happy she'd made me. "I was going to say this to you before your mother got sick." She was speaking quickly, breathlessly. "You know, maybe we should just forget about it until she gets better."

"Forget about it? Either you're coming over here or I'm coming over there. That's what happens next. But we're never forgetting about it."

She came over to my side and she kissed me or I kissed her or we kissed together. However I describe it, there was a whole lot of kissing going on.

42

It took me a minute to really believe Merry. I'd gone from Caron to Sabena so quickly I feared I was becoming a romantic spinning top, sure to tip over once the momentum waned. Instead of me being the aggressor I let Merry create the tempo and define the pace. I guess I took Tawana's advice. I wasn't the chaser, the man looking for conquest. With Merry I was the love object in a way I had never been before. Once I accepted her love on her terms, not pushing forward to some goal but as part of the natural flow of life, I felt surprisingly comfortable. I tried to put my balls away and stop juggling my life away. I haven't gotten there yet but my hands are moving slower and slower.

That winter of contentment brought other, equally radical changes to my life. Roberta and Stewart, bonded in front of glowing computer screens, joined in their respect for motherhood, and longing for a nuclear family, decided to move in together.

"Are you sure about this, Roberta? You've only been with him six months or something. Not even that. That is not a lot of time, girl."

"If Stewart was just another of the shiftless MFs I usually get hooked up with, I'd be dead wrong," she told me one evening as we packed up hairpieces into a storage box. "But you know, Stewart is not a nigga. He's a man—the kind that has already memorized, not just my birthday, but the birthdays of all the girls."

"Okay. So you got me over here to give my blessing to you and the supernerd?"

"No," she replied as she playfully placed a hunk of long, straight Naomi Campbell–type hair on my head. "I'm too old to be asking you or anybody permission to do anything about my love life. My personal decisions are mine. I got you over here to try on hair." She took off the Campbell hair and replaced it with some gold Lil Kim–type hair.

"Come on, Roberta." I pulled off the blond hair. "Come with it, 'cause I can feel an argument coming."

"Yeah, there is one thing I do need your permission for, something I need for you to agree with."

"And that is?"

"What do you think about letting Ma move in with Stewart and me?"

"Okay. You're about to embark on the most important love relationship of your life and have to deal with your daughters, his daughter, his baby's mother, and you also want to take in a sick woman who happens to be your mother."

"Rod-nee," she said like a troubled child, "Ma's recovering from the depression and Dr. Habibi and everyone else we consulted said the ulcer was a long-term problem that being in a happier environment would help. She'd be with the kids, with me, and in a real home again."

I shook my head in wonder at my sister's sense of love and charity. "What? Are you some kind of damn ghetto saint?"

"Rod-nee, I can't tell if you're making fun of me or supporting me."

I walked over to my sister and gave her a hug. Then I stepped back and looked at her. "Roberta, you sure you wanna do this? Even for a homegirl superwoman this is a lot to take on. Are you sure?"

Well, Roberta got teary eyed and her naturally feisty veneer fell. Suddenly there was this little girl I used to chase around the house staring at me. "You know, since Daddy died we've never been a whole family. You know what I mean?"

"Yeah."

"So I feel like this is a chance to make it all whole again. For me, her, and the girls."

Now I was feeling kinda teary myself. So I tried to play it off. "Roberta, I never knew you wanted to live on *The Cosby Show*."

"If I didn't love you," she said, raising her hand, "I'd smack the shit out of you."

"But you love me, Roberta."

"And you love me, Rodney."

"Okay. With Ma having access to a kitchen, maybe I'll finally learn her recipe for butter rolls."

"No, Ma won't teach you. I'll have Tanina do it."

"Okay," I said. "I'd like that."

43

It's not in any brochures, but it can get chilly in Los Angeles in February, reaching the mid-forties on particularly blustery nights. For many women in town such temperatures are nirvana, giving them the excuse to break out fur coats that are otherwise ridiculous possessions in the City of Angels. So when Joseph Kwanza's wife, Millie, came over to praise me for the Urban League dinner with a black fur wrapped around her slender arms, I just grinned and acted gracious.

After much deliberation the league had approved my concept for "Romance with Righteousness" for its Black History Month/Valentine's Day fund-raiser, under one condition—that I come on board and produce the event.

"We all agreed this approach to Black History Month was not simply novel, but a fine manner in which to highlight the need for family values, fidelity, and commitment to the continuing rebuilding of Los Angeles's sense of community." Joseph Kwanza was speaking at a podium before the tuxedo-and-evening-gown-wearing audience in the Beverly Wilshire ballroom. I was at the far end of the dais, feeling strange because I was in a tux and Kwanza, that once inscrutable man at the other end of the conference room, was now praising me before hundreds of the city's movers and shakers. "So I want to personally thank Rodney Hampton of Hampton Media for his creativity, persistence, and patience in making this event possible. Let me introduce Rodney Hampton."

Applause filled the room and I strode over to the podium, gave Kwanza a hug that I hadn't expected to give, and pulled out an index card. The last time I'd had such an audience was just under a year ago at Tim and Bernice's wedding. My remarks on this night were shorter and more heartfelt: "I want to thank the Los Angeles Urban League and, specifically, Mr. Kwanza for giving me the chance to make an idea reality. Whether it's poverty, lack of opportunity, or a broken heart— love of your fellow man, your neighbor, of your mate is the ultimate solution. And that is the theme of the presentation."

Every table had a bouquet of roses as its centerpiece. As the overhead lights dimmed, small lights under each bouquet came on, bathing the ballroom in a rosy glow. On a separate stage, captured by a red spotlight and garbed in a long scarlet dress, Kenya emerged and read three selections—one of Shakespeare's love sonnets, a poem by Carlos Fuentes in Spanish, and a poem by Nikki Giovanni.

Kenya then introduced a videotape of Angelenos—black, white, Hispanic, and Asian—attending the dinner. They were telling their wives, husbands, girlfriends, boyfriends, children, and family how much they loved them. I was even on the tape, as were my favorite lovebirds, Roberta and Stewart.

After that we upped the tempo. D-Vince came onstage to the cheers of the scattered hip-hop fans in the crowd. But by the time the soon shirtless D-Vince had done his thing, there were a lot of adult women wondering if his poster was on sale in the lobby.

The program ended with an all-star choir with members from several denominations from around L.A. County. It took a little doing to pull off but I had an ace in the hole—Amy Davis, who worked as my consultant and, somehow, slipped herself into the back of the choir.

Yeah, in many ways this was the night my life came full circle. In the process of organizing the choir Amy and I had built a real friendship. Belinda was invited but she had her own

Valentine's Day bash under way at Eden's Taste. "But," she assured me, "you are definitely on the list." Caron came with a date, a Mexican real estate broker named Ramon who looked like Andy Garcia. Caron was polite but, understandably, distant.

The funniest pairing of the night occurred backstage. While Circus sat at a table surrounded by car dealers from Encino, Kenya and D-Vince were bonding in the dressing rooms. Young and beautiful, with hormones popping like amphetamines, I watched them pass telephone numbers and smiled. For as long as it lasted I'm sure they'd both have fun.

The family was all there, including Ma, who sat with Tanina in her lap and Tawana by her side monitoring Grandma's tomato intake (and other acidy foods) as Grandma monitored their behavior. On the other side of the table sat Roberta and Stewart acting like honeymooners. I kept my fingers crossed and prayed nightly that it would all work out.

Despite all my hopes that this event would jump-start my career, I still wasn't prepared for the pile of business cards slipped snugly into my palm. Coke bottlers, video game manufacturers, book publishers, television syndicators—it was a bounty of contacts whose greetings were accompanied by praise for the evening's conception and execution.

In the long months I awaited the league's approval I fantasized about this level of success. Yet someone was missing. For most of the evening I was alone. I had a seat reserved between my ma and Tawana, but through the presentation it sat empty.

Merry was shooting a candy bar commercial outside Houston but had vowed to get to L.A. in time. Just before dessert, she entered the ballroom in a shoulderless black dress, black stockings, and black pumps. Her hair was short and shiny and she'd done something to her lips that seemed to make them glow. Whatever Merry had done, it was da bomb. I studied her stride, watched her slide between tables, and somehow intercepted her in the middle of the room.

"Word," I said in greeting.

She smiled and grabbed my lapels. "You still say 'word'?"

"It's a thing Tim and I have been doing since the eighties. It's kind of tongue-in-cheek."

"Kind of tongue-in-cheek? Listen, Rodney, either the tongue is in the cheek or it isn't. I don't believe in 'kind of' or even 'kinda.'"

"Okay," I said, "put your tongue in my cheek."

"Only there?"

"You gotta start somewhere." Then I said, "Ahhh," and opened my mouth.

"Have I told you I thought you were funny?"

"Stop gassing me up and kiss me. You know how."

"Real soft and gentle," she said, getting real close. "Just on the lips, right?"

"Word."